A NECESSARY

(Book 6 of 8 in the

Author: Jonathan Cox

First published NOV 2020

Publisher: JJ Cox Publishing Limited

All intellectual rights belong to the author.

This is a work of fiction and whilst influenced by the experiences and recollections of the author, no characters are based upon anyone living or dead and any similarities are purely coincidental. This book is sold on the condition that it is not re-sold, copied, or otherwise circulated without my prior consent. All intellectual and property rights belong to the author. This work has been registered with the Writers' Copyright Association.

The Nostrils Series

Book 1 – From Green to Blue

Book 2 – From Black to Blue

Book 3 – From Blue to Brown

Book 4 – When You Wear the Blue

Book 5 – We Don't Call Them Raids

Book 6 – A Necessary Fiction

Book 7 – Purple Cover

Book 8 – Never Yield

Prologue

18th June 2007

I'd been a Detective Sergeant on the country's busiest murder squad for five years so if anyone knew how to commit the perfect murder, it ought to be me.

I didn't take the decision to end my victim's life quickly. I thought through every argument for and against. I knew the easy option was to ignore the opportunity chance had presented and to get on with living my mundane existence. An extraordinary set of circumstances however had aligned, and a course, a purpose if you will, even a destiny, had illuminated before me. For the briefest of moments, I understood everything; even why I had been born.

I had one distinct advantage over other people who commit the ultimate crime, simply because contrary to what you see on your favourite T.V. series, ninety nine percent of murders are spontaneous acts of violence. As a result, the suspect unwittingly leaves a trail of evidence in the minutes, hours and days leading up to the crime. In contrast, I'd planned this murder down to the finest detail.

Another factor that weighed heavily in my favour was that I was the only person involved. I hadn't told anyone else what I was going to do and when the deed was done, I wouldn't confide in a soul, ever! I didn't require anyone's help or assistance. No one was driving me anywhere; or knowingly providing me with an alibi; or supplying me with a weapon or disposing of one; or laundering any ill-gotten gains; or making me a forged passport; or in any other way involved with what was going on. This operation was a sole enterprise.

When I set out that evening, I didn't take my mobile phone, and didn't take my own car anywhere near the scene. I had worked out a route devoid of any CCTV cameras, dressed in such a way that no one would take any notice of me and, from the moment I left the house, wore two layers of disposable clear plastic gloves to prevent leaving any fingerprints.

Nor would my internet browsing history give me away. I had entered nothing on my computer, or indeed any computer, that would suggest or hint at what I was about to do.

As an added bonus, this murder would be investigated by one of the smallest police forces in the country, which is never a bad thing for the suspect.

Finally, when my victim was found and the list of potential suspects drawn up, I'd be surprised if my name even appeared.

If for some unlucky reason I was stopped by police on route to the victim's house, I would surreptitiously lose my plastic gloves, produce my warrant card which would negate any further investigation or search, immediately return home and call the job off, permanently. As well as being a sole enterprise, this was also a one-shot operation.

The last five miles of my journey to and from the victim's address were made by bicycle, because unlike cars and motorbikes, this mode of transport has no registration marks. The only identifiable feature, the manufacturer's name and logo on the black frame, I'd covered up with black masking tape. What's more, while I did what I had to do, unlike a car, the bike could be parked up out of sight by leaving it at the end of a drive which the victim's drive with the neighbouring residence; except they didn't, because the neighbouring residence was for sale with vacant possession.

Once on the bike, I wore a long red jacket, which had the words 'Post Office' across the back. I figured out I would be most vulnerable riding a bike at three in the morning and there was just a possibility that some keen old bill would give me a pull. Of course, this wouldn't happen if the eyes of that eager police officer just saw a postman on his way to work. When do postmen work? Early in the morning, which is when I would be making my final approach. I could dispose of the jacket in a tip later in the day.

I'd found the jacket in a skip in Brighton some six months ago. I'd originally picked it up because I thought it might prove useful during surveillance, but I'd never used it. In the build-up to this operation, and to make sure it was completely free of any forensics linking to its previous owner, I'd put it through the washing machine half a dozen times.

I'd left home at three in the morning, driven to the middle of nowhere, where I'd got onto my bike to finish the last five miles of my journey to a little cul-de-sac and specifically a small two-bedroom residence at number nine.

If I was lucky, the person with whom I lived wouldn't even know what time I'd left the house, which would be really useful if I needed an alibi. Just to help things along, I'd slipped a 7.5mg Zopiclone into her night-time cup of tea. I was confident things wouldn't get anywhere near that far but if they did, an unblemished witness and my mobile phone signal would prove to a jury that I'd never left the house that night.

Of course, there is always the unanticipated. The car might fail to start or break down; after all it was over ten years old. I could have an accident. My bike might get a puncture, or the chain might come off. I could arrive at the address to discover there's an ambulance attending to an elderly resident residing next door who'd just had a heart attack. I was mentally prepared to pull out, if any of these things happened. I was determined not to be so focused that I would take a risk. I wanted the victim dead, and I wanted them to know why they were going to die before I killed them, but I was prepared to abort my mission if I had to.

As it transpired, the drive to the middle of nowhere was uneventful. It was a quiet night, and the rain was pouring down which was no bad thing. I left my car in a country park to the south of the town. I knew from a previous recce that on a clear night, I would have been able to see the castle overlooking the Thames Estuary, but not on that dark, dank night.

As I put the front wheel back on the bike, I'd had to remove this earlier to get it in the boot, I realised I was shaking. I must have been more nervous than I thought. I also needed a pee, but I wasn't going to leave any unnecessary forensic evidence anywhere, even in the car park of a country park five miles from the murder scene. I put on my rucksack in which were several items that were to play a key role in that night's events. As I did so, I realised this covered up most of the 'Post Office' label on the back of my coat. If that was the only mistake I'd made, I'd be very happy.

After a short ride, I joined the main road and headed east. A couple of miles later, I pulled up at a red traffic light before turning left. Under almost any other circumstances, at five in the morning and on a push bike, I would have ignored that red light and just cycled right through the junction but not that morning and bugger me, not five seconds after I'd stopped, a police car drew up next to me. Not for the first time, I knew fate was on my side. We were only held at the red light for a couple of seconds and as the police car drew away, I subtly glanced through the rear side window. There was only the driver, which was perfect because it meant there was no one sitting in the passenger seat who might have got a look at me.

There were only eleven or twelve houses in the cul-de-sac. I did a quick sweep up one side and down the other and couldn't see any interior lights on. The victim resided in the second semi-detached house on the right, number nine.

From the detached corner of the victim's semi, the telephone wire hung limply before crossing the street and veering upwards to the telegraph pole. I could reach it while still sat on my bike and my sharp pliers cut the thin wire at the first attempt. I alighted and carefully, slowly walked the bike to the end of the driveway and stood it in a dark corner near to the garden gate.

I suspected the victim had a panic alarm, but I also knew that these days, the device wasn't connected by the BT landline, but instead used a police radio signal that sent a set recorded message to the Control Room, twenty miles away at Essex Police Headquarters in Chelmsford. It was vital that the victim didn't get to that alarm when they realised what was about to happen.

I'm not the most agile individual, but I made short work of the four-foot wooden fence gate and was up and over in a flash. Once in the garden, which had a small lawn area and a fishpond to one side, I stayed motionless for several minutes and strained hard to detect any sounds from inside. I could hear a noise, but it was rhythmic, almost mechanical. I peered into several windows. My only purpose at this stage was to ascertain whether anyone else was in the property or, worst case scenario, a dog. I didn't see anything that worried me and established that the noise was the victim snoring.

I climbed back over the gate and removed my rucksack and long red postman's coat, which had in fact kept me remarkably dry, and left it on top of the bike. Underneath, I was suited and booted. I straightened my tie. I then took out several items from my rucksack, which included a red CID style notebook, my warrant card, several buff folders with the words Metropolitan Police clearly printed on the front and a green MPS Vehicle logbook. Finally, I took out the automatic pistol and put this in my inside jacket pocket, which I'd adapted just for that purpose by tearing the lining.

The occupant of number nine had tried to destroy my life but had failed. Now I was about to deliver vengeance.

I brushed myself down, took several deep breaths and knocked firmly on the front door with my tried and tested, 'this is the police, open up', knock.

Chapter 1

Six weeks earlier

Of course, I'd seen the News of the World headline, but I hadn't paid much attention to it. After all, the abduction and murder had happened a thousand miles away on a small tropical island off the Moroccan coast.

The case of the wife killing hotshot financier therefore was the last thing on my mind that bright spring morning as Julie and I walked the short distance from Patrick Dunne House down Sutton High Street to the café for breakfast. I'd been on the same South London murder squad for years and, if truth be told, was getting more than a little bored. For the first few years I'd got a real buzz whenever we got a new case but recently the gasp of excitement had become a sigh and I knew it was time to move on.

I'd applied for several jobs, one on Counter Terrorism, another on the Fraud Squad and a third as a police advisor based in Abuja, Nigeria. On all three occasions I'd been spectacularly dreadful on the board. The thing was, I wasn't any good at interviews. They never asked me what I knew, and I had quite a wide span of knowledge after twenty-five years in the Job. It seemed to me they only questioned me on things about which I knew absolutely nothing. When I went for the CT job, I'd revised everything there was to know about counter terrorism law and the Chair opened the interview with the sentence 'As you're not a CT operative, let me assure you that we won't be testing your knowledge of the highly specialist legislation'. Honestly, I could have screamed!

Several months ago, I'd discussed my frustration with my D.C.I., a nice guy called Justin Hansford, who said he'd have a word with a mate who was a staff officer for the Assistant Commissioner Crime and ask him to keep an eye out for anything that might be a bit different, like a special project or something. I didn't mind what I did if it wasn't, yet another, CCTV sweep or house to house schedule. In return, Justin asked me to clear out the murder squad property store at Arbour Square police station, where we used to be based. I accepted Justin's offer with excitement but when three months later nothing had come of it, I was resigned to staying put for the time being, whether I liked it or not.

I'd taken the Inspector's exam in March and was still waiting for the result. I think I did all right, but I wouldn't put money on having passed.

The thing is I was bored. I lived alone on a barge in the Docklands Marina; had an ex-wife, Jackie, an ex-girlfriend, Wendy, two girls, Pippa and Trudy, who I only saw one weekend in three, and an elder son from a much older relationship who I never saw. I had little money and even less inclination. All I had was work and that had lost its edge. On the plus side however, I'd been clean of heroin since 2003.

I'd worked with Julie for years; she was probably my closest friend. She'd been going out with a Flying Squad DS called Luke Pourgourides, they were getting married in the summer and Julie was arranging a big wedding.

"What do you think of this?" She asked, as we sat down.

"Luke thinks we shouldn't have sex for the next three months, you know, save ourselves to make the wedding night special."

"Does that include, well you know, self-satisfaction?" I asked.

"Apparently" She replied.

"So, Luke's not going to have a wank for three months, fuck off." I said, disbelievingly.

"That's the plan, besides, it's only two months, three weeks now." She replied.

"Mind you, I don't know why I'm sounding so disbelieving. I am living testament to not having sex."

As soon as the words left my mouth I grimaced, so to try to cover up my indiscretion, I quickly added …

"Only kidding."

Julie smiled kindly.

'You're not though, are you, babe?" She asked, quietly.

I shook my head and looked down at the table.

Julie looked around to check we weren't being overheard.

"Look, Chris, don't take this the wrong way but I might be able to help."

"I thought you were saving yourself for the wedding night." I replied.

"No, you idiot, I don't mean that, besides I've never found you the least bit attractive, that's why we can be such good friends, that's why Luke doesn't mind that we go out together."

"Thanks" I said, dejectedly.

Julie looked around again, so I started to realise she was serious about something.

"Are you going to suggest a blind date?"

"Well, yes." She replied.

"Go on, and for goodness sake, stop looking around, I'll let you know if anyone comes in."

"Look, Chris, don't be offended…"

"I won't be, go on."

"I have a friend, an old friend I was at infant's school with, her name's Cassandra, Cassandra Marsh. You saw her at our party last year, short dark brown hair, very attractive, small, slim build."

"Vaguely, but if I remember rightly, I did get pretty pissed. Wasn't she with some bloke that was driving a drug dealer's BMW you know, with all the windows blacked out, and some of the guys were like, 'who the fuck is he?'."

"Yes, that was her but that was her brother and he's not a drug dealer, he's a fireman and that's her BMW, anyway."

"She was quite attractive, I think. I don't understand, did you say you're not setting me up on a blind date or you are?" I asked, more than a little confused.

"Cassandra is lovely and very successful and, if I'm being honest babe, like West Ham and Dagenham and Redbridge."

"What?"

"Well, completely out of your league, babes."

"Seriously, if I laugh any more, I could make myself sick." I replied, sarcastically, not laughing at all.

"Listen, Cassandra runs her own business and might be able to assist you. I could put in a good word, see if she fancies a night out."

"Cassandra runs a dating agency?" I asked.

"Oh god no. The thing is, you need to know that Cassandra's a very, very …" Julie paused to maximise emphasis.

"… very, exclusive escort."

I was lost for words.

"Alright, close your mouth. Don't look so bloody shocked. The offer's there. You'd be a fool not to take it."

The truth is I was really keen. I hadn't had sex since I split up with Wendy in early 2004. There was a time, in my younger and less obese years, when I could easily find someone to go to bed with, but those days disappeared with my thirties and there were times when I wondered whether I would have sex again. But I was embarrassed to say as much to Julie, as I'd sound pathetic.

I wanted to say yes, but heard my voice saying…

"I'll be fine, thanks."

"You're a fool. She gorgeous and sexy and it's uncomplicated; and actually, she's great company. You've got nothing to lose."

"What, apart from my dignity, self-esteem and reputation?" I asked.

"Exactly, babe, nothing at all." Julie replied.

I swear it always happens, just as our breakfast arrived Julie's mobile went. She said just four words 'on our way back' and I knew we'd got a new job.

As we went to get up, I bemoaned that we weren't even in frame.

"Two jobs have come in, apparently, within an hour of each other."

Well, that explained that, I thought.

My own phone rang, and I assumed it was the Incident Room with the same message.

"I'm on my way." I said, before the caller could say anything.

"Gosh, that's impressive, I haven't even told you where to go, yet." Replied a voice I didn't recognise.

"Oh sorry, I thought you were someone else. Please, shall we start again?" I replied.

"Chris Pritchard?"

"Yes" I replied, in a deliberately controlled manner.

"It's Erling Kristiansen, here. I am the staff officer to A.C. Crime. I've got a little job for you; can you come and see me? Ninth floor at the Yard, room 918."

"Umm, yes, I think so, but my team's just picked up a new murder." I replied.

"Don't worry, I'll square it with Justin. How long will it take you to get here?"

"Running time from Sutton, boss. Probably an hour."

"Great"

The call was terminated, and I was left to explain to Julie that we would be going separate ways.

"Oh, that sounds exciting, babes. Let me know what it's all about, if you can, that is."

"Before we part, just how would it go with your friend, you know, Cassandra?"

Julie laughed.

"Just go out for a meal, nothing fancy. You might get to stay the night, babes."

Julie did a ridiculously exaggerated wink.

"After three years I won't need a night, perhaps a couple of minutes, maybe half an hour if we do it twice. Definitely not a whole night. And besides, what's that going to cost me? I've got no money, I've got an ex-wife and two lovely girls that I never see, but no money."

"She would normally charge two grand for an overnighter ... but I was thinking more of a date than a business arrangement. She's single and might like a normal night out with an ordinary guy." Julie replied.

"Two thousand pounds! Christ, I'm in the wrong job."

"She only does six or seven appointments a month and reckons she's on about a hundred and fifty k a year. She declares it all to the taxman; of course, she can offset a lot of what she earns like her car, her clothes, make up, meals out etcetera. She says she clears over ten grand a month."

"So, you think she'll give me a freebie." I asked.

"No, I think she'd just like a normal date night. Her last proper boyfriend was a bit of a nightmare. But that was years ago. There was stalking and restraining orders. You need some happiness in your life. We girls have agreed that we've never known anyone sadder than you. Since Wendy left you you've been like a lost puppy."

"Not just Wendy, Jackie too. One day I had everything, the next nothing. Look, I'm not moaning, you make your own bed. The thing is Julie, it used to be so easy with women but the nearer you get to fifty, the more difficult it becomes. And I know those happy days are never coming back, ever! Kill me, kill me now."

I smiled but in a rather weak and pathetic way.

She leaned in and gave me a hug. It was a nice thing to do.

"You'll meet someone, Chris. You never know that someone could be Cassandra Marsh."

"But a blind date with a desperate hooker? That's so sad."

"Trust me Chris, the last thing men that go out with Cassandra are, are sad; they're highly sophisticated businessmen. Oh, and normally quite a bit older. She gets a lot of Arabs and a few rich city types. They just want a great uncomplicated night out with an attractive and intelligent woman. I'll give her your mobile number and tell her to give you a call. As I said, I think she'd jump at the chance."

I nodded in agreement and headed off towards the train station.

A long time ago, I'd befriended a prostitute called Debbie. The whole thing didn't end well, and I'd learnt a valuable lesson about why police officers and hookers didn't mix. I hoped this new adventure would turn out better.

Chapter 2

"Read that." Detective Superintendent Erling Kristiansen instructed, as he gently threw a buff, unregistered docket across two desks towards me.

Erling was a tall white male, well-spoken and with a pleasant unassuming manner. I can honestly say, I took to him immediately.

I went to sit down.

"No, not here, take it to the canteen. Come back at twelve, the Assistant Commissioner has a fifteen-minute slot, he'll see you then. And bring some coffee back, that always goes down well; one latte and a straight black, no sugar." He replied.

I checked my watch, it was half ten, I had ninety minutes to kill, and the thickness of the files didn't suggest it would take particularly long to read.

Instead of heading to the canteen, I took the lift to the fourteenth floor and went to the library. I'd been going there for years and knew the staff intimately. We used to have a bit of a joke. It probably sounds lame, but I used to say I'd been on the squad looking for Lord Lucan since he disappeared in 1974. I was, I would tell them, the only detective left on the team and that it was my life's ambition to bring the murdering peer to justice. The lady who ran the library was white and in her early thirties; she had an older Asian lady assistant and a younger lad, probably just out of school. During one of my last visits, I'd been impressed to learn that the manager had a degree in being a librarian! I hadn't realised that was possible.

As I entered the room, I noticed a sign on the door announcing the library's imminent closure and my heart sank. Apparently, going forward the Met would only require one library, and that would be at Hendon Training Centre.

The atmosphere was sad, so I didn't bother with any of my usual banter and just asked them how they were all doing. Only the two women were in and they both looked close to tears. We talked about the closure and how it would affect them. They lived, they explained, in South London and relocating to Hendon was not an option so the decision to close had effectively ended their careers. I realised how lucky I was to be a police officer and as such, cocooned from such arbitrary HR decisions.

I offered my condolences and sat down to read the docket at one of half a dozen tables that were at the far end of the room.

The docket was entitled 'Operation Patella'. As you opened these dockets, the minutes sheet was on the left. This recorded the dockets movements and any decision making. On the right side were the principal reports and other documents and these were numbered consecutively. Their numbering corresponded to the minutes which referenced them. Both sets of papers were secured in place by the same orange treasury tag.

The first document numbered '1a' was a short letter written in a foreign language which I soon discovered was Portuguese. The next document, '1b', was a translation of the letter which was addressed to the Commissioner of Police for the Metropolis and read.

'Dear Sir,

The President of the Regional Government of Madeira respectfully requests the assistance of the Commissioner in connection with an investigation currently being conducted in the Republic by the Chief Officer of the Judicial Police department.

The investigation concerns a missing British citizen, Mrs Marcella Shannon Parker, who was last seen at the Porto Bay hotel in Funchal on 28th April 2007.

The President requests the appointment of a Metropolitan Police Officer to act as liaison between the law enforcement agencies of our respective countries and invites the appointee at their earliest convenience to attend a meeting at the Portuguese Embassy at 11 Belgravia Square, London. Contact details are overleaf.'

The only other documents were newspaper cuttings provided by Press Bureau.

I read through the minute sheet and discovered that the decision had been made to identify a suitable murder squad detective of at least

Inspector rank. Of course, I was only a Detective Sergeant and the role had originally been offered to my D.C.I. Justin, but it was noted he had a period of leave coming up and he recommended that I be approached and temporarily promoted to Detective Inspector for the duration of the enquiry. The note added that I had recently sat the promotion exam and it was anticipated that I would be successful.

While I was flattered, I immediately realised the financial implications. As a Detective Inspector I wouldn't be able to claim overtime which, even with a small acting up allowance, would still mean I was out of pocket by about five hundred pounds a month, maybe more.

Still, it was great that Justin had thought of me, so I wasn't going to disrespect my D.C.I. by turning down such a wonderful opportunity.

I read everything on the file twice, including the press cuttings, but it still only took me ten minutes.

When I looked up the librarian was standing opposite me. I smiled.

"You okay?" I asked.

She shrugged her shoulders and smiled.

"Have to be, won't I? Found Lord Lucan, yet?"

"Getting really close, any day now." I replied.

"What you gonna do, then?" I asked.

She shrugged her shoulders, again.

"You married?" I asked.

She shook her head.

"With anyone?"

She shook her head, again.

"Lesbian?" I asked.

She nodded.

"Thought so." I replied, with a ridiculously exaggerated nod, as if I'd known all along.

She laughed.

"You always make me laugh." She said and walked away.

The truth was, I had absolutely no idea whether she was being serious or not. It was only then that I realised she'd left a book on the table where she'd been standing. I leant over, picked it up and noticed that it was clearly brand new.

"The Upper Class Conspiracy – the story of Lord Lucan's escape."

I smiled.

Chapter 3

Detective Superintendent Erling Kristiansen led me into the Assistant Commissioner's office and introduced me. The Assistant Commissioner was John King, a tall white male standing more than 6'5" who had a formidable reputation for not suffering fools gladly. He was sitting reading some papers on his desk and didn't look up but waved his hand in the general direction of the coffee table and seating area. As the Detective Superintendent left, I sat down. It was at that point I realised I'd forgotten the coffee.

The rank of Assistant Commissioner only exists in the Metropolitan Police and equates to the Chief Constable of any other force. There are only two ranks above, Deputy Commissioner and Commissioner. As an A.C. you get a courtesy flat in London, a top of the range car and a dedicated driver. You also have a Staff Office, consisting of at least a Superintendent and a Personal Assistant, and often, but not always, an administrative officer to do the mundane jobs like copying and filing. John King was the Assistant Commissioner for Crime and, as such, the most senior detective in the country.

At least ten minutes passed. I spent the time studying the office which was nicely furnished without being opulent. Various 'end of course' photographs were on display and a large poster of Arsenal FC above which was the caption 'Stamp Racism Out'. I gave the A.C. a tick for political correctness.

I was still holding the docket and toyed with the idea of leafing through it once again, if only to make myself feel less awkward about sitting there like a spare phallus at a matrimonial ceremony but decided instead to place the file on the coffee table and act nonchalantly.

Eventually and apparently having completed reading whatever had held his attention for so long, the A.C. stood up and came over.

"Pritchard, yes?"

I was so tempted to respond by saying 'King, yes?' but decided instead to go with the more traditional …

19

"Sir"

"Have you read the papers?" He asked.

"Yes"

"Any reason why you can't undertake this role?"

"No, boss."

"Provide me with a two-page briefing make it no more than a page and a half, every fortnight. You need anything, speak to my staff officer; until further notice, you report to him."

I nodded, deftly.

"Nothing gets leaked to the press, understand?"

"Of course." I replied, with as much indignity as I could muster without being rude.

"And remember, you're representing this country, best behaviour, at all times. You're not having an affair or about to be exposed by the tabloids as being a paedophile, are you?"

I shook my head but the A.C. held my stare and looked deep into my eyes, as if he were trying to assess my character. If I'm being honest, it was a bit dramatic and more than a little ludicrous. Then all of a sudden, his expression changed, and he asked.

"Do I know you?"

"Don't think so, boss. I don't think we've ever met."

"Erling!" The A.C. called out.

His staff officer appeared at the opened door within a few seconds and the A.C. stood up. I did so too, realising our meeting was already at an end.

"Where do I know this officer from? I never forget a face."

Erling shook his head and quickly changed the subject.

"Just had the Commissioner's office on the phone, they want to know whether you've had the QPM?"

I knew the question was for the Assistant Commissioner, but it was too good an opportunity to miss.

"You can tell them I've already got it, but thanks anyway." I said.

For just a microsecond, a horrible moment, I thought I'd really fucked up as both the A.C. and Erling looked at me as if I was a total idiot and then the A.C.s face changed into a smile.

"Of course, you're that guy. You're the guy in the I.R.A. bombing in Stoke Newington. Must be twenty-five years ago, I was at training school when it happened. It had a profound impact on everyone in our class."

Clearly, like almost everyone, the A.C. mistakenly thought I'd been awarded the QPM. for my actions after the bombing but that wasn't correct. I'd got it for something else at about the same time, completely unrelated but it wasn't worth trying to correct the misconception.

"A long time ago, boss. You were at training school after me?" I asked.

He was a good ten years older than I was so I naturally assumed he would have much more service.

"I did ten years in the Paras before I joined the Met. Did you hear what happened with Barry Skinner, the terrorist that got convicted of the Preston Remembrance Day bombing?"

"I did." I replied.

"For murdering three children and seriously injuring a dozen more, he got just two years under the Good Friday agreement. When was the Preston bombing, Erling?"

"Eight-eight, I think." Erling replied.

"I know." I said quietly.

"Well, he also admitted being the Stoke Newington bomber and got another two-year sentence, concurrent." The A.C. added.

"I know. He was charged with the Stoke Newington bombing back in the eighties, but at the voir dire the Judge let him off on a technicality. Something about illegally obtained evidence. He admitted the offence, but the admission was captured on a cell probe and the Judge said because it was before he'd had access to legal advice, the admission couldn't be used in evidence." I explained.

"Listen to this, Pritchard. To cap it all, we've got to provide him with a new identity. You were badly injured, weren't you?"

"I was, boss."

"At training school, you were our complete hero. In fact, I remember now, we started a collection for the WPC's family."

"Dawn Matthews, her name was Dawn Matthews." I said.

"Of course. We lined the route of her funeral procession. The whole of training school from week one to week twenty was used. Full dress uniform, white gloves, everything – it was very moving. Were you there?" He asked.

"No, I was in hospital at the time."

"Yes, of course. You can still see your scar, on your head."

The A.C. held his own finger to his forehead just in case I needed reminding where it was.

"I know." I replied but smiled to indicate I wasn't being sarcastic.

"I still see Dawn's mum." I said.

"Do you?" He replied, appearing quite surprised.

"Every couple of weeks, sometimes less, but as often as I can." I replied.

"Do me a big favour, Chris isn't it? ..."

I nodded.

"... would you ask her if I can go visit her, unofficially?"

"I will, boss, but please don't mention that we're looking after the man that killed her daughter; that would really upset her. I tell you what, boss, Dawn's grave is about a mile down the road from where her mum lives, in Buckhurst Hill, take some flowers to the grave. Mrs Matthews would really appreciate that."

The A.C. turned to Erling.

"Can you arrange that?" He asked.

I felt a sudden anger, a real rush of raw emotion.

"Boss, either do it yourself or don't fucking bother."

I couldn't quite believe what I'd said but the words just came out. For a moment, no one moved, not an inch, it was as if someone had taken a photograph.

I waited for the A.C. to respond. Was I about to be sent back to uniform? He nodded once and, in that gesture, the slightest movement of his head, Assistant Commissioner King both acknowledged and conceded my point.

"I'll leave you the address of the church where she's buried." I said.

"Thank you, yes, of course." The A.C. replied, with more than a hint of contriteness.

"Anyway, back to the matter at hand. We're going to make you a temporary Detective Inspector, get your warrant card changed. We'll also order you an American Express card, for all your expenses. I'll give you carte blanche authority to travel to Portugal. Do you have a valid passport?" He added the question as an afterthought.

"I do." I replied.

Stupid as it seemed, I'd not thought for even a moment that I'd be travelling abroad; I just thought I'd be based in the U.K. This job had just got a lot more interesting.

***

A curious thing happened a few minutes later. I was sitting at the empty desk across from Erling's desk. The A.C. had been called down to see the Deputy Commissioner and the Staff Officer had popped down to the canteen to get a sandwich, leaving me with instructions to answer the phone if it rang and take a message. While I sat there, a white middle-aged officer whom I recognised as being a Commander from the laurel wreaths on his epaulettes, dropped a docket in front of me and said:

'Get the A.C. to sign this off, please."

Before I could say anything, he was gone.

The orange docket had one word on the front 'Expenses' and inside was a VAT receipt from the Caxton Wine Bar for seven hundred and fifty pounds. Attached to the receipt by a staple was a completed expense claim form 290 and an American Express credit card receipt for the same amount. Neither of these receipts listed what had been purchased but sitting loosely in the docket was the itemised bill. This was dated the previous day, for a table of seven and on it recorded a long list of alcoholic drinks, including six bottles of house champagne.

It didn't take a detective to work out what was going on. The senior officers had obviously been out on the piss and put it all on expenses. The irony was that as a police officer you weren't meant to even enter licenced premises, let alone drink on duty. I suspected that the A.C. had also been there, otherwise why would he be happy to sign it off?

Chapter 4

The meeting at the Portuguese Embassy was something I shall never forget. I was treated like a member of the royal family and introduced to the Ambassador herself. She was a lady in her late fifties with perfect poise, exuded class with every mannerism and who spoke perfect English but with a continental twirl that added a flair usually so absent in my native tongue. I felt intimidated but adopted the approach that the less I said, the less stupid I would appear. I think it worked.

After the meeting with the Ambassador, I was led into a side room where I met two male officers from Madeira, Adao Silva and Vincent Ferreira; both spoke reasonable English. They said they were from the Ministerio da Justica, which even I could work out to be the Ministry of Justice.

They had prepared a PowerPoint presentation on the case which contained photographs of the hotel and the victim's room, a map of the Island and photographs of all the main players; they delivered this slowly and carefully. Adao managed the laptop while Vincent read from a briefing sheet.

"The victim was a forty-five-year-old white female of British nationality; her name was Marcella Shannon Parker; her maiden name was Clifford. She lived on the outskirts of London in a village called Theydon Bois with her husband, Tristram; they had no children.

On 21st April 2007 the victim and three friends, Cheryl Penn, Lesley Gatz and Natasha Murray, flew to Madeira on holiday where they spent seven nights at the Porto Mare hotel, a luxury four-star resort located two miles west of the capital, Funchal. Their holiday appears to have been uneventful.

They were scheduled to fly back at 1100 hours on 28th April and had ordered a taxi for 0815 hours at the hotel to take them to the airport. Three of the four women met in reception at eight, but the victim did not appear. They called her mobile phone but after several rings, it went to voicemail. At 0825 hours, at the request of Cheryl, the lady working at reception rang Marcella's room but there was no reply. Lesley and Natasha took the taxi and Cheryl went to the room to get Marcella up, assuming she had overslept. Cheryl in fact ordered a second taxi before going to find her friend.

When she couldn't get a reply, Cheryl got a maid to open the door, but the room was empty. The bed had apparently been slept in and most of her belongings had been packed ready for departure. The victim's passport and purse were on the dressing table.

According to the hotel staff, at first Cheryl didn't seem overly anxious and just thought her friend would soon appear. After half an hour, Cheryl started to ask the whereabouts of a waiter called Miguel, and it didn't take long for the staff to put two and two together and work out that Cheryl thought the victim might have gone back to the waiter's room for sex. Just to complicate matters, the waiter didn't live in the hotel but in an apartment block about five miles away in a place called Camara de Lobos and he used a motorbike to get to and from work. The hotel dispatched one of the kitchen staff to his address with orders to bring him straight back.

In the meantime, Lesley and Natasha flew home without their two friends.

Several hours later, the waiter, who in fact hadn't gone home but to a friend's address instead, came into work and the hotel Manager took him to one side to question him. The waiter claimed to have spent the night with his girlfriend and to know absolutely nothing about the victim, other than to say he recalled her and her friends drinking in the bar the previous evening.

A thorough search of the hotel was conducted and then at 1520 hours, at just about the same time Lesley and Natasha were landing at Gatwick, the police were called.

By this time and without consulting anyone, the hotel had packed up the victim's belongings, stripped the beds and thoroughly cleaned the victim's room ready for the next guests.

The first officer at the scene, and by chance he was only a few days into his police career, took a missing person's report but didn't initiate any action and even forgot to circulate her description to colleagues.

Cheryl, by now distraught, tried to get hold of the victim's husband, Tristram, but he was travelling back to the U.K. from Malaga, where she believed he'd been on a week's golfing holiday with some friends. All she got was his voicemail service. She hoped that Tristram had heard from his wife but thought that unlikely.

Cheryl then got a taxi to the British Consulate but discovered it had closed at 1530 hours and didn't open until 1400 hours the following day. She returned to the hotel and made such a fuss that the manager again called the police, but they didn't arrive until early evening. It was a different officer this time, but he didn't take the matter particularly seriously, either. He did, however, circulate the victim's description, check the Missing Persons/Bodies Found Register, and contact immigration to ascertain whether she had left the country. Of course, that was highly unlikely as her passport was still at the hotel.

It was nearly midnight when Cheryl eventually contacted Tristram. He flew out to Madeira the following day. Both were subsequently interviewed by the police.

There being nothing else they could do on the island, Cheryl and Tristram flew back to the U.K. on 1st May 2007.

On that day the case was formally reclassified from a missing person enquiry to a criminal investigation and two detectives assigned to the case.

For two nights, new guests had been staying in Marcella's hotel room, so there was little point in conducting a forensic search, but they did so, nonetheless. They found traces of what could be blood on the carpet, not much, but enough to suggest someone had bled from a reasonably large cut. The sample was being tested at the laboratory.

The detectives thoroughly searched Marcella's luggage, and everything appeared to be where it should; no clues were found to assist the investigation.

Their enquiries with immigration confirmed that Marcella Parker entered the country on 21st April but there was no record of her leaving.

The police interviewed other hotel guests, although by then a great many who had been staying at the same time as the victim, had already left. The police also checked the hotel records on the night of the victim's disappearance to identify other potential suspects, without success."

I listened attentively to the presentation and made copious scribbles, so indecipherable that they would mean nothing to anyone else but me.

From the interactions between them, I worked out that Vincent was the senior of the two; his English was also better. I was also pleasantly surprised that they were quite candid about the initial failings that had been made. I had no criticism of them, the same could easily have happened in London, if a Portuguese tourist had gone missing. I wouldn't expect for one moment that we'd have immediately treated it like a murder investigation.

"Any blood pattern analysis?" I asked.

But both detectives clearly didn't understand the question, so I moved on.

"Have you done any financial enquiries?" I asked.

They had a brief conversation between them in Portuguese and then Vincent replied.

"No, because we have the wallet which has in it her credit cards."

"Off the record ..."

Adao quickly whispered something, and Vincent replied, and I guessed that Adao hadn't understood what I'd said and needed his partner to translate. He then nodded to me, as if to say, go on.

"Unofficially ..."

They did that whisper thing again and it was then I realised I needed to start using shorter words. The briefing, which was in near perfect English, had been read from a prepared script and did not reflect their own grasp of my language.

"Have you any idea what might have happened to her?" I asked, eventually.

They spoke together again, but this time for longer.

"We think she was taken from her room by force. At the start, we thought, maybe a kidnap. Because her husband, he has the money. But there was no asking for the money, no telephone call, nothing. Miss Marcella, she is dead. Thrown from the rocks in the north into the sea."

"In England, the newspapers say her husband, he had her murdered. What do you think?" I asked.

Vincent nodded.

"Now, we think, too." He replied.

"Why?"

"If no kidnap, why would anyone on the island want her dead? No one knows her. She not beautiful young girl, no rape, no stealing. The reason for what happened, it is here in England, not on the island."

I really couldn't argue with his logic.

Chapter 5

The thing was, over the years I had dealt with a few 'foreign' murders, and they were almost impossible to solve. In the last one, there was a big dispute in an extended family that mainly lived in Pakistan, but the quarrel culminated in the murder of one of the more distant cousins who ran a small grocery shop in Roehampton. At first, we treated the crime as a robbery that had gone wrong but as the months became years, we started to home in on the real motive, the family argument. Although, by then the investigative momentum had been lost and the clues were cold. Eventually, we were informed that the murderer had paid off the victim's family with a twenty grand compensation payment, so even they lost interest in assisting us and the case remains unsolved to this day.

I completely understood why my Portuguese colleagues thought this was unrelated to anything on their island, but I didn't necessarily agree, well not one hundred percent. The factor worrying me was Miguel, the waiter. While he might be completely innocent, I wanted to know how much investigation had been undertaken into his alibi. Had they done cell site on his phone? Had they interviewed his girlfriend? Had they conducted house to house at both his home address and his girlfriends? Did he have any previous convictions? Was there any intelligence suggesting criminality? Was the hotel aware of any occasions when he'd had a relationship with a guest? If this was my investigation then Miguel would be an early suspect, but it wasn't my case, so I had to go with the flow. What's more, I felt that so early in our relationship I couldn't go suggesting to them what they should be doing or thinking. I kept my mouth shut and my powder dry.

Within forty-eight hours of being assigned the case, I had a pass to the Portuguese Embassy, a Met American Express card, a MPS laptop and SIM card, and a warrant card that read 'Detective Inspector'. All of a sudden, I felt like I had a bit of a life back. That was one thing I really loved about the Job; you never quite knew what was coming next.

Just to bring me back to reality however, I received a phone call from Justin, my D.C.I., to remind me that I had agreed to sort out the property store at Arbour Square. I must confess to being less than enthusiastic, but a deal was a deal and I promised my boss to get over there in the next couple of weeks.

The Portuguese detectives asked me to interview Lesley and Natasha and gave me the statements from Cheryl and Tristram.

Cheryl's statement only went to four pages, which I thought was very short under the circumstances, and it didn't really contain any additional information to that which I had already received during the presentation.

Tristram's statement ran to a more credible ten pages and I spent the best part of the next day going through it with a fine-tooth comb. Most of the statement went into his background, domestic circumstances, his business, and family history.

Contrary to what the newspapers had said, Tristram was not an investment banker, he was in fact a hedge fund manager. Back in '98, he'd inherited £3 million from a distant relative which he used to set up his business, Skimmia Investments. Nearly 10 years later, the fund was worth over £700 million. Of course, this was client and company money not his own, but in his statement, he claimed to possess a personal wealth in the region of £75 million. His company was based in Canary Wharf and employed about sixty staff but the headquarters for tax purposes was in Gibraltar.

On the same day that his wife went to Madeira, according to his statement, Tristram flew from Stansted airport to Malaga to go on a golfing holiday with some friends.

The first time he knew anything was wrong was after he returned to the UK on the 28th and picked up a voicemail from Cheryl which asked him to contact her immediately. He called her back straight away and when he found out what was going on, made the necessary arrangements to fly out to Funchal the following day. Cheryl met him at the airport, and they went straight to the hotel. Tristram was surprised that the police weren't taking the matter seriously and he made several phone calls to 'people' back in London and, all of a sudden, the diplomats in Lisbon started to take the matter more seriously. Tristram also engaged a lawyer, a move which immediately aroused suspicion in the mind of the Portuguese detectives.

To make matters worse, halfway through his statement Tristram changed a significant part of his story. He had at first maintained the account that he was in Malaga on a golfing holiday with some friends but as the hours and days rolled by, Tristram realised that he'd have to come clean and admitted that he was in fact on holiday with his girlfriend. There were no mates and there was no golfing holiday - it was all a ruse so he could get a week away with his mystery. I don't think this endeared him to the two Portuguese detectives, who were, no doubt, devout Catholics, and good family men.

The girlfriend's name was Sonia Nicholson and she worked for a car dealership. No doubt I would be meeting her in due course, but I was a little surprised they didn't want me to see her sooner, rather than later.

I got the distinct impression that my Portuguese colleagues thought he was responsible. Things certainly didn't look good for the hedge fund manager.

Chapter 6

That afternoon was meant to be the office lunch, a quarterly ritual where everyone gets drunk, offends one another and, if you're lucky, avoids arrests for assault, drunk and disorderly and criminal damage. At one last year, events really took a turn for the worst. One of the DCs, a young lad called Kier, came straight to the restaurant from court, which wouldn't normally be a problem, except he was in possession of some exhibits from the case - twenty-two wraps of cocaine which obviously he should have first deposited in the property store. Twelve pints and four large brandies later, Kier thought it would be a good idea to try some of the class 'A' drug but the restaurant owner was less than impressed when he found him snorting the substance in the toilet and called the police. The whole incident had been caught on CCTV. Kier was arrested and subsequently convicted; he only got a bender, but of course, lost his job.

Today's office lunch had been cancelled because of the new job the team had just picked up, so I had the afternoon unexpectedly free. I'd read everything I could, several times, so I jumped in a car and drove over to Theydon Bois to have a look around. All the main players in this case lived in this village. For some years, I'd lived just down the road in Loughton and I'd been to the big pub opposite the village green several times, I think it was called The Victoria. I didn't know anyone who lived there.

I was particularly keen to see where Tristram and Marcella resided. As it transpired, this was at an address without a number, which I always considered to be an indication to expect something substantial. The house was very slightly out of town on the way towards Abridge. I might have had trouble finding it, however, a group of perhaps a dozen photographers were camped up on a small grassy knoll opposite the entrance, which gave the location away. Three T.V. cameras were standing on tripods, all pointing towards the tall gates. A clutch of predominantly white vans were parked on the verge about fifty meters along the road, several had large satellite dishes on their roofs, all pointing in the same direction.

The house itself was set well back from the main road and behind a large wooden fence topped with well-groomed leylandii, and was almost impossible to see, except for a vague outline. I chatted to several of the paparazzi, while holding a red book and pen, and I think they assumed I was from the local rag. One of them let me climb his stepladder for a better view; I was mightily impressed by what I saw.

The house was a new build, a very imposing detached residence over three floors, painted white and light grey. The upper right section of the house was particularly striking as this appeared to be a mezzanine room set over two floors which had elongated windows on three sides so, even from a distance, you could see right through the room. From the outline of the furniture, and in particular one distinctive lamp, that hung over what could have been a draughtsman's drawing board, the room was clearly a very impressive study come office.

I would've guessed there were at least eight bedrooms and my imagination saw a stunning swimming pool and gymnasium on the ground floor. To the right of the main house was a second substantial two-story building, the ground floor of which was three garages.

In the drive were three cars: a black Porsche 911 Carrera, a silver Range Rover Sport and a dark green Bentley Continental. I had to admire his choices, which I thought showed excellent automobile taste.

I didn't know much about house prices at this end of the market, but the place must have been worth an absolute fortune, perhaps somewhere between three and five million.

"Nice drum." The photographer said to me, as I descended his ladder.

He was a short white middle-aged man smoking a cigarette. At his feet were a myriad of cameras and lenses.

"I've seen worse." I replied, sarcastically.

"Not going to be much good to him now though, is it?"

"You reckon he's guilty, do you?" I asked.

"According to my mate's source." He replied.

"Trustworthy, is he?"

"Apparently, the geezer paid an Eastern European hitman to kill his missus. By the time anyone knew she was missing, the hitman was back in Poland counting his money."

I nodded, in a non-committal way.

"Any sign of movement?" He asked me, lighting another cigarette as soon as he'd finished the first.

"No; do you know if he's in there?"

"Saw him in the office earlier, perhaps thirty minutes ago." The man replied.

"Do you want one?" He offered me a cigarette, but I shook my head.

A taller white male joined us, I assumed they were working together, and took the outstretched cigarette that had originally been offered to me.

"You ponce." The shorter guy said.

"You snooze, you lose." The second guy replied.

"I heard the guy's a major drug dealer, and the murder of the wife was revenge for having over some North London crime family." The taller man said, with much conviction.

"He's a banker, isn't he?" I asked, innocently.

"That's how he launders his money, through his bank, or whatever." He replied, as if I was a bit stupid.

"Oh" I replied, as if some great secret had just been explained to me.

A third man joined us, and quickly a fourth and fifth, until we were quite a crowd.

"I heard he's a fraudster, a Ponzi scheme running to billions."

"He was having an affair and he didn't want to give his wife half."

"That's bollocks, it was his wife who was having the affair, that's why he bumped her off."

"I heard he's a distant relative of Winston Churchill, which of course means there's a Princess Diana connection, too."

"The Portuguese police really fucked up, they even cleaned the hotel room and put another guest in before they searched it for forensic evidence."

"Did they find anything?" I asked.

"A blood splattered wall; I heard it from a mate who works on the island."

"I reckon she's done a moonlight flit."

"Why would anyone want to leave all that behind?"

"I heard he did a lot of business with Russians. They're all criminals, well the ones with the money, anyway."

"Money's not everything, besides he was slapping her about."

"That's tragic."

"Is it?"

A round of guilty sniggers circulated.

"Of course, it is, why slap when you can punch?"

The sniggers grew both in volume and guilt.

I felt like I'd slipped back in time about thirty years.

"She's been abducted, raped and then murdered; it's the same old, same old."

"It'll be a stranger, some Madeiran Neanderthal. Wasn't that where the Neanderthals last lived? Madeira?"

"You're thinking of Gibraltar." I said.

"This case reminds me of the Sheffield case, back in 88; remember? The guy who had the yacht?"

On this point at least, everyone seemed to agree.

Two things became clear to me; firstly, these men, and they were all men, although from different media companies, knew each other well; and secondly, they knew absolutely nothing about what had actually happened to Marcella Parker.

I'd kept very quiet but just when the speculation started to wane, the short man who'd lent me his ladder turned to me and asked:

"Who're you with?"

A black Audi saloon pulled up at the gates before I could reply, the crowd dispersed, and cameras started to click in rapid succession. The driver got out and approached the intercom but before he got close enough to speak, the gates started to open, and he jumped back in the car and drove in.

I took the opportunity to slip quietly away. I'd learned precisely nothing from this pack of wolves.

Chapter 7

By the afternoon of the first day, I was sitting in Lesley Gatz's impressive, detached house in Theydon Bois.

Lesley was white, in her late thirties, unexceptional in a pleasant, ordinary sort of way and I took to her immediately. Lesley was tired, like she hadn't slept in weeks. She wore no make-up and her short brown hair looked like it had been somewhat forgotten, but more than anything, she looked sad, truly deeply sorrowful and it came across in everything she said and did.

She lived, as it was to turn out with all the people in this case, in the lap of luxury.

It was hard not to compare my current surroundings with my own humble abode. I lived on a barge called 'Starburst' which was moored in East London. It was nice enough, it was all I could afford after my divorce, but my galley was 8' by 6', so 48 square foot, not the 600 square foot that surrounded me now. I wondered what people did to have such a lovely house. Although more politely phrased, this was one of my first questions.

"I'm a housewife but my husband Keith owns an engineering company. They make components for turbines and other bespoke precision engineering." She spoke, without enthusiasm. I suspected it was an explanation she had recounted a thousand times.

"How did he get into that? Presumably he's got an engineering degree?" I asked.

It's a tactic which most good detectives use, to get your witness to start talking about neutral matters so they relax and don't feel like they're being put under pressure right away. I had a good mate who sold bedrooms and he said the same thing, 'try and find something you and the customer have in common, then talk about that rather than trying to sell'. This approach also gave you an opportunity to get to know your witness's non-verbal communications.

"Oh god no, it was his father's business. Keith left school at sixteen, started at the bottom and worked his way up. His dad had him making the tea and sweeping up the cuttings for the first year."

"Where's his company based?" I asked.

"They've just relocated, used to be based in East London but they're in Harlow now."

We chatted easily about nothing for another few minutes and Lesley's mood seem to lift slightly; then there was the tiniest of pauses as Lesley placed a cup of black coffee on the worktop in front of me.

"Did your husband know Marcella?" I asked, gently coaching the conversation towards the interview.

"He did, but only through me."

"What was Marcella like?" I asked.

I like a nice open question and that was, if I say so myself, just perfect.

"Was? So, you do think she's dead then?"

"We don't have any firm evidence to confirm that, but we have lots of circumstantial that suggests it is unlikely she is still alive." I replied, candidly.

"Couldn't she have been abducted? There was that case in America last year, you know, the fourteen-year-old girl who was kept in a cage by her abductor for fifteen years. It does happen." Lesley said.

"Possibly. We're looking at every possibility." I replied.

"Give me a percentage figure, what are the chances she's still alive?" Lesley demanded, but not in an aggressive way.

I think in some ways she was desperately trying to come to terms with everything.

"Fifteen, maybe twenty." I replied.

Lesley started to cry. I looked at the floor. As she wiped her tears away with tissues from a nearby box, she spoke through her sobs.

"I, I just can't believe I didn't realise something was wrong; can't believe I came back and left her there. I'll never get over the guilt. I know that's what everyone in the village is thinking."

"Tell me what happened that morning, the morning she went missing?" I asked.

"Well, it all happened so quickly really. We were in the lobby waiting for her; the taxi was there. We rang her mobile, but it went straight to voicemail. We got the woman on reception to ring the phone in her room, but she didn't answer. It was getting later and later and stupidly we'd not left ourselves a great deal of extra time. Cheryl said she'd go and get her and that we should take the taxi that was there, get in the queue at the airport, and her and Marcella would get another cab and join us in the queue. So that's what we did, except there wasn't a terribly long queue at check-in because we were late anyway and in no time at all we'd checked in. We decided to go through security and wait there, because we wanted to get a coffee and something to eat. Natasha and I kept calling Cheryl, the first few times she didn't answer and then when she did, she said she couldn't find Marcella anywhere. In no time at all, we had to decide, whether to board or stay and that would mean getting our bags unloaded and going back through customs. We spoke to the girl at the gate; she said we wouldn't be allowed to do that and that we had to get on the plane. And the rest is, well, history. The thing is, at every stage we genuinely thought Marcella and Cheryl would only be a few minutes behind us. We never thought, until right at the end, we'd be leaving Madeira without them, but even then, we thought they'd just be on the next plane or one tomorrow."

"Did you speculate as to where Marcella might be?" I asked.

Lesley took a deep breath and didn't answer immediately. She stared into her coffee cup. I knew only too well to let the silence hang.

"We thought she'd got off with the waiter." She replied, eventually.

"Okay" I replied.

"She'd been flirting with him all week; he was only a young guy, perhaps twenty-four, but she reckoned he looked a bit like some famous Spanish footballer who I'd never heard of. All week she said she was going to get him into bed on the last night, you know, she didn't want to do anything before then because she said it would lead to complications with him following her around the resort like a puppy, you know, if she made her move any sooner – she was only joking. She was only joking about the whole thing, really. But on the last night she dropped him a ridiculously big tip. We thought it was hilarious. But then you think a lot of things are hilarious when you've had a bit too much to drink, don't you? Of course, when she failed to show the next morning, it didn't take us long to conclude that they'd got off together; maybe even ended up in his room, or house, or flat or wherever he lived."

"So, were you a bit miffed with her?"

Lesley shook her head guiltily with a 'don't I feel like a piece of shit now' expression on her face. I had thought it strange that they'd come home without their friend but now she'd explained how the morning played out, it made perfect sense.

"The rest of the week, before the last evening, how was that?" I asked.

"Perfectly normal; we go away every year, it must have been the tenth time, maybe more. We went to Krakow last year, Prague the year before. We've been to Riga, Paris, Lisbon, and Barcelona. This year we just fancied a week in the sun."

"Had you been to Madeira before?"

"No, though I think Marcella had been there a few years ago on a cruise. No one else had. My parents have been, and they rave about the place. In fact, they recommended the hotel. It was lovely."

"Have you got any children?" I asked.

"Me? No. As you probably know, neither has Marcella. Natasha has two boys, twins in their late teens, but they're not hers, she's the step mum, and Cheryl has a daughter who's twelve. She was with her grandparents last week."

"So, what did you get up to, in Madeira?"

"We spent most of the time around the pool and went into town during the evening for a meal and a few drinks and then back to the hotel for a nightcap. Honestly, nothing of any significance happened. We had too much to eat, too much to drink. We read and relaxed and moaned about our fantastic lives. What else do you do?"

"Did you all get on?"

"Of course, we're not teenage girls. Yes, we used to moan because Natasha was always late. I got a little bit too drunk, most nights. Marcella packed way too much so her suitcases weighed in over her allowance at check in which caused no end of problems at the airport: Cheryl was the sensible one, always is. She organises everything and makes sure we find our way home but really, it wasn't rock and roll. It was just four middle aged women having a week in the sun."

"Does anyone else know about the waiter? Do you know whether Marcella met up with him?"

"I don't think so. I'm sure Cheryl would have told the police as soon as she spoke to them."

"But you don't know that for a fact?" I asked, a little surprised.

I'd assumed all three women had been in almost constant contact.

"I've spoken to Natasha, mainly. We haven't met up since we got back and if I'm being honest, I think we're all too stressed. Besides, it's a bit embarrassing, isn't it? You know, forty plus something married woman fancying a young waiter. Very Shirley Valentine."

"What do you know about Marcella's marriage? I mean, not what you've read in the papers. What did you know before all this happened?"

"Their marriage wasn't perfect, but then whose is? But she had a pretty fantastic life, so she put up with any downsides. Did she love him? No, probably not. Did she like him? Not a great deal. Did she want to leave him? I don't think so. Did they get on? Seemed to. If you saw them together, you'd think they were the perfectly normal couple. Marcella is …"

Lesley paused.

"… , was, really attractive. I mean, men would stare. Tristram's a good looking fellow, they were like Theydon Bois's Posh and Becks. Not so much these days, but ten years ago. They were comfortable financially, even by the standards of this village. Have you seen their house?"

"Kind of; well from a distance." I replied.

"Well wait until you do; and remember, there's just the two of them. Why would anyone want out of that situation? No, Marcella wasn't truly happy, but she wasn't doing too badly by any stretch of the imagination."

"You've read the papers?"

Lesley nodded.

"Do you think that Tristram had her murdered?"

"Well, assuming she didn't end up with the waiter that night; and if she had, it would have been the first time she'd have done anything like that in all the years we've been going away, I just don't know what could have happened to her? Although Tristram is an arrogant, male chauvinist pig – I never imagined he could do that. But then, I never thought Marcella would want a night of passion with a greasy waiter, so quite frankly, you should just ignore everything I say."

"Does your husband know Tristram?" I asked.

"Keith? Yes, but they aren't close. Tristram helped him with some investments last year. Something to do with shares and dividends, I think." She replied.

I spent the best part of two days interviewing Lesley and ended up taking a long statement. There really wasn't any clue as to what had happened to Marcella. Their week on holiday had been remarkably unremarkable. There was no grand revelation of secrets, no one was sleeping with someone they shouldn't be, no one was either desperately happy or dreadfully sad. What was clear was that although all four were good mates, Marcella and Cheryl were best friends, and Lesley and Natasha were best friends.

Could any of the women have been involved in the disappearance and murder? It seemed highly unlikely to me.

Chapter 8

Theydon Bois wasn't far from Buckhurst Hill, so when I'd finished with Lesley, I drove to see Mrs M.

Mrs M, or rather Mrs Matthews, who was Dawn's mother. Back in 1983, Dawn was my Street Duties Instructor, and she was killed by an I.R.A. bomb in the Arndale Shopping Centre in Stoke Newington. I was injured in the explosion but survived. Since then, Mrs M and I have been close.

Even though it was gone nine, I knew Mrs M wouldn't mind me calling but just so she didn't get worried I dropped her a text message to let her know I was on the way round. When I arrived, the front door was ajar and a cup of tea brewing in the kitchen. Mrs M was in what she always used to call, 'slops', that is to say, an old T shirt and tracksuit trousers. She was in fact not as old as one would have thought, as she'd had Dawn very young, but our relationship was maternal and that was exactly how we both liked it.

"I spoke to an Assistant Commissioner this morning, his name's Alan King, he wants to come and visit you. Would that be okay?" I asked, as I settled into my favourite spot on the settee.

"I met him about an entirely unrelated matter. He recognised me and then the conversation moved onto Dawn, and I mentioned that we were still friends."

"Friends?" Mrs M looked hurt.

"You know what I mean." I said, but obviously I'd disappointed Mrs M by choosing such an ordinary word.

"Anyway, he remembers the incident well and said he'd like to come and see you. He's a well-respected guy. It's nothing to do with him, what happened with Skinner, you know that, don't you? I'll tell you what though, you could use it as a chance to get it off your chest and have a right moan."

Mrs M shrugged her shoulders with a heavy degree of resignation.

"He can come if he wants; I'll have to tidy up a bit."

I looked around the living room, it was immaculate.

"Yeah, its's a right state, this place, you've really let it go."

Mrs M smiled; it was nice.

"I'm glad you've come around, I wanted to ask you something."

"Go on?"

"You're still living on the boat?"

I nodded.

"How's that going?"

"It's alright; it's all I can afford. It's better in the summer, winters are cold and damp and drying washing is a nightmare."

I thought I'd try to make Mrs M smile again.

"Look Mrs M, if you want to move in, you'd more than welcome on Starburst but I have to warn you, I'm pretty certain I snore and we're going to be sharing a very small double bed."

"We've done that before, darling."

I was quite taken aback. Many, many years ago we'd spent a night together, but we'd never mentioned or even alluded to it before. Mrs M was being quite daring.

"So, when are you moving in, then?" I said in a mock upbeat attitude, trying to ignore the reference to our secret liaison.

Mrs M smiled at me, like only she could smile at me. It made me feel warm inside.

"I think you should sell the boat and move in with me, permanently. You'll be nearer to your girls, too. I don't want any rent, just pay a bit towards your food. I'll cook for you; I'll do all your washing and ironing. And, I've not just thought of this, I've been thinking of this for years. Of course, if the idea isn't going to work for you, just say no. If you need time to think it over, that's fine."

I thought it was a great idea but there were one or two issues.

"What if I want to bring home a couple of gorgeous young blondes for a night of passion?"

"I thought you might ask that…"

Mrs M replied.

"… listen, you can bring home anyone you want, as often as you want. This will be your home."

"Are you sure?" I asked.

"Look, you're in your forties, I very much doubt it'll be a different woman every night …"

Mrs M paused.

"… or indeed every week, or month, or year."

She laughed out loud.

"I wouldn't be so sure, I mean …"

"Alright, be honest, Chris, when was the last time you had a proper relationship? Now, hang on, let me rephrase that. When was the last time you had any relationship?"

"You know." I replied.

"Wendy?"

I nodded.

Wendy had been my girlfriend and when my wife, Jackie, chucked me out, I moved straight in with her. Wendy had just fallen pregnant with someone else's baby but that's another story. At the first scan, she learned the foetus had died at about six weeks. That was really the end of our relationship. Within a couple of months, she'd started seeing her best mate's brother who was able to give her the family I couldn't, and she consigned me to the history books. I don't blame her, but it hurt.

There was barely a day that went by when I didn't think about her and I followed her life through information from mutual friends and contacts. Just occasionally, I saw her photograph in a job publication or I'd catch a glimpse of her at the Yard and my heart raced with more excitement than a seven-year-old waking up on Christmas morning.

It was sad and pathetic, and I hated myself for being so unable to move on. I think it's one of the reasons I've never found or even gone seeking anyone else because I just couldn't face being dumped again. In fact, now I come to think of it, every woman I've ever loved had left me – Dawn, Carol, Sarah, Jackie and finally Wendy!

"You really loved her, didn't you? I never met her, did I?"

"I could hardly introduce you two, could I? I was married to Jackie; you came to our wedding. You sat at the top table." I replied.

"I know …" Mrs M replied, gently.

"… but now I wish I'd met her. Life's too short, you have to do everything you can while you can."

"Ain't that true." I said, reflectingly.

"So, Christopher Pritchard, what's it going to be? Are you going to move back in with Mum?"

I laughed gently at Mrs M's use of the word 'Mum'. She'd never used it before but in reality, that's what she had been to me for the last twenty plus years. I had lost my own Mum when I was eighteen and Mrs M was a pretty good replacement. If I'm being honest, she was probably better than the original.

"I'd love to, Mrs M." I replied.

"Sorry?" She said.

"I'd love to, Mum."

She smiled.

"That's better."

***

Unless you'd been through what Mrs M and I had experienced, it's difficult to understand how natural it felt to move in with 'mum'. She'd lost her daughter at twenty-four, in the most awful circumstances. A daughter who, only two years before, had survived cancer that was, according to doctors, ninety percent certain to take her life.

I was an only child whose father died before I was born. My mother never recovered from my father's death, and over the next eighteen years, drank herself to death. Did she love me completely? Ever and always. Was she a good mother? Not really. As a consequence, I largely brought myself up, getting off to school when mum was still hungover in bed, and cooking for us both, when mum was in her late-afternoon drunken stupor. Only the family of an alcoholic can truly understand what I mean by the term 'late-afternoon stupor'.

It took me just a millionth of a second to take Mrs M up on her offer. Why wouldn't I? From October to April, I froze my bollocks off in my floating fridge. I was lonely, bored and generally pretty pissed off with the way my life had turned out. I had nothing except my job. As a result, I prided myself on being, or rather striving to be, the best detective in the Metropolitan Police. Of course, I wasn't, but I was a bloody good one.

In my private life, Mrs M had been the one constant. She had outlasted my family, partners, and friends – she was my North Star, always there and forever constant. I loved her like a mother, I can say no more.

As I drove home that night, I felt happier than I had in years. I knew I would take a loss on the barge. I'd paid eighty thousand but now I was selling, I'd be lucky to see sixty. Such is the way of the world. But I didn't care. I would have a home, and I'd be home, in that small corner of south-west Essex that I knew so well.

Despite what Mrs M had said, I wouldn't feel comfortable taking a woman home but that really was a moot point. I hadn't taken a woman back to Starburst in the four years I'd been living onboard, and I didn't suspect that anything was going to change any day soon.

It's funny how things turn. How the most ordinary day can hide a series of surprises and a wonder of new opportunities. They don't happen very often, perhaps half a dozen times in your life. But in the last two days I had a new job, a new home and possibly a new date. Well fuck me, my life was looking up.

Chapter 9

When I got back to Starburst the first thing I did, it was always the first thing I did, was to light the gas stove. This was the most effective way of heating the barge and, even though it was nearly summer, the weather was cold and miserable. I opened a litre bottle of supermarket branded scotch and poured a large glass. In fact, there were probably five pub measures and I topped it up with an equal amount of water until the tumbler was reassuringly half full. This was the very best part of any day; those few seconds before putting the glass to my lips. It reminded me of darker days, when I got a similar thrill out of preparing my first hit of H. But before I could raise the glass to my lips, there was a rock which indicated someone had stepped onto the side of my barge and a few moments later a timid, 'Hello, Chris', from the stern.

I recognised the voice immediately; it was Jackie, my ex.

Jackie and I had been happily married for about ten years and we had two lovely girls, Pippa and Trudy, who were now eighteen and sixteen. She'd kicked me out for a number of reasons, all valid. First, she thought I was still on the gear, although, ironically, I had just given up and had remained clean since; secondly, she knew I was over the side with Wendy; and, thirdly, she'd started a same sex relationship with a local gym owner, a female called George, who was, quite frankly, absolutely lovely. After we separated, we got on surprisingly well and still maintained a sort of love for one another which existed to that day. The divorce had killed me financially, which is why I was living on a barge, but I wasn't the only police officer to find himself in this position and besides, by and large I'd deserved it.

But Jackie's unsolicited and unannounced visit was very unusual, and it could only mean something quite serious was up. It didn't take me long to find out - George and her were splitting up.

"I was starting to have my suspicions ..." Jackie explained, sitting on my small couch with a cup of hot steaming tea in her hand.

"... so, I started checking up on her."

"What, like following her around?" I said.

"More like going through her computer and her phone, although she rarely leaves that unlocked. That was a big clue, I mean, she never used to have a lock on her phone. I can't really follow her, she owns like six gyms now, and they're all over the place."

"She's done well, hasn't she? I saw an article about her in a London magazine a few months ago." I said.

"She has, she's worth like three million, well her business is. In fact, she wanted me to give up nursing and just keep the home. I'm bloody glad I didn't do that, now."

"So? What's happened?"

"Well yesterday, when she was in the shower, I went through her handbag and found a rent book for a flat in Blackwell, just down the road from here."

"Whose name was the rent book in?" I asked.

"Brittany Styles"

"And when was the first entry?"

"In March this year, and fifteen hundred pounds a bloody month!"

"Ok, you can't know anything for sure, there might be an innocent explanation." I said.

"I do and there isn't." Jackie replied.

"Go on …"

"I've just knocked on her door."

"Oh, so that's why you're here, because it's just down the road."

"No, I came here first, but you weren't in. I texted you but you ignored me."

It was only then that I remembered I had seen a text from Jackie when I was at Mrs M's, but I'd ignored it because I thought I'd just call her tomorrow."

"I wanted you to come with me, you know, to the address."

"Oh …" I replied, but I was grateful she'd gone without me because the last thing I needed was to get involved in some domestic involving my ex and her lesbian lover's mystery.

"What happened, Jackie?"

"Well, it turns out Brittany is a nineteen-year-old, size zero, apprentice fitness instructor working at George's latest gym in Canary Wharf. She's young and pretty and everything I'm not. I can't compete with her."

"What did you say? How did it go?"

"It was the briefest of doorstep conversations. She said she knew who I was; that George told her I'd never find out; that they were completely in love; and George had promised her that one day they'd be together. To cap it all, she said, if I didn't leave she'd call …"

Jackie started to cry, so I leaned into her and pulled her head to my chest while simultaneously taking the cup of tea from her and putting it on the coffee table. I was quite impressed to pull off such a difficult manoeuvre with such aplomb.

"Was that it?"

She nodded.

"You did the right thing, getting out before she called the police." I said.

"Bloody hell, Chris, she wasn't going to call the police; she was going to call her dad!"

"Oh" I said, perhaps with too much ironic humour.

"How humiliating was that? I feel like I've been kicked in the stomach. The love of my life is seeing someone so young that they're going to call their dad on me!"

"How old is George?" I asked.

"Thirty-seven; she's six years younger than me."

"Does George know what you've done?" I asked.

"I've texted her and given her twenty-four hours to get out of the house."

"Has she responded?"

Jackie felt in her coat pocket, retrieved her phone, punched a few numbers, and handed it to me. I read a message from George.

How dare you confront Brittany like that, go within a mile of her again and I'll get an injunction against you. I'll be out of your house and your life by midday tomorrow. Never contact me again!

"Fuck me!" Was all I could say.

It probably sounds like hindsight, but I'd never liked George just because she was incredibly hard. And it seemed to me, the more successful she became, the more ruthless she became. With that said, I'd probably only met her about three times in the last two years.

"Are the girls at home?" I said.

"No Pippa is at her boyfriend's and Trudy is away with school for the pre-GCSE study week, remember?"

I nodded.

"You wanna stay here the night?"

She nodded.

"You have the bed. I'll kip down on the settee." I suggested.

She nodded, again.

"Can you take some time off, Chris. You know, spend the next week or so with me? Right now, I could really do with a friend."

Chapter 10

Sometimes it's difficult for civvies to understand. I wanted to, I really did, but I just couldn't take any time off. Was I meant to say to Assistant Commissioner King, or for that matter my Portuguese colleagues, 'oh I know this is really important, but I've got to take a week off because the ex has a few domestics'?

I did explain to Jackie what was going on, and I did say I would try to catch up with her at the end of each day, but that was as far as I could commit. She did say something that was good to hear. She said the girls wouldn't miss George like they missed me when I left. That was probably the nicest thing Jackie had said to me in a long time.

I drove over to Theydon Bois to take my second statement of the enquiry; this time from Natasha Murray who was everything I hadn't expected; six foot two tall and proud of it, full-bosomed and larger than life in every sense. She had bright purple, perfectly maintained hair, brilliantly white teeth and a sunbed tan which had a hint of orange.

Most surprisingly of all, when we met and I offered the usual handshake, she ignored my protruding arm and instead hugged me like a long-lost friend.

"Oh, my darling, Lesley has told me all about you and what you're doing. Isn't it just the most awfulest business, ever? Come in, come in, come in."

Natasha lived about half a mile from her best friend. She also lived in what estate agents would probably describe as a substantial and contemporary family residence offering in excess of 5,000 square foot of ultra-modern living space. From the family portrait that dominated the living room, Natasha's old man, Graham, was considerably older, perhaps in his late fifties, whereas Natasha was at the most, in her mid-forties.

"Lesley tells me you've got two boys." I said.

As usual, I wanted a bit of time to talk about anything except the actual reason I was there.

"Yes, the twins, Steven and Sebastian. They're off to Uni next month, I shall miss them dreadfully, the house will seem so empty. Do you have any children, Christopher?"

The conversation waxed and waned about children, marriage and divorce for longer than I'd intended but it didn't matter. Natasha had a lovely way about her, as if she was genuinely interested in my life. I soon found myself enjoying her company. Perhaps it was an indication that I was missing something, or rather someone, in my own life? Anyone coming in part way through our chat would never have guessed that I was meant to be there to interview her about her missing, probably murdered, friend.

Eventually, I steered the subject back to the matter at hand.

"Tell me about Marcella?"

"She was wonderful, honey. The perfect woman, beautiful, intelligent, really very intelligent. Funny, oh my god, she was so funny. I'm not sure about Tristram if I'm being honest, bit aloof, too full of his own importance."

"Have you seen what the papers are saying?"

"Of course."

"Do you think he's got anything to do with it?" I asked.

Natasha turned her nose up like there was a bad smell. I didn't know quite how to interpret the gesture.

"Is that you don't like him, or you don't think he could have done it?" I asked.

"I don't like him, Marcella's way too good for him. But how on earth my dear, would he arrange to have her killed while she was on holiday in a small island in the middle of nowhere? I mean, why not have her done in in the UK? Wouldn't that be simpler?"

That thought had crossed my mind, too; but the more I turned the whole thing over, the more I saw the advantages of having it done abroad. The most obvious being the incompetence of the local police. The local detectives, called the PJ or Judicial Police, just weren't used to dealing with murders. From my initial research I'd learnt that London traditionally has more murders than the country of Portugal, so I could only guess that murders in Madeira were extremely rare. What's more, the language and cultural differences and the lack of local CCTV coverage would certainly hinder any investigation. If the murderer flew in and out on a false passport, he could be anywhere in Europe by the time anyone realised there was a crime to investigate. I could therefore understand why a smart person would choose such a course of action. That didn't make Tristram guilty, but it kept him in the frame. I kept these thoughts to myself.

"Weren't you worried when Marcella failed to appear that morning?" I asked.

I knew the answer, and no doubt Lesley had told Natasha what she'd told me, but I still had to ask the question.

"My darling, Christopher, I thought she might have had some male company. She'd been getting on really well with the young bar guy, I thought, well, perhaps … well, you're a man of the world. And now of course, well, you've read the papers."

The 'papers' had referenced a long running affair Tristram had had with a Canary Wharf colleague; they'd said nothing about anyone else. I thought Natasha might have let something slip but decided to pop the information in my back pocket, for now.

"Even if she had spent the night with someone, shouldn't she have been ready to set off for the airport on time?" I asked.

"Absolutely, darling; very bad form to keep everyone waiting. But we weren't worried. Didn't think, 'gosh she's late she must have been abducted and murdered during the night'. Thought, Cheryl and her would catch us up at the airport. Then thought they'd be on the next flight. Never thought …"

Her sentence didn't need finishing.

"Tell me about the week itself?"

"Good, we had a lovely time. We go away every year, Christopher, must be our tenth trip, maybe more."

"Any arguments or disagreements?"

"Officer, you're not really suggesting one of us killed her, are you?"

"Of course not, but I need to ask these questions, I'm sure you understand." I replied.

"I understand, of course, I'm only teasing. No, we got on fabulously, always do."

"What will you miss most about Marcella?"

I knew that question wasn't in any Murder Investigation manual and inside a small part of me cringed. I had anticipated a quick spontaneous response, but Natasha was carefully considering her answer, like a contestant going for a million pounds on Chris Tarrant's quiz show.

"Her advice, yeah, her advice. Marcella was super smart, brighter than any of us, brighter than her husband, even; not that he'd ever admit that. If I needed a really sound, unemotional opinion on what I should do, I'd call her. She was great at working things out, just from the merest hint or clue, do you understand?"

"Give me an example?"

"Ok, if we were at a party, she might perhaps notice that my husband made eye contact with another guest across the room, and I'm not talking about an attractive female, let's just say another bloke that he shouldn't really know. Well, then later something else would happen and I'd be like 'my giddy aunt, what's going on?' and Marcella would say 'I reckon this or that because blah blah blah' and invariably she'd be spot on. I'm not explaining myself very well …"

"No, Natasha, you have, I get it, I really do."

"She was good at working out why people did certain things, things that didn't seem to make any sense."

It wasn't quite the response I'd anticipated when I asked my question. I was trying to solicit an emotional reaction; instead, I got a clinical one, but the reply was nonetheless illuminating.

"Can I ask you a question, Christopher?"

"Of course." I replied.

"Do we know for certain it wasn't the waiter?"

"I assume so. Bear in mind, I only picked this case up a couple of days ago and haven't seen all the details of the investigation that's been done in Portugal, so I'm a little in the dark myself. Are you suggesting Marcella did get off with the waiter?"

"Lesley and I left Marcella and Cheryl to have one last drink, although it wasn't that late we still had some packing to do, so I don't know, what does Cheryl say?" Natasha asked.

"The Portuguese interviewed her. I'd have to check." I replied.

"Although, unlike you two she has already been interviewed, so I assume the waiter thing would have come out then, if there was anything to come out." I replied.

"Have you not spoken to Cheryl since you've got back?" I asked, quite surprised.

"No darling, she's not returned my calls, but I assumed she's just too upset. Her and Marcella were really, really close. I still can't believe this has happened, it's like I'm in a dream, or rather a nightmare. How is it possible that she just disappeared into thin air? Poor girl, just glad she hasn't got any kids. In fact, now I think about it, both her parents are dead too, and she's an only child, good god. No one to mourn her, well, except us."

"What about Tristram, won't he miss her?" I asked.

She shook her head.

"I don't think so; he's free to get on with his life. Oh, he'll go through the motions, but I doubt it'll take long before she's just a dim and distant memory. They didn't have sex, you know."

I shook my head, inferring the thought had never crossed my mind.

"Sex is everything in a marriage. Once the sex stops, you might as well issue the decree nisi. I say to Graham, you can do anything to anyone if I'm involved. I mean, we're not naturally monogamous, are we. That's just a load of claptrap perpetrated by religion in one massive conspiracy to keep us all grumpy and therefore hopeful of a better life when we die. No darling, sex, sex, and more sex."

I was a little taken back, an emotion that my face clearly gave away.

"Gosh, you look shocked, my darling."

"I am not especially shocked. I suppose I'm just surprised that you're telling me. After all, that's quite private."

"And Marcella and Tristram? Did they share your liberal attitude?" I asked.

"I don't think Marcella would have been up for it." Natasha replied.

"Was Marcella faithful to Tristram?" I asked.

"Think so."

"Despite making a play for the waiter?"

"Now you mention it Christopher, that was a little out of character. It had never happened before. Not on any of the previous holidays. But if she wasn't getting it at home, perhaps she suspected Tristram was getting it elsewhere, which he clearly was, and probably just felt like a nice, hard fuck from a young good-looking man. Can't blame her, certainly don't judge her."

"No rumours about her seeing anyone else?"

Natasha shook her head.

"What did you know about Tristram's girlfriend?"

"Only what I've read in the papers. His business takes him away a couple of times a week. He was always over in Amsterdam, or Luxembourg, often went to Moscow, so getting away was easy for him. I suppose he used to take her on those trips, I'm only guessing."

"Did Marcella mention Tristram during the week away?"

Natasha looked like she was thinking hard and then replied:

"No, I don't think she did."

"Did you not spend the whole week moaning about your other halves?" I asked.

"No, not really. My Graham was looking after the twins, not that they need much looking after these days. Keith, that Lesley's husband, was working; he works really long hours, and Cheryl's Lloyd, well, come to think of it, I've no idea what he was up to."

"Did you know Tristram was on a golfing holiday?"

"I think so, darling; he usually goes golfing when we go away. Or of course, perhaps he never did, who knows?" Natasha replied.

"The papers are saying that Marcella does a lot of work for charity, what can you tell me about that? I asked.

"She does. Marcella is a trustee for Clean Water for the World, a charity that she first got involved with when she was at Cambridge University. They started twenty-odd years ago with a couple of dozen shops around East Anglia; you know Norwich, Ipswich, Cambridge. Now they're a worldwide organisation. She does accounts for them, her degree was in Maths, and sometimes flies out to Africa to meet with local officials when they're having trouble getting the money to where it was needed to finance a particular project. It's not a full-time role; she works two weeks a month, something like that, which suits her perfectly. She still earns like seventy-five thousand pounds a year."

"Fucking hell." I said, rather unprofessionally.

"That's not a lot, darling. Not in Theydon Bois world. That's hardly worth getting out of bed for." Natasha said, apparently unaffected by my swearing.

"Does she enjoy it, then?"

"There was a fraud or something a few years ago, some complication or other, and she was interviewed by representatives from the Charity Commission, but I don't know what came of it. Then she had some issue earlier this year, she kept having to go to meet somebody about it, lawyers I assume. When I asked her about it one day, she seemed a bit flustered and changed the subject. I must admit, I thought she might have made some sort of mistake. But she still worked for them after that, so it can't have been too bad."

"What do you think happened to Marcella, then. Give me your best guess?"

"Abducted. Possibly kidnapped" She replied.

"Do you think Tristram was involved?"

Natasha shrugged her shoulders.

"If she wasn't abducted or kidnapped, then perhaps, I suppose. No, actually, no. I don't think he was involved, I take that back."

Was Marcella's disappearance something to do with the charity? Probably not; but I just had the feeling I'd learnt something relevant but, as is often the case, it takes a few days for me to work out exactly what.

Chapter 11

In the late afternoon, I met up with Vincent, the Portuguese police officer, in a coffee shop in Loughton. He was short, perhaps 5'8", of medium build with a dark swarthy complexion and in his early forties. He wore dark trousers and an open neck white shirt, which made him look more like a waiter in the local Italian than a police officer, and I also noticed that he wore a gold crucifix around his neck.

The first few minutes, the queuing, the 'what do you want', 'do you take sugar', 'where shall we sit', stage – was a little awkward but eventually we settled into a far corner, slightly apart from the other customers.

"Where is Adao?" I asked, remembering to keep my words and sentences short.

"He goes back to Madeira because there is, how you say, a movement in the case."

"What's happened?" I asked.

"The laboratorio, they finds the blood in the hotel room. It is Mrs Parkers. On the tapete, the …" He fought to find the right word.

"… the floor."

"The carpet?" I asked.

"Yes."

"How much blood, do you know?"

"Pouca, pouca."

I didn't understand a word of Portuguese, but I thought 'pouca' was probably 'a little'.

"They arrest the waiter; they look in his house for her blood."

That seemed eminently sensible; I just wish they'd done that a little earlier. So far, they'd only treated the waiter as a witness. At last it seemed they were starting to view him as a suspect. Vincent's next line however made me change my thinking.

"The waiter, he not do this."

"No?" I said.

"No, no. Adao knows his family. They good people. His father is a high man. He nice boy. He has girlfriend, they marry next month."

"Are you and Adao from Madeira?" I asked.

"Adao, yes, me, no. I come from Lisbon."

The coffee shop was getting busier and the background noise increasing.

"Where are you staying?" I asked.

Vincent frowned.

"Where your hotel?"

"London" he replied.

"Where in London?" I clarified.

"The middle, Covent Garden underground. The Waldorf."

"Very nice." I said, guessing that was over three hundred pounds a night.

A group of young men who were standing in the queue were starting to get very rowdy. There were about six of them and they were effing and jeffing in a boisterous manner. Vincent looked at them and I could see the scowl on his face. I shared his dislike of such behaviour, but I hid my feelings better.

"You not say to them, 'be quiet'?" He asked.

"Only if I want to get myself into a fight." I replied, honestly.

"But you are police, you can tell them, no?"

"In England, no." I replied.

Vincent frowned and I suddenly felt quite embarrassed. Obviously, in Portugal, Vincent would have just wandered over and had a quiet word in their shell-like, and they'd have behaved, but it didn't work like that in this country.

Vincent looked around the rest of the café, studying each of the tables in turn.

"Everyone here is very …"

He couldn't seem to find the right word.

"Where are the old people?" He asked.

I shrugged my shoulders.

"All the girls, they have the dark skin."

He ran his right hand down his left forearm.

"They all have the long, white hair. All the same."

Then he looked at the floor.

"Why they all wear the …"

He clearly didn't know the right English word, so he created a gap between his thumb and forefinger to demonstrate a high heel.

"And the seios, the …"

He cupped both hands and held them to his chest, making what must be one of the oldest gestures known to mankind.

"They are …"

"Fake" I replied.

"And the young men, they are big …"

He rolled his shoulders forward to indicate a muscular upper body.

I nodded.

"They are dark, too. Are they all from Portugal?"

I smiled politely at his joke.

I'd spent the last three decades in and around Loughton, so Vincent's observations were quite interesting and not a little bit insulting. But when I looked around, he was right. All the girls were bleached blonde, with perfectly straight hair. They were all wearing high heels, many also had a platform sole. In fact, they looked like they were on a night out, but it was only four in the afternoon. The blokes were equally of a type: all weights animals who, when they weren't in the gym, must have been under a sunbed. But I noticed there was something else about everyone, something that Vincent had missed, they all had money – actually, they all had too much money.

"Have you been to England before?" I asked, keen to move the subject on.

"No"

I nodded; I had hoped for a little more. I guess Vincent sensed this because he added, a little too late:

"London is fantastic. Yesterday, I see the changing of the guard."

I spent the time it took to drink a second cup of coffee to fill Vincent in on the results of my interviews of Lesley and Natasha and I handed him copies of their signed statements. He read them carefully and commented how both agreed with Cheryl's version of events. It seemed therefore, that unless there was some massive conspiracy, the events leading up to Marcella's disappearance were pretty well established. There were tiny discrepancies, but my detective experience told me, 'tiny discrepancies', were often a good thing as they reflected untainted recollections. We agreed that none of the three women were involved. Although only small, that was at least a step forward.

"When you interview Mr Parker?" Vincent asked.

"You've already interviewed him, in Madeira?" I replied, surprised by the question.

"We didn't. The local police did. We request, please, you do a writing interview; we will give you questions to ask. We need you to do this for the extradition process."

"So, it wasn't you or Adao who interviewed him in Funchal?" I asked.

I had made that assumption when they'd first briefed me.

He shook his head.

"No, local police. They do not like him; they call him a …"

He thought for a few moments.

"… a pig. Can you ask him the questions?"

Vincent took out a folded piece of white paper and handed it over. It amounted to about twenty-five questions, written in perfect English, and many referred to the statement which Tristram had given in Madeira and sought clarity about what he'd said. I read through them quickly but carefully. They all seemed eminently sensible.

"Do you want to be present?" I asked.

"No, not allowed. When can you do?"

"I'll go to his house now and, if I can, set it up for next week. Would that be okay?"

He nodded.

"Tonight, you come to my hotel, we go out for a meal?" Vincent asked, quite out of the blue.

"Tomorrow, yes. Tonight no. I have to see my ex." I replied.

"X?"

"Wife, divorce, you understand?"

"Yes, yes." He replied.

When we left, Vincent got into a large black limousine which was parked up a little way down the street. He got into the back, so I assumed it was chauffeur driven. He seemed a nice enough chap, if a little unremarkable. But that was probably the language gap. I mean, his English wasn't bad, but he certainly wasn't fluent. Mind you, I couldn't speak a word of another language. That gave me an idea. Opposite was a WH Smith's, so I wandered over and ten minutes later left with an English-Portuguese dictionary and a CD entitled 'Portuguese for Dummies', which sounded just about right in every respect.

Chapter 12

It was a couple of days since I'd been to Tristram's drum. I noticed immediately that the press attention had waned because the throng of reporters and photographers had reduced to a small huddle. I parked up well down the road, walked up to the impressive front gate and rang the intercom. There was no response. I waited an appropriate time and rang again.

"Speak" A metallic voice commanded.

"Mr Parker, it's the police, please can you let me in? I'll hold my warrant card up to the camera thingy."

I did so.

"What's your name? I can't read it."

"Detective Sergeant, I mean Inspector Christopher Pritchard." I replied, momentarily forgetting my temporary promotion.

"What are you? A Sergeant or an Inspector? How can you be both?"

"Mr Parker, please open the door." I said, using my very politest voice.

"Have you got a warrant?"

"No"

"Wait there, I want to phone my solicitor."

The green transmit light went out and I gathered that Mr Parker had hung up.

One or two of the press photographers had started to take pictures of me and a reporter wandered over.

"Who are you then?" He said, in a not unfriendly manner.

"Guess" I replied, with a grin.

"I suspect you're from the SCOT team at the Yard."

"Close but no cigar. And I think the SCOT team is now called SET." I replied.

"SET?" He queried.

"Special Enquiry Team" I explained.

"Jesus Christ, the job does love an unnecessary change."

I thought that was a strange thing for someone not in the job to say.

"You look familiar." The journalist said.

I couldn't believe it! No one recognised me anymore and then two people in two days.

"I don't think we've ever met." I replied.

"I do know you."

I didn't reply but pushed the intercom button again, more out of impatience than hope.

"Wait" A curt voice responded but before he terminated the call, I could hear the tiniest snippet of his conversation with his solicitor 'Of course I won't sign anything ...'.

"I know where I know you. Don't you recognise me?" He asked.

I looked him up and down. A white, male hack in his mid-forties wearing indeterminate clothing and smoking a cigarette. He could have been anyone.

"We worked at Tottenham together. I was a permanent custody officer: you were a DS in the office. Dave Johnson, PS 36YT."

He put out his hand.

I think I did remember him, just; I knew his name more than I recognised his face but that might have been because he must have lost four stone in weight. I put my hand out and we shook hands.

"Hello Dave, what the fuck are you doing as a journalist? That's a long way from a Custody Suite in Tottenham."

I have to say, while we did know one another back then, we were never more than colleagues whose paths very occasionally passed. We'd say hello, but apart from professional interaction, that was about as far as our conversation would stretch. I remembered something else that I'd subsequently heard about him but couldn't quite put my finger on it. It was grief, he'd dropped in the shit somehow.

The intercom light lit up again.

"Hello, come in"

There was a buzz, and I pushed the pedestrian door in the gate open.

"I need to go, Dave."

As I turned to walk through, Dave reached into his pocket and thrust a card in my hand.

"Call me when you're through."

I must have frowned because he immediately followed up by saying.

"Don't worry, I'm not going to break your balls about this case, I'd just love to catch up. Call me later, I'm staying in a B&B in Loughton."

I nodded and closed the door behind me.

The front door was ajar, so I pushed it open, called out and went in. I'd got a few steps into the impressive, galleried hallway when Mr Tristram Parker stepped out from a doorway and said curtly:

"Take your shoes off. What sort of manners were you taught?"

I slipped my shoes off, placed them back by the door and bit my lip. Police officers don't take their shoes off, for obvious reasons, but I decided I would at least try and make an effort to strike up some rapport with Mr Parker.

"Kitchen" He said, as if he were barking orders to a dog.

I followed him into the kitchen, a single room across the entire back of the house. He walked to the other side of an island and sat on a stall; as he hadn't invited me to sit down, I stood opposite him and put my daybook and folder on the work surface. I still had my coat on. I took it off and popped it on the back of a stool.

"Make yourself at home, officer." He said, sarcastically.

Mr Tristram Parker was a white male in his late forties, he could have been older. He was about the same height as me, slim, with immaculate hair and crisp, precise features.

"Now, what do you want? I gave a statement when I was in Funchal."

"I've been appointed to liaise with the Portuguese police; they have asked me to ask you some questions to clarify certain matters."

"That'll have to be done with my solicitor present. I'm not saying anything or signing anything without her present."

"Let me ask you a simple question, I'm not accusing you of anything, I've not cautioned you, I just want to know one thing?"

He nodded curtly.

"Where is your wife?"

"I have no idea."

"Are you worried about her?"

"I can't win, whatever I say. If I say I am, that suggests I think something awful has happened to her; if I say no, I sound heartless and as if I already know what's happened."

"Did she ever threaten to leave you?" I asked.

"I'm not playing this game, Constable. I'll give you my PA's details, you can arrange an appointment and my solicitor will be present."

I was getting nowhere fast and wasn't going to gain anything from staying but it had been useful to meet him, if only briefly. It gave me a measure of the man. I picked my coat back up.

"Tomorrow?"

He nodded.

"Is there anything you'd like to ask me?"

"Yes"

"Fire away."

"You can remember the way out, can't you, Constable?"

I knew he was trying to get under my skin by calling me Constable, but I didn't bite. Besides, whatever rank a police officer attains, he still retains the powers of a Constable, and therefore, to describe him or her as such isn't entirely inaccurate.

I made my way towards the door and didn't intend looking back, but Mr Parker called out from the kitchen.

"Actually, I have got some questions for you."

I stopped and turned around.

"Why on earth would anyone want to be a police officer?"

It wasn't what I was expecting, so I hesitated.

"I mean, if you're ambitious you'd have gone into the city; if you were bright, you'd be a lawyer, even brighter and you'd be a doctor or a vet. If you had a degree but didn't know what to do with it, you'd be a teacher. I conclude therefore that you've got little ambition, no qualifications and very little up here …"

He pointed to the side of his head.

"You're about as charismatic as my teapot and as articulate as a bus. You have, Constable, very little to commend you to the world. Despite all these shortcomings, the state allows you to wield a considerable amount of power, which is quite frankly, ludicrous, ridiculous, and quite frightening …"

I looked him straight in the eye while he delivered his diatribe.

"…if you worked for me, I'd have someone of your education and intellect ordering the stationery and you'd probably get that wrong. And you, you …

He pointed aggressively.

"… dare to come to my house and ask me about my missing wife, as if I'm some two-bit criminal. As soon as you step out of that door, I will get my investigations team to dig into every facet of your life. By the end of the week, I will know more about your life than you do. If your wife is concubitio with the milkman, I'll know; if your child farts during gym class, I'll get a phone call; if your daughter goes down on her music teacher during her private clarinet lesson, there'll be a video on the internet by the end of the day.

Let me make one thing crystal clear, if you go against me, or try to harm me, in any way – I will use this information to destroy you, I will destroy your career and I will decimate whatever sad, little family life you have. I will make sure you regret being appointed 'liaison officer' until the day you die. Do I make myself clear, or was I using words that were too elongated for a police officer to understand?"

When he'd started, Tristram had been quite steady, quite controlled but the longer he went on, the more strained and uptight he became. It told me a great deal about the man I was dealing with, and I can't say I was particularly struck by his charm and wit.

As I left, I said:

"Just so you know, I've officially reported your wife missing. I've completed the description, as best I can, but if she had any birthmarks or other peculiarities, I'd be obliged if you'd let me know. Oh, and at some stage, please can you let me have the details of her doctor and dentist."

I spoke crisply but with a detached air of professionalism.

Tristram opened his mouth, and I would have bet money on him saying something but to my complete surprise he said nothing.

I turned on my heels and left.

Chapter 13

I hadn't been in the house more than five minutes. When I emerged, a couple of the photographers took some pictures, but I kept my head down and made my way to my car. Once inside, I pulled out Dave Johnson's card and called his mobile. Thirty minutes later, we were sitting in The Crown in Loughton High Street.

"I'm going to have to admit something, mate, I know you were called Nostrils, but I can't remember your actual name?"

"Chris, Dave, Chris Pritchard. I was on a CIPP team with Colin Harte, Dot MacDonald and Bob Clark …"

"Wasn't Bob Clark the guy who tried to set himself alight, down on the south coast somewhere?" Dave asked.

"Yeah, that's right. I was only there a couple of years and then I went on to the A.M.I.P. Tottenham was a great place to work but nowhere near as busy as Stokey."

"Didn't you have some run in with a black DI, she was only there a few months? Kitty Young?"

I nodded.

"She's a Commander, now. On the Race and Diversity Command; actually, she might be a D.A.C." He replied.

"How do you know that? You've left the job?" I asked.

"I never knew her in the Job but she lives in the same street as me."

"Where's that?" I asked.

We live in Hornchurch; Berwick Avenue." He replied.

"You're joking. What number? My brother used to live there." I asked.

77

It was a complete lie, but I was genuinely curious to discover where my old nemesis lived.

Twelve. Kitty's at nine. Where did your brother live?" He asked.

"Twenty-eight, I think." I replied.

"I think you've got the wrong road, Nostrils. Anyway, I only discovered she'd move in a few months ago because I've got a mate who's doing some research on her. It was her boyfriend's place originally. I let my mate use an upstairs bedroom to do some obs and take a few photos. He's got a source who reckons she's tied up in some big expenses scandal involving Emu. Apparently, they had a big jolly to the States to go to some international conference for various Black Police Associations and charged all their expenses to the Association."

'Emu' was the A.E.M.O. or, to give the organisation it's full title, the Association of Ethnic Minority Officers but everyone just called it Emu.

"Well, they would, wouldn't they?" I suggested.

"Not first-class BA tickets, bottles of Cristal champagne, caviar meals, trips up Golden Gate Bridge and, to cap it all, a two thousand dollar a night escort agency. Apparently, in five days, three of them spent fifty thousand pounds. There is even a suggestion they bought three Rolex, ostensibly as presents for their hosts, but funnily enough, they forgot to present them and bought them back to the UK. In fact, they ran up so much on their Emu credit cards that there isn't enough money in the organisation's bank account to cover the spend. They've just put the monthly membership fee up to redress the shortfall."

"Was Kitty one of them?"

"No, but she's the treasurer of Emu so she had to approve the expenditure. The guys she moved in with, the one that lives in my street, is one of the three guys that went, and he wasn't even a member until like the day before the trip! Anyway, some of the honest members are furious and one of them is touting the story to the press. My mate's doing the research to see if there's enough to publish. He wanted photographic

78

evidence linking Kitty to the guy that went but, as I said, I don't think he lives there anymore. I can only assume, she's now renting the place."

"Oh, interesting but hardly surprising. It feels like Emu can do just about what they like, and no one dare challenge them otherwise they'll shout racism." I replied.

"Of course, because racism is their raison d'etre. If they managed to eliminate it, they'd have to disband, and all go home. Why would they want that to happen? So, they have to find it everywhere."

"I agree completely but discussing the subject winds me up." I said, hoping he'd change the subject.

"Last I heard, her boyfriend's moved out and she's living there now. That's what the gossip on the street is, anyway."

"Do you know for certain she's still there?" I asked.

"Yes, because her driver picks her up at seven most days. He drives a black Jaguar."

"How high the mighty have risen." I replied.

"Anyway, what happened to you? Custody Officer to journalist, how did that happen?" I asked.

"It's a long story."

"Go on." I said.

"But it's less of a leap than you'd think. My degree is in Journalism and my older brother, he's a lot older, is the Features Editor at the Mail. When I lost my job with the Met, it was an obvious option."

"How did you lose your job? Were you sacked?" I asked.

"Not exactly, I resigned before they could sack me."

"Go on." I said, again.

"About the time your colleague was setting himself on fire, a new WPC arrived on Street Duties from Hendon. She was in her thirties, so quite a late joiner and married with three kids, which was unusual. She was Welsh, I think, with bright red hair."

"Crumpet?"

"Very short, average looks, a bit lumpy but she was really bubbly and very friendly. And she was a bit of a lad, if you know what I mean, she farted and talked about sex and everyone thought she was okay."

"Go on."

"She went onto A relief and rumours started to circulate that she was sleeping with an Inspector from another relief. Then someone else, who's sister was a trainer at Hendon, got very drunk at a Christmas do and let slip that this woman had slept with most of her class at training school and half of the instructors. In fact, on the coach on her way home from their end of course dinner and dance, she gave one of the PCs head in front of everyone."

"Sounds like just my sort of girl! Was her husband in the job?" I asked.

"No, he was a garage hand somewhere."

"What was her name?"

"Hen, short for Henrietta. Anyway, one day she brought a prisoner into me and they'd just introduced those handheld metal detectors. I was showing her and a colleague how to use it, you now, adjust the sensitivity, stuff like that, and I ran it up her leg as part of the demonstration. When it got level with the top of her leg it beeped, and I said, jokingly; 'my dear you really must take those love balls out before you come to work'. Everyone, including her, laughed and she replied; 'how do you know it wasn't my suspenders?'.

Anyway, a few weeks past and I got a one six three for sexual harassment and was put on restricted duties. I was completely blown away. The story I heard was that she wasn't bothered, but her boyfriend, the Inspector, heard what had happened, obviously from her, and started to see pound notes. He was about to leave his wife for her and perhaps he thought a few extra grand would come in handy. I went sick a few weeks later and never went back."

"I'm sorry, that's all quite sad." I said, with genuine empathy.

"How long did you do in the end?" I asked.

"Only ten, I was in the Royal Navy before then, so I carried my pension over."

"And now you're Fleet Street's finest reporter." I said, raising my glass in a toast.

We clinked.

"Wapping, actually, Nostrils." He replied.

We both took a few gulps, and I was just wiping my lips with my coat sleeve when Dave said:

"The wife killing Investment Banker, any thoughts?"

I smiled. I knew all the rules about not talking to the press and I'd stuck to them throughout my service, but Dave had been clever. He'd told me his story and opened up, and to some extent it was incumbent upon me to return the compliment. More than that though, as I genuinely knew very little that wasn't already in the public domain, I thought perhaps I had more to gain from this conversation than lose.

"Dave, I took the job yesterday and I'm only in a liaison role. I'm yet to have a briefing from the Portuguese police, I was just asked to reach out to Mr Parker so we could get his wife officially reported as missing. If you know anything more than I've read over the last few days in the papers, then, honestly, you know more than I do. I'm not saying I won't find out more, but today, I know practically nothing about the case. Sorry, Dave, I know it's not what you wanted to hear but it's the truth."

It wasn't the whole truth, but mostly accurate.

"Fair enough, Nostrils. Will you let me know if you get anything?"

"Fuck me, it's difficult, Dave."

"We might be able to compensate you?" He suggested.

"I can't do that, mate – that's borderline corruption. I've got way too much to lose and besides, it's just not my style."

"Plenty of your colleagues do." He replied, sipping the last mouth full of his pint.

"Not me, Dave, sorry."

"Do you want another?" I asked, hoping he'd say no, but he didn't.

When I sat down again, I told him about the day before when I'd chatted to the journalists outside Tristram's house and the various theories they were discussing.

"That's pretty typical, it's all bullshit. If any one of us did discover anything tangible the first person we'd be speaking to is our editor and the last would be our rivals from other outlets."

He downed half of his second pint in one go and sat there, looking at me, while obviously mulling something over in his mind.

"If he did kill her, I might have a motive for you."

"Go on."

"I think she might have been in another relationship; I think old Mr Investment Banker might have found out. Apparently, she was meeting someone every week in Pimlico."

"Source grade?"

"E4" He replied.

I shrugged my shoulders, an E4 intelligence grading was from an untested anonymous source – in other words 'dog shit'.

"But even if she was, why kill her? He's over the side, too. It might have been quite convenient if she had been, too." I countered.

"We have another source in his company, they've no idea what happened to the wife but they're very happy to dish the dirt on him. You don't get that successful without pissing a lot of people off. In fact, there was a story building about his company before all this happened. Something to do with tax evasion, or avoidance, one of the two. Our financial guys had got a sniff of an FT investigation."

"Is this the same E4 source that told you about the affair?" I asked.

"No, completely different. This is a B2."

A B2 grade was known and reliable.

"Will anyone formally speak to me?" I asked.

"Give Laura Shewan a call at the FT, she might, she's reliable and completely trustworthy."

I made a note of her name, my memory for such details which used to be so reliable, was fading the further I got into middle age.

Chapter 14

I was in a bit of a dilemma. Dave Johnson had provided me with two pieces of information; one, about Marcella having a relationship and two, about some dodgy goings-on at Tristram's company. Both needed to be formally submitted on a report, but I could hardly say my source was a journalist from The Mail Group. I used a tactic most detectives employed on such delicate occasions and made a quick, anonymous call to Crime Stoppers. It would take a few days for the report to come through, but it should land on my desk within a week and then I could act upon the information without fear of questions about the provenance.

I made the call to Crime Stoppers from a TK in Debden which I selected because it wasn't covered by CCTV and then drove over to Jackie's to see whether George had vacated and find out how Jackie was getting on.

Although I went there regularly to pick up or drop of my girls, I hadn't been inside my old marital home for several years, so it was quite strange being invited in and not kept waiting on the doorstep. They'd certainly done a lot of work and spent wisely – there was a huge double level extension at the back which transformed this tired, small three-bedroom mid-war semi into a decent size four bedroom, with a bathroom ensuite and an orangery, which I understood to be a posh conservatory. I guess Jackie couldn't afford all this on her nurse's salary and my maintenance payments, so George must have financed most of it. Now she'd left, I wondered whether she'd be wanting any of her money back.

Jackie was still in a state of shock; she looked like she hadn't slept for days, wore no make-up, and had cried for so long her eyes were a misty bloodshot red.

Pippa was still at her boyfriends, where apparently, she spent four or five nights a week, but Trudy was in her room, so I went in and sat on the end of her bed for a chat.

"Hi darling, how was the school trip?"

"Fine. Then I come home to this."

"Sorry, darling. I don't really know what to say, I thought your Mum and George were really happy together."

Trudy pinched her nose up.

"Oh"

Trudy shook her head; I think more to stop herself saying any more than to demonstrate a negative.

"Will you miss George?"

Trudy shook her head.

Sometimes sixteen-year-old girls can be so uncommunicative! I thought I'd give it one more go.

"How are you doing?"

"Fine" She replied.

"Is there anything I can do?"

She shook her head.

Her mobile phone beeped; she picked it up and read a message.

"Is that your boyfriend?"

"Don't be stupid, Dad."

She started to type a message using both thumbs with impressive speed and dexterity.

"Anyone I know?" I nodded towards the phone, thinking it might be a message to her sister.

She shook her head.

"So, no news for me?"

She shook her head again.

"Have you got any questions for me?"

For just a moment I detected a slight pause in her fingering.

"Like what?" She asked, almost in amazement.

"You know, like, 'how's your work going, Dad?' perhaps?" I suggested.

"Your work's so boring."

I took a deep breath, perhaps she was right.

I stood up, leaned over and kissed her on the forehead. She didn't flinch or acknowledge the gesture.

"See you, darling."

I think I heard a grunt as I closed the door.

Back downstairs, Jackie had poured herself a large gin and tonic and made me a cup of tea.

"I didn't know you were a G&T girl?" I said, having only ever seen her drink wine.

"A George legacy, I'm afraid. Her brother works for a beverage company, and he reckons it's going to be the next big thing. He used to bring round testers and samples of different flavoured gins and we'd fill in a form giving some feedback. You still drinking scotch?"

"Too much." I replied, candidly.

"Have you seen anything of Wendy?" She asked.

"Only the odd chance meeting, nothing other than that." I replied.

"What did happen there?" She asked.

"When you threw me out …"

Jackie went to interject but I gave her a look to suggest she should just shut up, which she did.

"… I moved in with Wendy. She was pregnant …"

"… not from you, you'd had the snip."

"No, from someone else." I replied, without divulging that the 'someone else' had been Matthew Starr, my nineteen-year-old son from a former relationship.

"What a lovely girl." Jackie said, sarcastically.

"Are you sure you don't want me to get you a saucer of milk instead of that G&T?"

"G&T's fine, thank you. Go on, you were talking about your slutty girlfriend."

"Look, Jackie, she wanted to get pregnant, I couldn't help so she tried some alternative methods. Anyway, she had a miscarriage at six weeks."

"Six weeks? In the trade we call that a heavy period." Jackie, the nurse, retorted.

"Anyway, when she lost the baby, and knowing that she was desperate for one and that I wasn't going to be of assistance, she dumped me and started going out with her best friend's brother. Of course, her best friend had been suggesting that course of action for years, and I'm sure he was a nice fellow, so she made the right choice for her."

"And has she had a baby now?"

"Yes, a boy; he must be three, so all's well that ends well, eh?" I said.

"But not for you?" She observed.

"I got what I deserved." I replied, stoically.

"Sorry, Chris, I wish it had worked out, I do."

"I wish George had worked out for you." I replied.

"Didn't even know you liked women; says a lot for our marriage, doesn't it?"

"Most women are a bit bi. I loved you Chris, but there was too much baggage. The bomb, the kidnapping, your terrible heroin addiction and then to cap it all, Wendy. There is only so much weight a wife can bear."

I could have taken issue with her, I could for example, point out that she was the first to go over the side, not me. But what was the point?

"What happened to Matthew?" She asked.

"That was a very difficult situation. After staying with Wendy, he decided he didn't want to go to university but to join the Old Bill. His mum and real dad went apoplectic because his whole life had been geared up to going to Uni, you know, private tuition and a public-school education. Anyway, he dipped the job interview, they told him he needed more life experience, which was undoubtedly true, and he went off to Exeter University as planned, so it all worked out all right."

"Do you see much of him?"

I shook my head.

"He's got his own life, and a fantastic set of parents, doesn't really need me. I think, well, I know, he's glad he tracked me down and understood a bit more about who he really was, but he'd been brought up in rural, middle-class England and I was, I think, a bit too rough. I keep in contact and send cards and everything, but the last couple of times I asked him to come and visit, he made some excuses and declined. No one stays with me for very long."

"Oh Chris, don't say that. What about Mrs M?"

I laughed gently.

"That's true, there'll always be Mrs M. In fact, I'm moving in with her next week or maybe the week after. She asked me and I'm tired of living onboard Starburst."

"You seemed all right last night, I thought it was cosy."

"You wouldn't say that come January when the ice forms on the inside of the windows!"

"You'll only be down the road. I'm glad you've got Mrs M, Chris."

"Me too." I replied.

Chapter 15

The following day was largely admin. I confirmed the interview with Tristram for next week at his solicitors in Epping, and then prepped for it. I was very surprised to learn Tristram wasn't using a top London firm but instead had chosen a popular local company with a solid reputation as a family focused business. In fact, I'd even used them when I got divorced. I drafted a briefing for the Assistant Commissioner and met up with Vincent at the Embassy to see if there had been any developments on the island that would impact upon the interview, but there hadn't.

I got the impression that the investigation in Madeira had come to a stop and that they saw no more lines of enquiry. I pushed Vincent about the waiter, but he explained he was not a suspect in any way, shape or form, pointed out he had cooperated at every stage and that his alibi checked out.

Vincent said that the airport police had checked every flight out of Madeira from the night before Marcella's disappearance and for the subsequent seven days, and that she had not left the island. They had also checked the ferry routes, the principal one running to an island called Puerto Santos, but that too had returned a negative outcome. I did learn that you didn't need identification to board that ferry so, technically at least, Marcella could have travelled to Puerto Santos and then flown from there to Lisbon. I pointed this out to Vincent, who said he'd make some more enquiries. As we were about to part, Vincent asked.

'Mrs Parker, why would Mrs Parker run away?'

He was right, of course. Why would Marcella run away? What from? She didn't have the perfect marriage, if such a thing existed. She had loads of freedom, excessive amounts of money and a very comfortable life – nothing therefore suggested she had anything to run away from.

So, if she didn't run away, she must be dead. And if it wasn't the waiter, and it didn't seem like it was, then someone else. But no one else on the island had any connection to her, unless it was either of the three women, Cheryl, Lesley, or Natasha. Now I hadn't met Cheryl, but Lesley and Natasha were the most normal middle-class English women you could ever meet. Why would anyone want Marcella dead? And even if it was one of them, what did they do with her body? Following that logic, it had to be Tristram, not in person of course, but someone, or perhaps two people, acting under his instructions. He certainly had the money to arrange it, but I couldn't see a motive. Why not just divorce her? It would cost him, but people like Tristram have most of their money out of the reach of the Inland Revenue which, I suspect, makes it out of reach of the divorce courts, too.

It was also clear that whilst Lesley and Natasha didn't have much time for Tristram, neither of them thought he was responsible for what had happened to Marcella.

Nothing here made much sense, maybe after next week's interview the mist would start to clear.

With that said, I wasn't the investigator, something I had to keep reminding myself of; I was just the liaison officer.

While I was out with Vincent, I took a call from the Essex Coroner's Officer. They were opening a case and asked me to attend and give evidence at the opening hearing. It was scheduled in six weeks. I made a mental note to add this to my briefing for the Assistant Commissioner.

The Portuguese Embassy is right in the heart of Belgravia, one of my favourite parts of London, and home to one of my favourite drinking holes, the Nag's Head in Kinnerton Street. This pub is in an old mews, only a hundred yards from one of the busiest roads in London but a million miles away in atmosphere. I doubt the interior of the place had changed in a hundred years and several of London's most infamous murderers were amongst its previous customers, including John Haig, the acid bath murderer.

I took Vincent for a drink there; his face was an absolute picture when we entered. I also insisted he drank proper British bitter, much to his initial disgust. Truth be told, I suspected he was a wine drinker who dabbled with the odd half of lager on a hot sunny Portuguese summer day, so a pint of warm, flat London Pride was a new experience. After two, he started to relax and after four I had to put him in the back of a black cab giving instructions to the driver to take him straight to his hotel. It was a pleasant enough two hours, but it was still work with both of us being incredibly polite and equally discreet. It was also a little tricky at times because his English wasn't quite what it needed to be to converse on equal terms.

Only after the cab had turned out of the end of the road, did the grumpy old landlord emerge from the pub with what I immediately recognised to be Vincent's brown leather attaché case. He'd apparently left it in the toilet after his last visit.

I took it with gratitude and immediately rang his mobile but when the case vibrated, I knew it also contained his phone.

I realised I'd have to make my way to his hotel to return it, so I walked north to the Cromwell Road and flagged down an eastbound Hackney carriage.

It couldn't be helped, as old bill I am just curious, that is, after all, one of the attributes of a good detective. When I was in the back of the cab, I flicked on the light and had a cursory glance through the contents. Of course, all the paperwork was in Portuguese, but he also had an A to Z of London and several calling cards for West End escorts, which he must have collected from T.K.s. He wasn't quite the good catholic son, after all. I really wasn't bothered, I have never been one to judge other's morals, probably because I am aware that, over the years, mine have been appalling. What was interesting were several still photographs of an empty hotel room, apparently taken from a covert camera. That was interesting as it probably meant they had Tristram's hotel room in Funchal probed up, but what was more curious was that they hadn't mentioned that to me during their briefing at the Embassy. Why would they keep that to themselves? Then I saw an I.D. card with a photograph of Vincent. It was issued by an organisation called Servico de Informacoes de Seguranca. The thing was, I was sure Vincent's surname was Ferreira, as in a Portuguese version of the famous Italian Formula 1 team, but this I.D. said Vincent Alto. The logical assumption was that the name he had given me was a covert identity – but why?

I dropped Vincent's attaché case off at the hotel reception and was about to jump on the rattler when my phone rang.

"Christopher Pritchard?" Said a pleasant, almost seductive, female voice.

"Yes, who's this?"

"My name's Cassandra, I'm a friend of Julie. She's asked me to give you a call."

I'd completely forgotten about Julie's proposal; it had only been a couple of days ago but so much had happened in those forty-eight hours.

"Oh, hi, Cassandra. Listen, I'm embarrassed, honestly you don't have to do this. I thought Julie was joking when she said she'd set me up with you. Honestly, hang up and we can both pretend this never happened."

"No way, Mr Pritchard. You're not getting away that easily."

"Okay, okay. I'd love to have an evening out with you, Cassandra …"

I deliberately chose the word 'evening' as opposed to 'night'.

" … Julie suggested a nice meal? I thought, maybe the theatre?"

"Bugger the theatre, bores me stupid, though it's a damn sight better than the ballet or opera. How about a meal and then back to mine and we can cuddle up by the fire?"

"Do you have a fire?" I asked.

"I'll have one fitted between now and Saturday." She replied.

"Sounds perfect then. Where abouts do you live, I'll find a restaurant nearby?"

"I live in Notting Hill; just off the market." She replied.

"I've got to confess, that's a part of London I don't know. Other than what I've seen in the film, I wouldn't recognise the place at all."

"I was in that film."

For the shortest second I thought about making a joke about Julia Roberts and her role as hooker in Pretty Woman but fortunately the conversation moved on.

"I was an extra, and the back of my head appears in the scene where Hugh Grant throws juice all over Julia Roberts."

"I hope they pay you royalties whenever they show the film."

"No, they made a one-off gift to a charity of our choice. Anyway, there are loads of lovely restaurants within two hundred yards of where I live. Come over Saturday, I'll book one, pick me up from my flat at eight and we'll have a great night out, I'm sure."

"Sounds good." I said.

"I'll text you my address, stay over."

And with that Cassandra terminated the call.

A new job, a new home and, potentially, a girlfriend. Everything was coming up roses.

Chapter 16

The following morning, I was rudely awoken at seven by a call on my mobile phone. It was the reporter from the Financial Times, Laura Shewan. I'd left her a message the previous day but never really thought she'd call me back. Her manner was brusque but just about courteous.

"Have I woken you up, Mr Pritchard?"

"No" I lied.

"I was just brushing my teeth." I lied, again.

It was an excuse I often used in these circumstances.

"You wanted to speak to me about Skimmia Investments? I presume it's in connection with his missing wife?"

"Yes" I replied.

"Did Dave Johnson give you my details?"

The question blind-sided me a little. Was it alright to admit that it was Dave, or would I be dropping him in the shit? I took a shot.

"Yes, I know Dave from old. He said you were worth reaching out to."

"I'll be at Canary Wharf in an hour, I'll meet you under the clocks. I'll be wearing a red coat."

And with that she hung up.

Canary Wharf was only a short walk from Starburst, but I hardly ever went there. On the rare occasion I had, the place seemed like a different world – everyone was young, and the women were pretty and wore short skirts and high heels, and the people were rich and the drinks expensive. As a forty something old bill I felt like a piscine out of H2O, so I gave it a wide birth. I suppose on some levels I was jealous, and it was hard to see so many with so much when you have so little. That morning however, I put these misgivings to one side and at eight I met Laura Shewan just outside the main entrance to the enormous underground station. She was young, immaculate and beautifully spoken.

"Shall we get a coffee?" I suggested.

"At this time in Canary Wharf? Only if you want to spend twenty minutes standing in a queue. Let's walk and talk. I assume we're off the record?" She asked.

"Yes, I'm sure we are. Tell me, Laura, what exactly does that mean?"

She laughed, but kindly.

"It means that while I will make a record of our meeting and what is said, I will not publish the content of the meeting or reveal you as my source."

I was a little taken back, I thought I was interviewing her, not the other way around which, for a police officer involved in such a sensitive enquiry, would mean I was breaking about six of the Met's disciplinary codes in one go. I needed to clarify the situation quickly or end the meeting.

I stopped walking to emphasise the point I wanted to make.

"Laura, I'm here because I thought you might have information to assist my enquiry into the missing Marcella Parker, I'm not here to leak anything to the press."

"I know." She replied and started walking again.

I was a little confused but decided to go with the situation I found myself in.

"Dave Johnson told me you were looking at Tristram Parker's business activities before all this kicked off with his wife. Is that right?"

"I was. Well, I still am but my sources are no longer talking to me. I think Mr Parker's company makes its money by exploiting holes in the tax laws. And the whole scam has been hijacked by the Russians, who are desperate to get their money into London."

"Isn't that what they all do?"

"Yes and no. All the big banks say they don't exploit tax loopholes, well that's the trend, at the moment, to be, or at least appear ethical. And yes, there are ways wealthy individuals can avoid tax and some companies that specialise in these schemes."

"Help me, Laura. I'm not financially minded, give me an example."

"Professional footballers get their wages paid into offshore companies; the offshore companies pay less corporation tax than individuals pay in income tax in the U.K. and then the offshore company lends the money to the player. Well, if money is a loan, it's not income, so it doesn't attract income tax, or National Insurance for that matter. Doing this a footballer can pay twenty percent tax as opposed to the highest rate, what's that, fifty percent at the moment, plus National Insurance at twelve percent. And of course, the loans are never repaid because the footballer is the owner and sole director of the offshore company."

I did understand it, only briefly, but I got the concept.

"Is that what Skimmia Investments does?" I asked.

"Definitely not." Laura replied.

I must have looked surprised.

"You asked me for an example of a tax avoidance scheme and that is one. That's not what's going on at Skimmia Investments. It's something else, something more sophisticated, something no one else is doing. There was a rumour circulating that only a dozen people know exactly how it's done, and the Inland Revenue are completely stumped but they're keeping it quiet because if they make a fuss, and the loophole gets out, they'll lose like billions of pounds worth of revenue a year."

"Can they just make the activity illegal?" I asked.

"It's not that simple because, like all the best tax avoidance schemes, it's international and therefore, outside the jurisdiction of U.K. tax laws."

"Let me try to understand. Tristram Parker's company is a hedge fund, right?"

Laura nodded but before I could speak, she asked:

"Do you understand what a hedge fund does?"

I shook my head; I didn't see the point of bullshitting.

"It's an offshore based investment company. They take their clients' money, place it with other clients' money, and then buy derivatives or other financial products that they calculate will return a profit. Often, they offset a particular investment against an opposite position, so they might go long in green energy but short in oil. If one loses badly, the loss will be offset by a profit in the other; hence the name 'hedge'."

"As in 'hedging your bets'?" I suggested.

"Exactly. A hedge fund is only as good as its intelligence and its ability to understand and interpret that intelligence." Laura explained.

I thought it sounded awfully like policing, but I kept that view to myself.

"Give me another example, Laura?"

"De Beers owns ninety percent of the world's diamond minds. Let's say, Skimmia Investment's have a contact at that company who tell them that De Beers surveyors have just discovered a huge new diamond deposit, so big, that it will likely devalue the price of diamonds by one percent. More diamonds in the world the price drops, you understand?"

"With you so far."

"Skimmia Investment's inside contact informs them about this discovery, for a price, of course …"

"Of course." I interjected, just to demonstrate that I was following.

"… and they go short in diamonds."

Laura looked at me.

"Go short means they anticipate a stock will fall, so they sell the stock before they've actually bought it."

"How do you sell something you don't own?" I asked.

"That's what a derivative is." Laura replied.

"So, going long means?"

"You buy a stock in anticipation that it's price will rise." She replied.

I felt that I should have been confused but I wasn't; in fact, I kind of got it.

"So, in your example, because Skimmia Investments know there are going to be more diamonds in the world, they know the price will fall, so they short them. A bit like insider trading." I suggested.

"Exactly" Laura said.

"But what's that got to do with tax avoidance? And what's happened to his wife?" I asked.

"I don't know, but I do know the tax avoidance thing is a massive national scandal. We're talking about billions of pounds of lost tax revenue, and it just could be the reason why, despite everything, this country's rich just keep getting richer and richer. Maybe his wife was going to blow the whistle?"

"Perhaps" I replied.

"But where do I go from here?" I asked.

"For a start, you need an experienced F.I. One who is prepared to bend the rules a little. In the meantime, if I hear anymore, I will let you know?" Laura said.

"And what do you want from me?" I asked.

Laura looked thoughtful and then replied.

"Nothing"

"Thank you." I replied, genuinely impressed that fate had put me in touch with a decent and honourable member of the fourth estate.

Chapter 17

I'd made a few phone calls to trusted confidants and was told the person I needed was a PS Bruce Franklin, who was based at Hornsey police station. I arranged a meeting for the following day at the Old Star opposite the Yard. According to my contacts, Bruce was not only the best Financial Investigator the Met possessed, but he was also mightily pissed off with the job, at the moment, having been returned to uniform under tenure after eight years as a DS at six.

'Six' was the colloquial name for the Metropolitan Police Fraud Squad, a name derived from its location in the organisational structure, Special Crime Directorate Six.

I made my way to the Portuguese Embassy for a twelve o'clock meeting with Vincent. I was really early, so I wandered around Harrods for an hour. I couldn't afford anything the shop sold but I just loved everything about the store, and it was a great place to waste time.

Vincent met me in the Embassy reception; he was grinning from cheek to cheek.

"Thank you so much for finding my bag, Christopher. I was not well."

He rubbed his hand in a circular motion in front of his stomach.

"I was on the toilet. I not drink that beer again, not good for me."

He laughed.

"But my bag, thank you, thank you."

"It was my pleasure, my friend." I said.

"The Ambassador, she wants to meet you." Vincent said.

"What about? The bag?" I said, with some disbelief.

"No, no, no. About the investigation." He replied.

I was a little surprised. I hadn't expected to meet the Ambassador again, especially so soon.

"She wants to ask you to do something for us."

"Okay" I replied, tentatively.

I was acutely aware that, as a lowly temporary Detective Inspective, I would have to refer a request of any weight to the Assistant Commissioner. Since looking through Vincent's attaché case, I was also cognisant of the fact that they weren't telling me everything they knew.

Meeting the Ambassador was fine in principle but in reality, it meant we were waiting for nearly three hours until she was free for a meeting that lasted precisely two minutes.

"Thank you for coming to see me, Christopher."

I smiled as warmly as I could.

"We are interviewing Mr Parker next week, yes?" She asked.

"Yes, Wednesday, Ma'am. I have written to his solicitors, and we intend to conduct the interview at their offices."

"And you have interviewed the other two ladies who were on holiday?"

"Yes, Lesley Gatz and Natasha Murray. Ma'am, I would also like to interview Mr Parker's girlfriend, Miss Sonia Nicholson."

The Ambassador looked at Vincent who nodded deftly.

"Yes, of course."

I was just starting to wonder what she was going to ask me to do, when she said.
"We request that you search Mr Parker's house for evidence."

"Okay …" I replied, a little tentatively.

While it seemed a sensible request, in reality this was really going to complicate matters.

"Thank you, I am obligated for your time, Detective Inspector Pritchard."

And with that the Ambassador stood up, shook my hands and left.

***

I made my way over to the Yard and to the Assistant Commissioner's office on the ninth floor. Although I had little hope of seeing him without an appointment, I did want to speak to his staff officer, Detective Superintendent Erling Kristiansen.

Erling's office was adjacent to the A.C.'s and although he was obviously in, he was away from his desk. I stood at the window looking down on the entrance to the Met headquarters. A steady river of people entered and left the building through the recently built security gates. I wondered just how many people worked here?

Occasionally I would see a person I recognised and a specific memory which I associated with them would burst briefly to light in the back of my mind. And then I saw her. She was standing outside Clippers of the Yard, a barber's shop in Dacre Street, talking to another woman. My Wendy, the girl I'd moved in with when I left Jackie. The girl who I still loved with all my heart. Did this mean she was now working at the Yard? I touched inside of the double-glazed window, because that felt like I was just a little bit nearer to her.

"Chris" A voice said from behind and I physically jumped with surprise.

Erling laughed.

"You were obviously miles away, sorry, didn't mean to surprise you like that."

"I was, miles away I mean." I replied, a little embarrassed that I'd reacted that way.

When I glanced back down, Wendy was gone.

"How's it going with the Portuguese?" He asked.

I took a seat at an empty desk immediately opposite his own.

"Yeah, it's fine but I got a little ambushed today by the Ambassador, so I need to run something past you and the boss."

I nodded towards the A.C.'s office.

"She wants me ..."

"Who's she?" Erling interrupted.

"The Ambassador, Guv'nor." I replied, smiling inside at Erling's diversity failing.

If he'd said that on a promotion board, even if he'd worked remorselessly hard for his whole career, that one slip would have failed him – such was the over sensitivity of the Met, these days.

"She has requested we search Mr Parker's home address."

Erling picked up a bundle of photocopied press cuttings and threw them across the desk. Every day, Press Bureau at the Yard went through every newspaper, identified any story that might have a connection to the Met, copied the article, and then put together a bundle of papers which were circulated to all the most senior officers.

"The story has still got traction; it's in every paper. Someone is feeding them stories."

I must admit, I hadn't looked at a newspaper in days, perhaps I should have. I felt inclined to respond by saying 'it's not me' but quickly decided such a denial might come across badly, so I ignored the comment.

"Have you agreed to the search?" Erling asked.

"I think so." I replied.

He shook his head.

"I know; I should have said I'd need to take advice but she, well, sort of bamboozled me."

"That's why she's an Ambassador, I suppose." He observed.

"Guv'nor, it's not a bad call. I mean we really should, shouldn't we?" I replied.

"I don't disagree, but it's going to get complicated." Erling said.

"I agree; I think the same. I'm going to need a Section 8 PACE warrant; I'm going to need a team 'cos I can't do it on my own; I'll need somewhere to store anything we seize; the press will go into a frenzy, so I'll need to do them some lines; Mr Parker is going to go apoplectic, and he's got enough money and power to make a very powerful enemy; and finally, can I assume, anything we do find will be admissible in a Portuguese court? Because I really don't know."

"Well, you'd better get on with it." Erling said, with a smile.

And then I saw a wonderful opportunity.

"Are you okay if I take an F.I. along on the search, just in case?"

"Of course; thought you would anyway. Do you know one?"

"I do, he's been tenured back to uniform, but he wants to keep his accreditation up, so he has to do at least one case a year. His name's Bruce Franklin, he was at S.O.6 for years."

"Crack on." He said.

"Will you brief the A.C?" I asked.

"I will, and use the Special Enquiry Team, they're based over the road at Wellington House. I'll drop their D.C.I. an email."

"Who's that?" I asked.

"Dave Walby." He replied.

I knew Dave of old; he was the business.

Chapter 18

I met Bruce Franklin at the Old Star as we'd arranged. Although I'd never met him, I recognised him immediately. He was a white male, in his early fifties with a round face and round features and he was standing outside the pub with a pint in one hand and a roll-up in the other. He looked a little untidy, his hair needed a cut, and his clothes were a little dishevelled, but he was every inch the Fraud Squad detective. I took a punt and without even asking, held out my hand and said:

"Hello, Brucie boy."

"Hello, Nostrils." He replied.

I'd never met him before, so his use of my old nickname surprised me; a reaction which he clearly read.

"My girlfriend used to work with you at Stokey." He said.

"Who's that?"

"Sarah Thompson, used to be best mates with Dawn Matthews."

I did remember Sarah, well, everyone called her Tommy, she was an ex-judo champion or something.

"I remember Tommy …" I laughed.

"… hard as fucking nails." I added.

"That's her, she's put on a bit of timber since you knew her, but she's still coaching the kids."

"Haven't we all?" I said, patting my belly.

I bought Brucie another pint and got myself a large whisky. We stayed outside, the weather was just about warm enough and it was obvious that my new friend was a chain smoker.

"How's life back in uniform?" I asked.

"Cunts"

"What? Your new colleagues?"

"No, no; they're fine; well, they're very young, Nostrils. I mean the senior management who tenured me are complete and utter spineless cunts."

"What happened?"

"I got shafted because I was investigating Emu."

"What? The credit card thing, the trip to San Francisco?" I asked.

"That's the one. I'd been on it for over a year, had the case just about wrapped up when fucking D.P.S. swooped and said it was their job."

"But it probably was, wasn't it?" I asked.

"Fuck me, Nostrils, I tried to give it to them when it first came in, but they weren't interested. I would have quite happily handed it over but no, it didn't meet their acceptance criteria, or some bollocks, because everyone had been off duty on the trip. But just when I'm about to send my file to the CPS, they call me down to Jubilee House and take everything I've got. And my mate down there, a DI on the. F.I.U., says he's been told to kill it. It's a complete cover up because the job's shit scared about being called racist. Yet, it's the honest members who blew the whistle and wanted something done. Honestly, I ain't that bothered about losing the job, it was getting moved back to uniform that really pissed me off, matey. At six, I was used to dealing with multi-million-pound frauds, so the Emu job was, by comparison, loose change."

"Who came forward?" I asked.

"A guy Tommy knew through Judo, Colin Harte."

I knew Colin well; I'd worked with him at Tottenham about ten years ago.

"Didn't Tommy and Colin go out for a bit?" I asked.

"They had a kid, didn't they? She's thirteen." Brucie responded.

"So, how long have you and Tommy been together?"

"Couple of three years, we don't live together. Anyway, what's this piece of work you've got for me?"

"First, the good news. I've got A.C. King's sign off to use you."

"Fuck me, Nostrils, I'm impressed. It must be an important job; will it get me off earlies, lates and nights for a few weeks?"

"I should think so. It's attracted quite a lot of publicity, it's the hedge fund manager's wife that's gone missing in Madeira. Do you know the one I mean?"

"I'd guessed as much. Mr Tristram Parker, big city whiz kid, an absolute cunt, apparently."

"Have you met him?"

"No, but I've got contacts, mainly retired old bill that ended up doing AML for the big banks. I'll tell you what I do know for sure, RBS I think, closed his bank accounts because they weren't able to identify the source of some of his funds and thought it was dodgy Russian money."

"What personal funds or his business?" I asked

"His business, I think, Skimmia Investments, right?" Brucie said.

"Can you find out more? Any contacts at the S.O.C.A.? They deal with Suspicious Activity Reports, don't they?" I asked.

"One or two. You need me to find any financial links to the missing woman?"

"It's a difficult one, mate. Of course, it's a Portuguese investigation but we do have some jurisdiction because the Essex coroner's opening a court case."

"Which of course he's quite entitled to do, as it's a U.K. national." Brucie added.

"I'm working in a liaison capacity, not an investigator, but we've got to spin his drum and I'll need you along on that." I said.

"I would have thought the Portuguese might have done some F.I. work but they haven't." I said.

"That's hardly surprising, Nostrils, all the relevant accounts will be U.K. based, so they won't be able to get access."

"Oh, fair enough." I replied.

"Do we know for certain Mrs Parker is dead?" Brucie asked.

"No"

"But the Portuguese are making that assumption?" Brucie said.

"Absolutely"

I didn't know whether to share with Brucie the fact that they'd deployed intrusive surveillance on Mr Parker.

"Let's start with her. Get me all her details and I'll get a Production Order on all her accounts. Let's see what we can find out from there. I'll come with you on the search, just let me know when it is."

"Of course. There is something else, something 'off the record'." I said.

"Oh, jolly good, that's what I like to hear, matey." Brucie replied.

"I've got some intelligence to suggest Mr Parker and his investment company, Skimmia Investments, might be involved in some big tax avoidance scheme."

"Oh, the plot thickens, Nostrils. Are the scheme and the missing wife connected?"

"How the fuck do I know?" I said, with mock indignation.

"Oh, no problem, Nostrils, we'll soon get to the bottom of this case."

"It'll be a piece of cake." I replied.

Chapter 19

The next weeks were manic, both work and my private life. I had my date, if that's what it was, with Cassandra Marsh at the weekend to look forward to. I put my barge up for sale and started moving things in at Mrs M's. She gave me keys to the house so I could come and go as I pleased. I kept in daily contact with Jackie to make sure she was all right. She seemed to be, but I was surprised, and if I'm being honest, a little disappointed to learn she'd taken a month off work sick with depression. I don't remember her having a minute off when our marriage fell off a cliff.

The biggest problem I had was getting the search warrant, which I hadn't anticipated.

As it was a Section 8 PACE warrant, I had to go to Horseferry Road Magistrates Court where the Magistrate is one of London's few stipendiaries. That's to say, fully qualified legal professionals as opposed to the local teacher, or doctor or bank manager, who are referred to as lay magistrates. As a police officer, this often makes them easier to deal with, but not on this day.

To get a warrant, you must present two parts: the warrant and the information. The warrant itself, is easy enough. You type it up and all the Magistrate has to do, is sign at the bottom. It's one page in triplicate and takes about ten minutes. The more challenging part is the information, basically the grounds which you are setting out justifying the issue of the warrant. You must sign the information and then swear under oath in the presence of the Magistrate that what you have presented is the truth. If you do this process before a lay magistrate, they read your information, you take the oath, they ask you if it's true, you say yes, and they sign the three copies of the warrant. However, if you do this before a Stipendiary, then you might be asked some questions about what you've said in your information.

I thought I'd completed a comprehensive information, which ran to nearly four sides of A4 but as I was typing it, I did start to identify some potential weaknesses. However, as the story had been front-page news in most of the tabloids, I never thought for a second there'd be any problems getting the warrant. I was wrong.

"Detective Inspector, I've read your information carefully. I have a few questions."

I smiled, as nicely as I could.

"Is there any evidence Mrs Marcella Parker has been murdered? Because I certainly didn't see any in your information?"

"No evidence, your Worship, but I believe there are grounds to suspect."

"Her passport was still in her hotel room?"

"Yes, Sir."

"But people can get two passports."

I didn't say anything; one, because I didn't know whether they could or not and two, because it wasn't a question.

"Well, Officer?"

"I don't know, Sir."

"Has she used any bank account since her disappearance? There's nothing in the information about financial enquiries."

"They've only just been commissioned." I replied.

"Why?"

"Because this is primarily an investigation being conducted in Portugal by the Portuguese authorities. They have no power to make such a request. I've only recently been appointed to assist them and one of the first actions I took was to commission the financial investigation here in the U.K."

I was stretching the truth a bit.

"So, for all we know, Mrs Parker could have purchased a villa and be living in Spain?"

"I strongly suspect she is not, your Worship. Her husband would surely be aware if that was the case?"

"Does your wife always know what you're doing?"

I was quite taken back by the question and perhaps, under different circumstances, I would have challenged it, but this was a court and in a court the judge or magistrate is god.

"I'm not married." I replied, nicely side stepping his point.

"I also note from your information an absence of communications data. What has been done in respect of her mobile phone, and that of her husband, Mr …"

The Magistrate checked the information.

" … Tristram Parker?"

Now I was buggered. I hadn't even thought about comms data. I'd been really fucking busy, and it had never crossed my mind. I felt embarrassed and conflicted. I should lie, and just say 'I recently commissioned comms data enquiries, but I was under oath and, strange though it may seem, I had never lied under oath.

"Mrs Parker's mobile phone was recovered alongside her passport in her hotel room." I replied, but I knew that wasn't enough.

"But nonetheless Officer, there must be vital information on it? What have the enquiries into Mr Parker's phone solicited?"

"They are yet to be undertaken." I replied.

The Magistrate huffed loudly; clearly his patience with me was starting to wear thin.

"If you want to raid someone's home, Detective Inspector Pritchard, you really need better grounds than these." He said.

"We don't call them raids." I replied, meekly.

"I'm on the cusp of turning your application down, Detective Inspector Pritchard. It sounds like a fishing expedition. You've come here half cocked. Is there anything else you can tell me that might change my mind?"

"There is an international dimension to this enquiry that makes it quite unusual ..."

"Unusual for who? You, perhaps, but not the Metropolitan Police, surely. In their long and illustrious history, they must have dealt with hundreds of similar cases. When you stand in this court Officer, you are the Metropolitan Police so please don't start to tell me this is anything other than business as usual."

I was losing and I knew it.

"Sir, with respect, you've wrongly anticipated what I was about to say ..."

"I apologise, go on."

"The international dimension means that the investigation moves slower than others with which I have been involved. I have been asked to provide the highest level of service and cooperation to our Portuguese law enforcement colleagues and have met their ambassador on several occasions. It was the Ambassador herself who asked us to assist by arranging for Mr Parker's home address to be searched. They are convinced that he arranged for his wife to be murdered. I have found no evidence to challenge their assertion. I ask you, if it is within your remit, to consider the wider diplomatic issues, alongside the information which I have provided. Cooperation across borders is going to become increasingly important, as the guise and nature of crime becomes, ever more, international, and this is a great opportunity for this country to demonstrate our commitment to supporting that important objective."

In my twenty-four years of policing, that was, verbally at least, my finest moment. I was far more eloquent than usual, and my words just rolled together. I'd heard senior officers speak eloquently and I'd always grudgingly admired them. It was nice, just once, to get it so right myself.

"Application declined." The Magistrate declared. He got up and walked out of the court.

***

I felt like shit. I came out of the court a little numb. I crossed over the road and into a small garden area, which I once read, used to be a burial pit for plague victims. I flopped down on a bench, a couple of winos were sitting immediately opposite me, losing themselves in what looked like a large bottle of white cider. I put my head in my hands.

"You alright, mate?" One of the wino gentlemen said.

For a few moments I didn't realise he was talking to me.

"Oi, you alright?"

I looked up, caught his eye and nodded.

"You wanna drink?"

He held the bottle towards me. I smiled and shook my head.

"Thanks, though." I replied.

"Wife left you?" He asked.

"No, she's come back." I replied.

They laughed and their attention turned to other matters involving someone called 'Roger' who 'had a fucking attitude', apparently.

It was the first time, in all the years I'd been in the job, I'd had an application for a warrant turned down. Was it because the Magistrate was a Stipendiary? Was he being especially awkward, had he got out of the bed on the wrong side this morning? Was my information lacking? I turned everything carefully over in my head and came to the definitive answer – I had badly fucked up. Of course, I should have requested both Tristram's and Marcella's itemised call records, that was a no brainer.

Should I have checked with the Passport Office about a second passport? Of course, I should have done. Had I sufficiently challenged Vincent about why they were so adamant Mr Parker had arranged to have his wife killed? No, I sure he had? No. But in fairness, you don't have to be one hundred percent certain to get a warrant, that's why you get a warrant, to confirm or deny your suspicions. But I'd let myself down. I think I was so excited about being involved in something a bit different, a bit special, I'd stopped thinking like a proper Detective. And then it hit me. Since my temporary promotion I'd got SOS - Senior Officer Syndrome!

Chapter 20

I'd nearly cancelled Cassandra Marsh on at least three occasions. I was so busy at work and started to get a little stressed by the thought of my first date in four years. To make matters worse, I wasn't sure what sort of date it was, exactly.

I called Julie for reassurance.

"Hi, babes." She said.

"I want to cancel; I can't go through with it." I said, urgently.

"Oh, hi Julie, how are you? How's your week been?" She said, sarcastically.

"Sorry, Jules, how are you, how's your week been?"

"Why?" She said.

"Because it's such a sad and lonely thing to do." I replied.

"No, it's not. Since you split up with Wendy, have you been out with anyone?" She asked, putting an exaggerated emphasis on the last word.

"No" I said, quietly.

"Do you know what Wendy's done? She's moved in with her new partner, had a baby, got pregnant with a second and is getting married next month and going on honeymoon to the Maldives."

I felt gutted.

"Pregnant again?" I said, in the most pathetic loser voice imaginable.

"Yes, three months, she's just had the first scan. And you haven't even had a date. Not one! Get your arse in gear, darling, and take Cassandra out."

"Have you spoken to her recently?"

"Who? Wendy or Cassandra?"

"Cassandra"

"Yes, babes, yesterday. I've bigged you up; she's looking forward to a fun night out. But I want a full report on my desk on Monday."

"Yes, Ma'am." I replied, submissively.

***

That evening was my first official night at Mrs M's. She cooked a roast dinner, the first I'd had since I left Jackie. It was absolutely fantastic. Over dinner, we chatted like we always did. Mrs M liked it if we talked about Dawn, but sometimes I couldn't deal with it. Nonetheless, as I hadn't asked for a few weeks I enquired whether she'd been to the cemetery.

"Only twice this week, it's been such miserable weather for late May. There was a lovely new bunch of flowers. I bought the message home to show you."

She handed me a small printed 'Thinking of You' card, which I turned over and read the handwritten inscription.

> *'Dear WPC Dawn Matthews,*
>
> *You will live forever in the hearts of your friends and colleagues.*
>
> *Thank you for your sacrifice.*
>
> *So dreadfully sorry for your family's loss.*
>
> *John King*
> *Assistant Commissioner – Crime*
> *M.P.S.'*

I gave A.C. King a big tick for such lovely words and a small tick for writing the card himself.

"Wasn't that lovely?" Mrs M said.

"Yes, nice."

"Do you know him?"

"I'm kinda working for him at the moment; he's given me this murder in Portugal, but I've only met him once, a couple of weeks ago. He's got a good reputation amongst detectives; he's tough and uncompromising."

"He's written to me; he's invited me to dinner at Scotland Yard with some other relatives …"

She let the sentence hang; I knew what she meant.

"Will you go? You always refused before. You said until they bring Dawn's killers to justice. Remember when they wanted to name that police building after her and you told them where to go?"

Mrs M sighed.

"I might go this time. What do you think?"

"Why the change of heart?"

She shook her head and shrugged her shoulders.

"I don't know, I think I just feel different. Have they invited you?" She asked.

"No, I made it clear many years ago that I didn't want to go to anything like that." I replied.

"You'd get too upset, wouldn't you?"

"I'd bawl like a baby, Mum." I replied.

She smiled kindly.

"What do you fancy for dinner tomorrow?"

"Oh, I'm out; I've got a date."

"Gosh, wonderful I mean; who is she?"

"I've never met her, don't even know what she looks like, it's a blind date set up by Julie, one of my team."

"Are you excited?"

"Terrified!" I replied.

"Where are you going?"

"Somewhere in Notting Hill, she's booking it."

"Notting Hill? I loved that film?"

"Well, apparently, she was in it."

"You're teasing me, Christopher."

"I'm not, she was an extra, the back of her head made a starring role in one of the market scenes." I replied.

Mrs M howled with laugher and I'd no idea why. She was trying to say something but giggling too hard. When, eventually, she spurted the words out I was more than a little taken aback.

"I bet you hope the back of her head features again, tomorrow, don't you, darling?"

Chapter 21

I had to work on the Saturday morning because I'd promised my old D.C.I. that I would sort out the property store at Arbour Square. I decided to pack my going out clothes, a towel and an overnight washbag and drive straight from Arbour Square to Notting Hill in the early evening. There was a shower which I could use at the factory to make sure I was nice and clean for my date.

Property stores at any police station or department are a nightmare, but they're even worse at Murder Squads because there's a risk in disposing anything that might eventually become evidence. With the discovery of D.N.A., many cold cases came back to life and exhibits seized thirty years ago are sending criminals to prison. Had someone like me, say fifteen years before the development of D.N.A. evidence, thrown away that pair of knickers or that blood-stained knife, no conviction would have been possible.

With that said, you cannot keep everything simply because there's not enough room to store it. What's more, as most searches are done and therefore most exhibits seized at the very beginning of an investigation, it necessarily follows that many exhibits won't ever be required. And it's not uncommon for a murder squad to deal with a suspicious death that turns out to be natural causes and therefore nothing seized during the investigation needs to be retained.

The rules are that if you seize an exhibit, you are responsible for disposing of it. But officers are lazy, we all are, and years later they move onto other roles without ever having sorted out their property. As a consequence, property stores become overcrowded with thousands of exhibits that no one needs, and no one wants.

It fell to me to sort the mess out. To do so, I had to go through every exhibit one by one, cross reference it to a particular operation, see the status of the case and the role of the exhibit played, and if it was no longer required, either contact the owner or, if the owner was dead, locate a relative to whom to return it.

If the property was worthless, say for example, a piece of wood, a tile of lino, a knife, or a settee, then I could authorise it to be disposed of. This meant filling in a form and taking it to the Prisoner's Property store in Mandela Way if it was substantial, or if not and it was safe to do so, just take it to the local tip.

It was a nightmare job and in reality, I needed about a month to make any meaningful progress, but I would make a start and then I could at least tell that to the D.C.I.

The place was deserted which meant none of the other teams were on that weekend. I was a little surprised because there were about four private vehicles parked in the rear yard, which would normally mean one of the teams was in. You were only allowed to park your own cars in the yard at weekends, otherwise the place would be gridlocked.

It was unusual to be in the place on my own; it even felt a bit eerie. I made a coffee and then logged on from my desk to see whether I had anything exciting in my inbox – I didn't. I stood up to go down to the basement where the property store was located but as I did so, heard a 'beep, beep, beep' from the back yard. I moved casually over to the window to have a look and see what was going on.

A large white lorry was reversing into the yard and two DCs from one of the other teams were making sure the driver didn't reverse into anything, for which I was most grateful as the rear nearside of the lorry looked awfully close to the front of my own car, although it probably looked worse from the angle I was looking at.

I recognised the lorry. My team had used it last year to move a family into Witness Protection. It was also used when a large number of exhibits had to be moved, for example, taken to the Old Bailey for a trial. It was in fact a police vehicle, usually kept at Lambeth, and you have to book to use it. I was a bit pissed off because it almost certainly meant a load of new exhibits were about to be deposited in the property store which I was charged with clearing.

I kept watching from two floors up. The lorry pulled to a halt and the driver got out. He was a DS from the same team as the other two. Then all three walked over to what I could only assume to be their own cars and opened the boots and back doors. It was all very strange.

Then the DS opened the rear of the lorry and three of them started to transfer whatever was in the back of the lorry to their own cars. I didn't need to be a detective to realise something very dodgy was going on.

I stepped a little back from the window just to make sure they didn't see me if they looked up. It was like watching a scene from the Great Train Robbery where the thieves transfer the mail bags from the carriage to their trucks.

On one of the nearby desks was a pair of binoculars which I put to use to see exactly what they were carrying. The ploy worked almost immediately – booze and fags. Crates of beers, cases of wine and spirits and almost endless cartons of cigarettes. What the fuck had they done? Robbed an off-licence?

The whole operation was carried out with military precision and not ten minutes after I heard the beeps of the lorry reversing, I saw boots slam, doors close and the roller back of the lorry pulled down. Then something curious happened, the DS knelt by the tailgate and picked at something then, whatever he'd picked off, he threw into one of the large metal bins.

I gave them twenty minutes to make sure they didn't come back for something they'd forgotten and then went to the bin to retrieve whatever it was the DS had deposited.
It was a circular yellow sticker with the black GB letters. It was the plate you have to put on the back of your car when you take it abroad.

The penny dropped.

***

I decided to start with the oldest property, which was on a top shelf right at the back of the store. Everything was covered in dust, and I doubted anyone had been back there for years. On a top shelf at the very back of the store, I found several exhibits, mainly items of clothing from the late 80s; that was nearly twenty years ago! When I looked up the operation name, it wasn't even on the system, so it must have been before H.O.L.M.E.S., in the days when murder enquiries were conducted using an indexing system based on roller cards.

Then I noticed something which made me smile. Lying on a nearby desk amongst a load of old toot, was a handheld metal detector. It was made of plastic, about eighteen inches long, and was in the shape of a small tennis racket. On the handle was a small button which you pressed to activate. It reminded me of Dave Johnson's story about the WPC and her love balls. I ran it up and down my arm to see if it beeped when passed over my watch and it did. I was like a kid with a new toy and went around testing it on things. But just like a kid, after ten minutes I got bored and put it to one side and got on with the actual task at hand.

The next item on the top shelf was curious. It was a small safe, no more than fifteen inches square. Still, it was incredibly heavy, and I struggled to lift it down. There was a single keyhole in the door, a small handle, which didn't budge, and an ornate maker's livery. The safe had never been bagged, and a faded orange label had been stuck on with sellotape which had now mostly perished. On the label was faint writing and I could only just make out the operation name 'Pickford' and a date from 1992.

A few typing strokes later, I found the case on H.O.L.M.E.S. It had only lasted a few days and a quick glance through the closing report told me it was a suicide which had at first been treated as suspicious, until they found the suicide note. From what I read, I discovered the safe had been seized because the victim, who had hanged himself, had used the safe to stand on before putting the noose around his neck and stepping off.

I wondered whether the metal detector would indicate on whatever was inside, so I gave it a go, which was pretty stupid, as the whole object was made of steel.

I would have thought no more about it if about an hour later, I hadn't come across a large empty suitcase which records showed belonged to the suicide victim. I checked it thoroughly, there was nothing in it; but then, I decided to test my detector again, and I ran it around the inside. As I passed it over one particular bit, I kept getting a beep, so I tore a small hole in the lining and poked my finger through. Stuck to the inside of the case and hidden behind the lining was an old intricate key. I took it out and examined the item closely. It was old and very distinctive in appearance, and I knew exactly where to put it.

Chapter 22

Just before I was about to leave, my mobile rang. Before I'd even looked at caller I.D. I'd worked out Cassandra Marsh was cancelling.

"Hi, Chris Pritchard." I said, in my most 'I'm really so busy' voice.

"Hi, matey."

It wasn't Cassandra but I didn't recognise the voice and the number wasn't in my contacts.

"Who's this?"

"Brucie, Nostrils."

It was the Financial Investigator from Hornsey.

"Did you get the warrant? Have you got a date, yet?" He asked.

I felt really embarrassed.

"No, the fucking beak bounced it."

"Oh, you peckerhead." He said.

"Peckerhead? You mean dickhead." I said.

"I'd never call a D.I. a dickhead, Nostrils, well, not to his face. Where did you go for the warrant?"

"Horseferry Road."

"Well, that's your first mistake?" He observed.

"Why's that?"

"Theydon Bois is in Essex and it's the Essex Coroner who is dealing with it. So why the fuck didn't you go to Epping Magistrates? You'd have been before a lay bench; they'd have never said no to a Scotland Yard detective."

"Of course, you're right. Never crossed my mind."

"Listen, I spent seven years getting Production Orders, the further away you are from London the better. I had a weekly slot reserved for me at Newcastle Crown. The journey was a bastard, but the judge never turned me down."

I assumed he wasn't being serious.

"I can't go to Epping Mags, now, can I? Not after being turned down at Horseferry Road?"

"No. What was his beef, did he tell you?"

"He wanted more evidence that Mrs Parker had been murdered and not just done a moonlight."

"Well, I might be able to help you, there." He said.

"Since the evening before she went missing, there is no record of her spending even a penny from any of her bank accounts or credit cards. And fuck me, could that woman spend. I've done you an analysis, I'll email it over. Her average monthly spend, when she's not on holiday, is eight thousand pounds. It makes interesting reading. There is something else ..."

"Go on."

"Who does she know in Pimlico?" Brucie asked.

"No idea, why?"

"Over the last six months, she goes there quite regularly; lots of debits in coffee shops and restaurants. She's meeting someone there, usually during the day."

"That's interesting."

"Yeah, take a look, it's all on my analysis."

"Thanks, Brucie, that's great. I'm waiting for comms data to come back and when that shows Mrs Parker hasn't made any calls from her mobile, I'll go back for the Section 8."

"One more thing, matey."

"Go on."

"Been asking my contacts in the city about that tax avoidance scheme ..."

"Go on."

"No one knows much but I've asked them to put some feelers out; but at three this morning I had a call from a withheld number which I answered. For a good thirty seconds, I could tell someone was there but not speaking. Just as I was about to hang up, a female voice with a foreign accent, didn't give a name, said something like, 'listen carefully', the caller then told me where I lived and the names of my three children and then where each of them went to school'. I was like 'what the fuck' 'who the fuck are you?'. She said, 'one more question about tax and you'll never forgive yourself'. Then she hung up."

"Fuck me, Brucie, you alright?"

"I was a bit taken back, matey."

"Have you reported it?"

"Not yet. I mean, the tax thing is a little off piste, isn't it? I didn't want to compromise you."

"Fuck me, do we need to meet?"

I could see my date for that evening fading before my very eyes.

"No. Let's do nothing for now. Whoever is trying to scare me, well, I've got bigger balls. I don't know what you've uncovered, matey, but it's fucking upset someone."

"But I didn't discover it, I know fuck all about tax affairs, it was a journalist who told me, so it isn't the secret of Castle Rackrent, not if half of Fleet Street knows it."

"I don't think half of Fleet Street does, matey."

"What do you want to do?" I asked, very conscious that it was poor Brucie and his family who were being threatened, not me.

"Nostrils, I've been coppering for twenty-eight years. I took an oath 'without fear or favour', remember. Whoever that cunt was, she picked the wrong old bill to threaten. I don't scare, not when I'm working for Her Majesty, not ever. All he's done, is make me more fucking determined."

"Respect" I replied, quietly.

There was a pause.

"Thank you." He replied, with dignity.

"So, where do you go from here? I mean, none of your contacts knew anything specific, did they?" I asked.

"No, but someone they know, did. Or how else did the message get through?"

"Any idea who might be the link?"

"One of the guys I called, we worked together at six, works at one of the big city auditing firms. When I called, his company had just audited Skimmia Investments, so I suspect that's the touch paper."

"Who is it and can he be trusted?"

"His name's Steve Kibble. Yeah, he was good old bill. We were mates and did a few trips abroad, once we spent six weeks in the U.S. on a long firm job. He's straight. At least he was. I'll go back to him."

"Be careful."

"Careful? It's my middle name. Or is it Norman?"

And on that ridiculous conversation point, I told him to keep in touch and we hung up.

Chapter 23

Don't ask me why I did it; I don't know. I don't think I'll ever know.

It was stupid, but not as dangerous as it seems.

While as a Detective Inspector, I might be stopped driving my own car: while I might even be fined for speeding or arrested for drink drive, honestly, no police officer in London was going to conduct a thorough search of my car. On that very fact, I would bet a million pounds.

The fact was, at six p.m. that Saturday evening, I was driving from Arbour Square to Notting Hill, with the contents of the aforementioned safe, hidden safely under the driver's seat.

There was a plan forming in the dark, deep recesses of my sub-conscious.

Chapter 24

Parking anywhere in Notting Hill is a nightmare. I ended up leaving my car in an NCP at an extortionate rate, but I calculated it would be worth it. Not having sex for four years puts trivial things like a twenty-eight pound a night parking charge into perspective.

Of course, I didn't know exactly what to expect but I enjoyed guessing. I mean if Cassandra Marsh could charge a client two thousand pounds a night, she was, one, even more expensive than the parking and, two, certain to be stunning.

Cassandra lived in the flat at the very top of what would have been, when it was built, an enormous single occupancy, Victorian terraced house. It was still impressive but 'single occupancy' had been converted into five large flats, one for each floor. I was buzzed in and, after five floors' worth of stairs, reached Cassandra's front door more than a little out of breath. About half-way up, I realised I should probably have brought some flowers.

The front door was ajar, so I gently pushed it open.

"Come in, come in." Said a voice from a room to the left.

The flat was tastefully decorated and, in this location, must have cost a fortune. I entered the lounge, a wooden floored room that looked like something out of a glossy magazine.

As I walked in, Cassandra was just putting on her coat. She came over, smiled, and hugged me.

"Christopher, I am delighted to meet you."

Cassandra was, well, pixie like. She looked really young, possibly in her mid-twenties, was white, petite, almost tiny, with short black hair cut close to her head. She was attractive but pretty and tidy, rather than stunning. She spoke with the tiniest hint of an Irish accent. In fact, in just about every regard, she was exactly opposite to everything I'd imagined a high-class escort would be.

She wore blue jeans and trainers and a plain white blouse; her coat was a brown leather jacket.

"Where are we going?" I asked, desperately trying not to look too disappointed.

"A little bistro in Portobello Road, it's only a few minutes' walk away, and they do the most fantastic food. It's very popular and you have to book weeks in advance."

As we descended the five flights of stairs which I had only just ascended, the first thing to cross my mind was that people were going to think I was going out with my daughter. If Cassandra was in her early twenties, she was at least twenty years younger than me. What's more, what was my mate Julie doing being friendly with such a young woman? But then, Julie spoke as if she'd known Cassandra all her life. They seemed a strange pair.

Ten minutes later, the evening took a turn for the worse when I discovered to my angst that the Portobello Road bistro was not only bloody vegetarian, but they didn't serve alcohol. Cassandra couldn't have chosen a worse restaurant for me; I'd rather have gone to McDonalds.

Cassandra, to her credit, was smiley and chatty despite the grey cloud hanging over my head. If she sensed my disillusionment, she didn't let it show. I made a conscious decision to snap out of my mood and to make the best of the evening.

"How do you know Julie?" I asked.

"We were at school together." She replied, to my amazement.

"I'm sorry?"

"We were at school together."

"You've got to be kidding? You're much, much younger than her."

"Julie never told me you were so smooth." She replied.

"I'm serious. You're telling me you're the same age as Julie? What is she? Forty-two?"

"I'm the school year below, and then I'm an August baby and she's a September – so there's just short of two years between us. At school, Julie was the most popular girl, and she took a shine to me, which was great because I was getting bullied. Whatever you do, don't tell Julie you think I look younger."

"Honestly, Cassandra, I thought you were like, in your twenties."

"I know I look young. I get I.D.'d, whenever I buy alcohol."

"Is that annoying?"

"Yes, when your nearly forty! I know I look young; I'm a size six, I'm small and I have very young features. But trust me, Christopher, underneath this childhood exterior, lies the heart, mind and libido of a forty-year-old woman."

The use of the word libido was quite daring; I mean we hardly knew one another. Yet, I was sitting opposite a high-class hooker, so what did it all mean? I decided to be entirely candid.

"I hope you don't mind, but can we have an honest conversation? I'm too old for games and guessing."

Cassandra smiled and visibly relaxed. Then she smiled again, deeper, almost to another level. She looked into my eyes with a friendliness and sincerity I think I'd rarely witnessed before. It almost took my breath away. But she didn't say a word.

"I don't know what we're doing here, I mean ..."

I suddenly felt quite nervous.

"... Julie set us up, but what are we on? A blind date? Or ..."

Cassandra didn't say anything for a few moments.

"We are on a date." Cassandra said, eventually.

"Julie told you what I did for a living, didn't she?"

I nodded.

"Well, I'm not doing that this evening."

"Good, I think." I replied, completely honestly.

"Oh, just because I'm not doing that, doesn't mean we won't be having sex."

"Do you fancy me? Or is it just that you haven't had sex since 2003?" Cassandra said, mischievously.

"So, Julie has told you everything? Thanks, Julie."

"She's told you everything about me." Cassandra replied.

"She didn't really, she told me what you did for a living; didn't go into any details."

"What do you think I do?" She asked.

That was a challenge. How on earth was I going to describe a high-class hooker nicely?

"I think you go on dates with men in exchange for money."

"Nicely put." She said.

"But that's right, isn't it?"

"Sort of, but let's get this on the table …"

She lowered her voice.

"Twice a week, or thereabouts, I work. My work involves sometimes socialising with wealthy men. Well, that's not strictly true; sometimes but

135

not always it's goes beyond socialising, to include some form of sexual activity. They pay me a great deal of money because ..."

She lowered her voice even further, so I had to lean forward to hear what she was saying.

"... I perform a role, an acting part, and I play it very well. And I only do business with a very small niche of exclusive clients."

"Exclusive? As in??"

"Exclusive as in rich."

"Aren't you interested exactly what roles I play?" She asked.

"Only if you're comfortable telling me?"

"Are you easily offended?" She asked.

"I doubt it. I've been a policeman for a long time; honestly, I don't think you could shock me." I said, trying to be both nonchalant and cool.

Chapter 25

In fact, I had a good evening with Cassandra. That is, once we'd left the world's most boring restaurant and went to a pub. She was quite extraordinary and had a fascinating life story.

The holder of a first in English from Loughborough, she made her first million writing erotic novels, while still at university. When her imagination ran out of stories, she settled down into a comfortable life, using her money to buy run down properties and then project managing the refurbishment. She decided early on that she didn't want the conventional nine to five jobs, and so she moved, with some success, from one money-making venture to another.

She had a close friend from university who was a psychiatrist specialising in the treatment of severe sexual deviances. This friend would hear from her clients, the most extraordinary fantasies, some were extreme, a few bordered on illegal, but most just slightly weird. Cassandra found the things she heard fascinating and, with her astute business brain, realised there were a breadth of opportunities to be exploited.

She spent a couple of years setting up a tranche of websites until she had perfected precisely the right one. After sending two thousand pounds, paid in advance into her bank account and from a bank account, the latter was important for security reasons, the client got to design his dream evening; well fourteen hours to be exact. He did so, by completing a really detailed online questionnaire, and from his answers, Cassandra would design the perfect night out. Often, clients just wanted the GFE, which I learned stood for girlfriend experience. Cassandra would play the role of the perfect partner, holding their hands, kissing their cheeks and whispering 'I love you' into their ears.

Every client would request something different, but usually they were all a variation on the GFE theme. The client might want Cassandra to pretend she was the wife of a close friend, apparently that was quite a common request. Sometimes they would want to call Cassandra by a specific name. Invariably, the evening ended back at a hotel room. As our evening progressed and Cassandra opened up even more, she did admit that having a very young-looking face and build was probably an advantage as she could play the role of a younger person. I suspected I knew to what she was eluding but I didn't want any details.

She had a website through which she conducted her business and a legitimate limited company, so she paid her taxes and national insurance like everyone else.

Driving home the following morning, I'd only been in the car a few moments when Julie rang.

"Well, how did it go?"

"Christ, Julie, I'm still technically in Notting Hill, give me a chance?"

"Spent the night, then?"

"I did."

"Where did you go, what did you do, how did you get on, tell me everything?"

"Look, Julie, I had a great night, well once we'd left the fucking vegetarian restaurant that didn't even have a liquor licence, we got on well. She's super bright, bubbly and, well, lovely, but I'm not sure there's anything long term."

"Did you shag her?" Julie asked.

"I didn't." I replied, honestly.

"What?"

"We didn't shag. She'd only had a couple of three Long Island iced teas, and she was quite pissed."

"Cassandra doesn't really drink, Chris. Three Long Island iced teas? No wonder she was a little drunk; I bet she was slaughtered."

"She fell asleep in the lounge, so I carried her to bed, tucked her in and slept on the settee."

"Oh no! Pop straight round and I'll sort you out, babes."

"Won't the old man mind?" I asked.

"He's playing golf."

I laughed.

"Seriously though, babes …"

"You mean you're not going to sort me out? Un-fucking believable! You're such a prick tease."

Julie laughed.

"You wouldn't have said that if you knew me at training school. Honestly Chris, no. You know that catholic leader guy, lives in the Vatican?"

"The Pope." I replied.

"You've got more chance if you pop round to his."

She laughed.

"But you still had a nice night out, though. Even though your soldiers remain confined to barracks, so to speak."

"My soldiers are going out on exercise the minute I get home. As for Cassandra, she's nice, she is, she really is, but I'm not sure."

"I must admit, I thought you'd end up having sex, but I've known you both for years, you're both alone, so I thought you might be ideal. If not forever, at least for a fling for a couple of months."

My phone started to beep to indicate someone else was calling. I glanced at the screen; it was Cassandra.

"Cassandra's calling." I said.

"Answer her, then call me straight back."

Julie hung up.

"You've left, I was going to make you breakfast." A very tired, very hungover voice said.

"Good morning, Cassandra. You were so fast asleep; it would have been a sin to wake you. I've got a busy day. I've got to finish moving my stuff and I'll need to do about four trips back and forth; remember I told you?"

"Call me tonight, after your busy day." She suggested.

"You're working later, remember?"

"Oh gosh, yes, sorry. Call me tomorrow, then. Bye."

I called Julie back.

"That was quick. Everything ok with Cassandra?" Julie asked.

"Yes, fine. Look, Julie, I don't really see any future in it."

"Oh, I am sorry, babes, why?"

"Firstly, she lives fucking miles away! Buckhurst Hill to Notting Hill is like the journey from hell."

"Get the train!"

I ignored her.

"Secondly, honestly, she's not really my type. I like them blonde and full bosomed. And thirdly, even if I did fall in love, I'm not sure I'd like her going out and sleeping with other men - even if I believed, which I do, that it's just business. And tenth …"

"You can't count!" Julie interjected.

"... and tenth, I didn't feel 'it'; you know what I mean? Oh, and forty-seventh and forty- eighth, she's vegetarian and doesn't really drink!"

"But she's so lovely, and rich and you're so ..."

She paused, but I guessed what she was going to say.

"Desperate, go on, say it."

"I was going to say sad, but desperate will do." Julie said.

"How come she hasn't already got a boyfriend?" I asked.

"Probably, babes, for all the reasons you've just said. She did have a bloke a couple of years ago, maybe four of five, but it turned into a nightmare; there was stalking and injunctions and loads of grief. It's taken her a couple of years to pluck up the courage to go out with someone and now you're going to dump her after just one date! All men are bastards." She asserted.

"I'm not dumping her, that does not count as dumping!" I asserted, firmly.

"Babes, gotta go, another call." Julie said, and she hung up.

Chapter 26

Monday saw the start of another busy week, which contained three key events; firstly, I had to try for a second time to get the Section 8 warrant from Horseferry Road Mags, for which I had a 1.45 pm appointment with the same beak. Then I had to pull together a team to do the search, probably on the Wednesday. Finally, and assuming Mr Parker wasn't arrested as a result of anything we found during the search, I had an appointment on Friday to interview him under caution at his solicitors.

I tried to get hold of Vincent but could only get his voicemail which might have been telling me something important, but as it was in Portuguese, I couldn't understand a word.

I got a call from Brucie, who offered to come with me to Horseferry Road; it felt a little embarrassing, like he was offering to hold my hand, but I said yes.

As it transpired, I got the warrant granted immediately and the beak even thanked me for taking onboard his previous comments so readily.

I made a quick phone call to an old friend, and Brucie and I walked over to Wellington House. On route, the two of us chatted about the threatening phone call and what it could mean. Brucie smoked several roll-ups, which he kept in a small Café Crème cigar tin.

The Special Enquiry Team were on the third floor, right at the back of the building and, I confess, I'd never had any dealing with them before. Having managed to get through the security door by showing our warrant cards and signing in a visitors' log, we were ushered into a small office at the rear and met by the D.C.I.

"Nostrils, you old cunt." Dave Walby said, using the most traditional Met detective to detective greeting.

"Hello, boss." I replied, in deference to his rank.

I introduced Brucie. We were told to sit down, and when orders for hot drinks were taken, Dave disappeared to the kitchen.

"You two clearly know each other." Brucie observed.

"We go way back. Worked together as DSs at CIB back in the late eighties, early nineties. You not met him before?"

"Don't think so, matey." Brucie replied.

"As good as they come, I owe him my life." I said.

Brucie nodded.

When Dave came back, I talked him through the job, showed him my recently acquired warrant and asked for some officers to assist me on Wednesday.

"Oh, the Investment Banker's mysterious missing wife case, eh?"

"He's a hedge fund manager. Come on, Dave, fucking sort your life out."

"Pardon me for fucking living, Nostrils. What's the difference, anyway?"

"I would explain but you'd never grasp it." I replied.

"Whatever the difference, one thing's still for sure." Dave said.

"What's that?"

"You're still a cunt, Nostrils." He replied.

"Can't argue with that." I replied.

"How long you been working with him?" Dave asked Brucie.

"Feels like years." He replied.

"And how long is it?" Dave asked.

Brucie looked at his watch and feigned adding up with his fingers.

"About forty-eight hours." He replied.

"That long? And you haven't nearly been killed, or kidnapped, or blown-up?" Dave asked.

"No, just the odd death threat." Brucie replied.

"Is that all? You have done well." Dave replied.

"Who's your top cover?" Dave asked, addressing the question back to me.

"John King" I replied, considering it unnecessary to give his rank.

"Oh, that old shagger." Dave replied.

"Really?" I asked, quite surprised.

"Fuck me, yes. We were at Carter Street as PCs, back in the days of Bernie Mullet. I think he made a bet with someone one New Year's Eve about who could sleep with the most WPCs the next year. Anyway, he was a nightmare."

"Did he win?"

"Well he got off to a good start, but his competitor realised he didn't stand a chance, he circulated the story about him having the clap and the WPCs quite literally, shut up shop to him."

The three of us laughed, and then looked around guiltily, in case anyone had heard us.

"That was a sneaky thing to do?" Brucie said.

"I didn't have a choice; he was beating me hands down!" Dave replied.

We laughed again.

"Is he still a shagger?" I asked.

"Apparently, my mate's his staff officer …"

"Erling?" I interjected.

"That's it. He reckons so. There's some bird, a posh civvy, Tina Klopp or something, works in the Commissioner's Office. Erling reckons there's been one too many late-night meetings between them. Nothing definite or confirmed. Anyway, about this warrant; I can lend you four DCs, ones an F.I., and a DS. Do you want them to arrange Ghostbusters?"

"Yes, please, but I'm hoping Mr Parker will be in and just open the door. Brucie's my F.I. so if yours can act as the exhibits officer, that would be great. Can I have them for two days, just so everything is properly topped and tailed, and their statements are done?"

"Two fucking days? You cheeky cunt! If it was anyone else, Nostrils, I'd tell them to fuck right off."

"Thanks, Dave, much appreciated."

"Still no reconciliation with the gorgeous Jackie?" Dave asked, changing the subject completely.

"No, she doesn't really like men anymore." I replied.

"Not surprised after sleeping with you for a few years." Dave replied.

I turned to Brucie and said.

"When earlier I said Dave was a close friend, when I said 'old' I meant 'rotten' and when I said 'friend' I meant 'cunt'."

"I'd heard a rumour that your missus had left you, I assumed it was because of that other bird you were shagging, what was her name?" Dave said.

"Wendy. And no, I'm not seeing her anymore." I replied.

"She works over the Yard now; often see her going out and in." Dave observed.

I nodded.

"I know."

The meeting ended and Brucie and I stood outside the rear entrance to St James tube station while he had another oily. For about a minute, we stood together in silence watching the world go by, when out of the blue, Brucie said.

"Tommy says hi. Reckons she was the first person you ever met at Stokey."

"She might be right." I replied; these days I couldn't remember much about yesterday, yet alone all those years ago.

"I had a call." Brucie said, almost absentmindedly.

"What another threatening call? Why the fuck didn't you mention it?"

"No, matey. I had a call from Steve Kibble, the guy at the auditors." He replied.

"We went for a few jars in Canary Wharf. Apparently, when they did the Skimmia Investments audit, they found what appeared to be wash trades on an unprecedented scale. They employ Steve on the AML side and they called him in to see if the activity had any connection to money laundering."

"Wash trades?" I asked.

"A wash trade is ostensibly a pointless transaction which has the benefit of increasing turnover, and therefore make a company's books look healthier. So, your own bank account, what, you have an income of fifty k and in a year, you spend all that, so roughly, you'll have an account turnover of one hundred k, fifty in, fifty out – get it?" Brucie explained.

I nodded.

"Well, if every day, you went to the cash point and drew out two hundred and fifty spondoolies; and then, every day you went into the bank and paid that money immediately back into your bank account, you'd be turning over another monkey a day, that's, what, one seventy k a year, in addition to your existing hundred, so your account turnover is now nearly three hundred thousand."

"Why, why would anyone want to do that?" I asked.

"Because if you're a business, or an investment company, your books now look much stronger because it appears; you're doing a great deal more business than you actually are. And if you're doing such a great level of business, your chances of making even more money are higher. Enron used that tactic; well, it was one of many."

"Are you saying there's a fraud going on?" I asked.

"No"

"Was it money laundering?"

"Steve said no. It turned out to be legitimate business."

"So what's the problem?" I asked.

"Because there was a great deal of Russian money, which is never great, and although it was legitimate business, it was all related to tax avoidance and isn't that what your journalist was looking at."

"How does wash trades link to tax avoidance?" I asked.

"Now that is the secret of Castle Rack-rents. Steve's no idea and neither have I." Brucie replied.

Chapter 27

When we did the warrant, I honestly thought Mr Tristram Parker was going to explode but, to his credit, he kept his temper and read every word on the document before refusing to sign it. It always made me smile when people, usually suspects, refused to sign for things, like their own property, for example, because it's such a meaningless gesture. I just wish I had a pound for every time I'd written the phrase 'refused to sign' in a signature box.

We went in early morning, not ridiculously early like you would with a firearms warrant, but by six o'clock we were starting to search the biggest house I'd ever been in, let alone spun.

And to my surprise, Mr Parker was already up and training in his gym, so he answered the front door covered in sweat and breathing heavily.

He tried to call his solicitor but of course, his solicitor was still in bed. Then he tried to insist we postponed the search until his solicitor was present, but I explained that wasn't how it worked.

I assured him that if he had nothing to hide, we wouldn't find anything, and that we would treat his home with respect.

I think I always knew he'd end up suing, so I was more conscious than ever to do everything by the book.

When we seized his computer, I genuinely felt sorry for him but that soon disappeared when he decided to repeat the assertions he'd made when I first met him about destroying me. I treated it a bit like a game and the nastier he got, the calmer I remained.

We found absolutely no evidence that linked to his wife's disappearance, but we did find evidence of an extraordinary level of wealth. He had a cabinet full of new Patek Philippe watches, there must have been thirty; he had a wine storage unit containing case after case of Chateau Petrus; in a wall safe he had ten 1kg gold bars. Laid out on his desk, were a series of sales magazines for large motor yachts for anything from £1.2 million. It was like nothing I'd ever seen. He even had several original Lowry's. I had never seen wealth like it.

The only thing we took away was his wife's toothbrush, for DNA analysis, and two Apple computers, a desktop and a notebook. The search took four hours, quite a short time considering the size of the house, but that was because we only took three exhibits.

Mr Parker was vile, but I still wasn't convinced he'd arranged to have his wife murdered. There would just be too much to lose, surely? If he was that unhappy, why not just divorce her?

I'd been on the case for nearly three weeks and hadn't got any closer to the truth. Mrs Parker's disappearance was a genuine mystery. If she had been abducted and murdered, her body really should have turned up by now. I know my Portuguese colleagues thought she might have been thrown into the sea, but in my experience, murderers weren't always that efficient. Having raped the poor woman, or whatever he did to her, experience taught me that suspects panic and usually dispose of the victim's body quite carelessly. The fact her hotel room had been cleaned several times and reoccupied by new guests before any forensic examination took place was an unrecoverable loss of evidence.

Mr Parker didn't seem to be helping matters. If he was innocent, his hatred towards the police in general and me in particular, wasn't helping him. In fact, he was acting like he was as guilty as a puppy sitting next to a pile of poo. But perhaps that was just his character? I got the impression that he had had a charmed life; that everything, at every opportunity, had always gone his way. I mean, he inherited millions when little older than a teenager – not a bad start in life. Then he invested that money and made even more money. Then he made money for other people, thereby making even more money for himself. From what I saw in his house, he certainly knew how to spend it, but very little was wasted. The finest watches, wines and bullion, all seemed pretty sound investments to me.

I was home early. Mr Parker's house was only a few miles from my new home in Buckhurst Hill. When I got in, I drafted a briefing for the A.C. on my job laptop but I couldn't get the bloody thing to link to the internet for love or money. I was just about to throw it out of the window when Julie rang.

"Hi babes, did you call Cassandra?"

"No, I've been really busy, Julie. And besides, I'm sorry but I'm just not feeling it. Have you spoken to her?" I asked.

"Of course, she called me on Sunday morning."

"She alright?" I said, rather meekly.

"I think she's waiting for you to call. She said she had a lovely evening."

"Julie, I don't know what to say."

"Babes, she fabulously rich, she's really attractive, slim, what's not to like?"

I felt a little cornered and the easy way out was to agree to call, which would of course lead to a second date. I was about to concede when Julie said.

"And why did you lie to me?"

"What are you talking about?"

"You did have sex, Cassandra told me." Julie said.

I was stunned. We most certainly did not have sex. Why on earth would Cassandra claim we had? That made my mind up for me.

"Sorry, Julie. Thanks for setting it up, I mean that, but I'm not going to call. If you really, really love me, you'll do me a favour and tell her."

"Okay, your decision. I'll give her a ring. What do you want me to say?"

"Just be honest, tell her …"

I hesitated, unsure how to best put it.

"Tell her, I'm so busy at the moment, I just haven't got time to do a new relationship justice."

"Jesus, babes, I won't say that. I'll think of something less offensive instead."

"Like what?" I asked.

"Like she smells really bad and is hideously ugly." Julie replied.

Sometimes I really didn't understand women!

Chapter 28

The next day I delivered my briefing to Erling on an orange docket, duly minuted. Once again, as soon as I arrived, Erling took the opportunity to vacate his desk and pop down to the fourth floor to get a sandwich and a coffee.

"Anything comes in, just take a message. Could be a job for you here once you've done with the Portuguese enquiry."

I didn't mind, it was only ten minutes. I couldn't log on because Erling had left himself logged in, so I sat there just fiddling with the documents, letters and files which littered his desk, desperate to have a good nosey around but equally eager not to get caught doing so. One file had the heading 'Client 321' and I opened it a few inches, just to peak inside. There was an expenses form and an invoice for a three-figure sum. I suspected that the senior officers had had another night out on the job, and I wanted to see what they'd put on their Met Police American Express cards this time. I opened the docket further while simultaneously straining my ears to make sure no one was coming

The actual sum was five hundred and twenty-six pounds, and the invoice was from a company called Eastwood Electrical. I looked closer; the document detailed the supply and installation of a washing machine and tumble drier at an address in Essex. The customer's name was Ruislip Associates with an address in Ruislip, North-West London. What was an invoice for a private company doing in the A.C.'s in tray? And why would the Metropolitan Police be paying to install someone's domestic appliances. I'd never heard anything like it. Having found the document with the expenses from the senior officer's night out, I was starting to seriously question whether I had uncovered some corruption. I suspected some senior officer was purchasing their kitchen appliances courtesy of their police credit card. I got out my phone and took several photographs of the paperwork. I'd just finished and closed the docket when the A.C. emerged from his office. I hadn't even realised he was there! It was a mighty close call.

"Christopher"

"Boss" I replied, with due reverence.

"Where's Erling?"

"Getting a sandwich, boss. He asked me to sit in for five minutes."

"Tea"

He nodded towards a kettle and a few cups sitting on a tray above a fridge.

I knew full well he was telling me to make him a cup of tea, but the lack of a 'please' pissed me off. Besides, I'd stood up to him once and survived.

"That's very good of you, boss. White, no sugar, please." I said, keeping my face absolutely dead pan.

He had started to turn away, but my reply made him check and he turned around to look me square in the face. I held his stare with a cheeky smile. I didn't know which way this was going to go and then his face burst into a smile.

"I like you, Nostrils. You're a cunt, but I like you. You've got balls, but then you always were my hero. Now make me a fucking tea, white, no sugar. And make yourself one and join me. I need a chat anyway."

"I invited Mrs Matthews to the Police Widows and Orphans Annual Charity Dinner. I hope she comes."

"I know she mentioned it. I hope she goes but she doesn't usually. She's never got over the fact that her daughter's killer walked free. She says the job is still investigating racially motivated murders from twenty years ago, so why isn't it pursuing her daughter's murderer?"

"He didn't technically walk free but I understand; I really do. Anyway, listen, Christopher. I'm picking up some vibes that you're ruffling a few feathers amongst the great and good."

"Boss, I have no idea what you're talking about." I replied.

I assumed the A.C. was referring to the Portuguese matter but all I'd done was make a few discreet enquiries about the suspect's business in order to tease out whether there was any link between those and the missing wife.

"A colleague of mine, a senior colleague of mine, arranged for a certain DS to be returned to uniform and sent to the far corner of the Met, and then the other day, she sees him drinking with you outside the Old Star. She is convinced there's a conspiracy going on."

I'd obviously taken a stupid pill that morning because for a few moments I had no idea what the A.C. was talking about. Although, in my defence, I did think he was going to be talking to me about the tax avoidance investigation.

"D.A.C. Young is convinced you're behind the Emu investigation and are trying to set her up."

"Boss, I've had nothing to do with that, ever, although I suspect half the Met knows about it. And the F.I. I'm using on the Portuguese enquiry was on that previously, but he's not on it now; not that I know of. He's making a few financial enquiries for me to see if Mrs Parker's disappearance is connected to her husband's business affairs."

"Make sure you don't give Ms Young any ammunition, Christopher. You don't want to make an enemy of her, she's highly likely to be the next Commissioner."

If Kitty Young became the next Commissioner, then my career was over but how could I possibly prevent an event so completely out of my control?

While the A.C.'s advice, not to make an enemy of Kitty Young, was sound, I thought that ship had already sailed.

***

When I left the office, Erling was back at his desk.

I said 'goodbye' but as I was about to leave, turned around, as if to make out I'd just remembered something.

"Oh, while I was in your chair, someone from Ruislip Associates rang and asked whether you'd got the invoice."

"That'll be Simon. Yes, I've definitely seen it. I'll get it before the A.C. to sign off."

"Who's Ruislip Associates? Why are we paying their invoices? I haven't discovered some corruption?" I said, half-jokingly.

"No, that's the name used by the Witness Protection Unit when they need any work doing by contractors or whoever. Simon's covert role is to be the company's CEO but in real life, he's the Unit's D.C.I."

"Oh" I said, as if I was already bored with the conversation.

"See you, Chris." Erling called out, as I walked off.

At least that expense claim seemed genuine.

***

The mention by the A.C. at yesterday's meeting of Kitty Young unsettled me. Kitty and I had history. She'd been on my relief at Stoke Newington back in the early 80s. She lasted about three weeks before going sick with work related stress and then suing the Job for racism. Halfway through the Employment Tribunal the Job offered her eighty thousand pounds and an apology, which she accepted. The day before, I had proved beyond all reasonable doubt that she'd committed perjury and conspiracy to pervert the course of justice, but what did that matter?

Then fifteen years later, our paths crossed at Tottenham. She tried to fit me up by planting racist material in my desk. I sidestepped that bullet by a small stroke of genius and a substantial dollop of luck. When I retaliated and applied pressure, Kitty went off sick, again.

In the ten years since I last seen her, Kitty had done two things remarkably well. First, she'd accelerated through the ranks at light speed and secondly, every other day she appeared on T.V. telling the world how racist the Met was and how she was striving to drive change from within.

If I thought about her too long it actually made me ill, so I pushed any memory of Kitty Young to the back of my mind and kept changing the channel.

I wasn't racist. I'd worked with many great black and Asian officers and the only people that gave them a hard time were those from their own communities. My best friend of all time was a black officer who'd died of AIDS many years ago. There wasn't a day went by that I didn't miss him.

Kitty Young however was an officer I can honestly say I hated. I used to fantasise that I could rid the world of her without getting caught.

***

There are times, not many, in your life when you just have a brilliant idea. There are many more times when you think you've had a brilliant idea, at the time. I hoped, this was one of the former.

I can remember the exact moment it arrived, when, after the meeting with the A.C. I got into a packed downward travelling lift on the ninth floor of the Yard.

It was a decent line of enquiry. I should have already thought of it and had it been a normal murder investigation, I'm pretty sure I would have done so, or even if I hadn't, one of my team would have suggested it.

When I was first briefed at the Embassy, Vincent mentioned that they'd checked the hotel records for the night of Marcella's disappearance and hadn't identified any other suspects. How would they be able to do that? The vast majority of the guests would not have been Portuguese, so, for example, how would they have been able to undertake PNC checks on their British guests? Was it possible that in the room next door to Marcella had resided a prolific sex offender who'd lusted after her all week and then climbed into her bedroom that final, fateful night? Alright, that would still leave a few obvious questions unanswered, like what did he do with her body? But it was an obvious line of enquiry.

I loitered outside the Yard and made several calls; the first, was to Vincent to get a copy of the hotel manifest so I could start to do some PNC and CRIMINT checks on the other guests. If they were foreign nationals, I needed to find out how to do those checks, so my second call was to an old contact I had in Interpol, Sergeant Bellamy. I'd known him forever. He'd long retired but when he did he walked straight into an admin job with the International Criminal Police Organisation.

Sergeant Bellamy was probably the oldest friend I had in the Job.

Chapter 29

I was making my way to meet Vincent at the Portuguese Embassy and get a copy of the manifest. I'd just got to the westbound platform at St James Park when my phone rang. St James Park is one of the few London underground stations near enough to street level to be able to get a signal, albeit a weak one.

"Who is it?" I asked politely.

"It's Ray." Replied a vaguely familiar voice.

"Ray who?"

"Raymond Stickleborough-Crompton"

"Alphabet, how are you mate?"

I had known Alphabet for years. He was a lovely fellow; very posh, very bright and slightly out of place as a police officer. He'd gone to Special Branch early in his career and our paths had rarely crossed, but I had fond memories of our time together on the Crime Squad.

"I'm good, Nostrils. Listen, you're doing that hedge fund manager's missing wife job, aren't you?"

"Yes, mate." I replied.

"You need to come and see me. I have some intelligence to break out."

"Where do you work now?" I asked, assuming he was still at SB.

"I'm at the Confi Unit; fifth floor of the Yard, Victoria block." He replied.

Although I'd never actually had anything to do with the Confi Unit, I was vaguely aware of what they did. They transferred secret and top-secret intelligence between agencies and then processed that intelligence through a sterile corridor to protect the source. So for example, if an informant reporting to HM Customs & Excise told their handler information unrelated to their business but very relevant to another agency, such as an impending terrorist attack, the Custom's Confi Unit would cleanse the intelligence of anything that might identify their informant, and then transfer the report to the MPS Confi Unit who would pass it to SO13, the Met's counter terrorism unit, for action. Amongst other things, the process off-set any disclosure issues downstream. The Confi Unit concept developed in the early 90s from issues arising from the NCIS Line Room – where they intercepted telephone calls. And yes, Confi was short for Confidential.

"I can be there in a few minutes, I'm opposite the Yard now." I replied.

"Brilliant" Alphabet said and hung up.

As I emerged from the station, the Evening Standard seller was just setting up and his papers were still bundled together by blue cord and lying on the pavement by his stall. The headline read 'Banker Faces Imminent Deportation', so I bought a copy and thumbed quickly through the article, but it didn't tell me anything I didn't already know and, I thought quite interestingly, no reference was made to yesterday's search.

It was lunch time at the Yard. As most of the pedestrian traffic was leaving, it only took a few moments to slip through the recently erected outer security gate and then the airlocks. I took the left set of lifts, as these served the lower floors.

To get to the Victoria block you could either cut across at the fourth floor, through the canteen, or via the conference rooms on the fifth. On the latter floor were paintings of all the previous Commissioners. I chose the latter which by sheer coincidence meant that as I got out of the lift, I walked straight into my old girlfriend, Wendy. I was completely taken aback.

"Hi" I said.

Only a one syllable word but the desperation in my voice was palatable, and in that moment, I knew I was still in love with her, and so did she.

"Oh, hello." She replied casually, as if we'd seen one another only few hours ago.

And then she stepped into the empty lift, pushed a button and was gone.

I don't think I could have been more hurt, if she pulled out a gun and shot me. I actually felt physically sick and when I looked at my hand it was shaking. The fact was that in the three years since we'd parted, I'd not stopped thinking about her, almost every hour of every day. I'd not been out with anyone else, I'd barely looked at another woman, unless they physically reminded me of her. It was pathetic and I knew that, but the heart wants what the heart wants, and it felt like I just couldn't move on.

'Oh hello', was that really all I was worth? After nearly four years of my life!

Just 'oh hello', from the woman who declared, over and over again, she would never leave me, who described her love for me as all-consuming and who, only a few months into our relationship, wanted to purchase a house in the street adjacent to mine just so she could feel even closer to me.

After a few minutes loitering by the Met's previous leaders, desperately waiting in case Wendy decided to come back, I composed myself and made my way to the Confi Unit.

I hadn't realised when I'd taken his call, Alphabet was now a Detective Superintendent, something I learnt when an attractive young WPC showed me into his office and passed the sign on his door. We greeted one another like the very old friends we were, with a firm manly handshake – this was England, after all.

Alphabet indicated four seats round a coffee table, and we sat opposite one another. The WPC, who I learnt was called Kelly, took our drink order and as she left Alphabet asked her to get 'Cola' to join us.

"Fuck me Alphabet, a Superintendent? I always knew you'd go places." I said.

"Not bad considering I failed the board last year, is it?" He replied.

"So, you're only on temporary promotion then, wasn't it a bit dodgy getting the sign for the door?" I asked.

"No, the promotion's permanent. Didn't you hear what happened with last year's Superintendent's process?"

I shook my head.

"About seventy of us went for it and thirty were appointed. Then one of those that failed bumped into the Commissioner at a glass ceiling event, pulled him to one side, and managed to convince him that they'd been hard done by and should have been promoted. The old Commis went in the next day and gave the order to promote her, which as Commissioner, he is quite entitled to do and wham, bam, thank you ma'am, she's a Superintendent.

News rapidly spread, and the Superintendent's Association put in appeals on behalf of the other candidates arguing that they should all be promoted, or at least those that scored higher than that officer at the assessment centre. Well, it only turns out, that women had come last, so they had to promote everyone, or face being sued for sexual discrimination. I couldn't believe my luck."

"I never knew, that's unbelievable. What's a glass event?"

"A glass ceiling event, it's an initiative to encourage female officers to seek promotion and improve their representation in the senior ranks."

I was somewhat perplexed. Every other senior officer I met was a woman which was fine but when you considered they all joined twenty years ago and in those days most recruits were male. The fact that there were now so many must be a result of discrimination against males.

As a white male in the Met you felt right at the bottom of the pile. At the top, of course, were the black and visibly ethnic minority officers and then came the women. Overtaking the white men were the gay and lesbian officers, who were right on trend and who some thought, might ultimately be better positioned than the female officers. And so, as a white heterosexual male, you felt pretty undervalued and very overlooked. Not that white males were any better than anyone else, they certainly weren't, but we thought we at least deserved equal opportunities.

A blonde female in her mid-thirties entered the office and Alphabet introduced us. This was Cola, short for Nicola, and she carried a single piece of A4 paper which, as she sat down, I recognised as a CRIMINT intelligence report.

"NDA?" Alphabet asked Cola.

"I'll print one off."

As quickly as she'd come in, Cola was off again.

"You still married?" Alphabet asked.

"What sort of question is that? How many other professions ask one another such a presumptuous question?" I asked, only half-jokingly.

"Well?" Alphabet asked, and I saw a hint of a cheeky smile.

"That's not the point." I replied, with faint indignity.

"Divorced then?"

"Yep"

He laughed; I smiled and shrugged my shoulders.

"Last I heard you were shacked up with that Greek bird, the tall one, works as a staff officer on the eighth floor." Alphabet said.

"She's long gone, mate. Gave her the big E …"

I made a slow exaggerated gesture with my right arm indicating that I was elbowing someone aside.

"She dumped you, did she?" He asked.

"Yep" I replied.

"I've just seen her, actually."

"Oh nice." Alphabet replied, but I could tell his interest in my love life was waning and I can't say I blamed him.

"You still gay?" I asked to lighten the mood and move the conversation on.

The moment the words left my mouth something from the dim and distant past pinged at the back of my brain.

Alphabet smiled but not unkindly and I knew I'd made a faux pas.

I grimaced.

"Sorry, I remember now." I said, contritely.

Fortunately, Cola chose that moment to return. She placed a blank Non-Disclosure Agreement on the table between us and I signed and dated it.

"Thanks" Cola said, and she replaced the NDA with the intelligence report.

I looked at Alphabet who nodded towards the table. I picked up the intelligence report and read it.

Intelligence suggested Skimmia Investments was, and continues to be, involved in laundering the proceeds of crime for senior Russian politicians and diplomats.

The intelligence was graded B2; that is to say it was assessed to be reliable and from a credible source. I quickly scanned the document looking for a source but of course all it said was MPS Confi Unit.

I turned the paper over sarcastically, as if to indicate that I wanted more information, and hoped this would be printed overleaf. I placed the paper back down with deliberate fussiness, squaring the bottom edge off to make sure it was exactly parallel to the side of the table.

"I'll pop back down to the Russian Embassy and ask them what the fuck's going on." I said.

Alphabet shrugged his shoulder as if to say that he was as baffled as me.

"You gotta tell me more than that?" I said.

"I can't. You know how it works. The intelligence came from one of our partner agencies."

"Do you know which?" I asked.

"I could easily find out, but I still couldn't tell you, so there's no point, Nostrils."

"Why Nostrils?" Cola asked.

"It's a long, old and boring story." I replied, but not unkindly.

"I'd love to know more?" Cola said.

"When I was a young P.C., an armed blagger aimed a sawn-off shotgun at my head and discharged the weapon. Fortunately, I ducked just in time. Nostrils is slang for a sawn-off shotgun. I've been 'Nostrils' ever since. Though, if I'm being honest, it took me months to understand why." I explained.

"I see." Cola replied, the outside of her lips turning upwards to form the beginning of a smile.

"Alphabet, I'm not sure what I'm meant to do with this intelligence?" I said, turning to face my old Crime Squad partner.

"I know mate, but you know, we receive intelligence, and we pass it on; it's kind of our job."

"If its source led, can we task the source?" I asked, hopefully.

"I genuinely don't know whether it's source led." Alphabet replied.

"Okay, help me here. I understand that you gather and disseminate sensitive intel with other Confi units. Which partner agencies are those units from?"

"I'm not sure I can ..."

"Oh, for fucks sake, Alphabet, sorry, I mean Detective Superintendent, that can't be a state secret, surely?"

"Sorry" He replied, slightly apologetically.

"MI5, MI6, NCIS, the line room ..." I said.

"They're called SOCA now." Cola corrected me.

"Ok, SOCA, Cuzzies, HMRC, The Prison Service, other police forces, foreign police forces, Post Office investigations ..." I went on.

"Who?" Cola asked.

"Never mind. Basically, this intelligence could have come from anywhere?" I asked.

Alphabet and Cola nodded.

"I can tell you something for definite, Nostrils." Alphabet said.

My hopes raised.

"It definitely wasn't ..."

He paused, for dramatic impact.

"Go on ..." I encouraged him.

"... from Post Office investigations."

I didn't want to, but I did laugh. He was, in a nice way, taking the piss.

"But if its B2, it can't be off a line, can it? Because that would be A1, right?"

"That's not quite true." Cola interjected.

"I don't know what to say, guys. I'm a bit bamboozled by it but I'll certainly pass it on to my F.I. Is that alright? I've signed the NDA so I can't really mention this to anyone, can I?"

"We'll give you another NDA, just get your F.I. to sign that, ok?" Alphabet suggested.

"That'll work." I said.

"If the case was being prosecuted in this country, this would go on the MG6d as sensitive unused and be the subject of a PII, if necessary. But none of that applies as this is a foreign prosecution." Alphabet explained.

"I know." I replied.

"Does this intelligence fit in with anything else you've heard?" Alphabet asked.

"Yes and no. I am not absolutely convinced the suspect arranged the murder of the victim, there's significant doubt in my mind. Yes, true, he had all the money in the world to finance the project and yes, there is no evidence, intelligence, or suggestion that anyone else would have wanted her dead. If it was a random attack or a spontaneous sex offence, the suspect would have left the body in situ but whoever did this killed the victim and then removed and disposed of the body. That might suggest this crime was planned down to the finest detail. Did Tristram Parker hire a contract killer of the highest order to murder and dispose of his wife while he was six hundred miles away with his girlfriend? I really don't think he did but, and it's an important but, I've been wrong before. In fact, over the years, my old partner, I've made rather a habit of it.

D'you know, if he was standing trial in this country, we would struggle to convince a jury, but I think there'll be a good chance in Lisbon where conviction rates are high. And that makes me worried, Alphabet."

"Sounds like an interesting job?" Alphabet commented.

"This is my seventh year on the murder squad, and I can honestly say I've never investigated anything like it. But then it's a bit strange because I'm only assisting the Portuguese guys."

"Is it on HOLMES?" Cola asked.

"No. And we searched his home address last week but nothing."

"I did hear something about Skimmia Investments and money laundering, but then apparently, whatever that was, wash trading I think was the term, in fact turned out to be something else. Something to do with tax avoidance."

"Cola, can you give Nostrils and me two minutes, please?"

A moment's hesitation flashed across Cola's face but in the next instant she smiled kindly and left the room. I guessed she was concerned that her boss was about to reveal more than he should. I hoped she was right.

Alphabet waited until Cola had closed the door. I didn't speak, I thought it wisest to let him say whatever he needed to first.

"Look, Nostrils. I don't know the source and I haven't got a clue as to the provenance, but B2 is about as good as you get these days, it really is. Nothing is graded A1 because that confirms the product has come from a telephone intercept. As you've said, this isn't your run of the mill murder enquiry because although the suspect and victim and most of the witnesses are English, the offence took place abroad. There was quite a debate about whether under these circumstances you should have been told about this intelligence. I decided you should."

I was tempted to say thank you but decided to hold out to see whether he was prepared to impart anything important. After all, he'd hardly have asked Cola to leave us alone if that was all he had to say. Instead, an awkward silence hung in the air for what felt like minutes.

Alphabet glanced towards the door, perhaps subconsciously checking that it was still closed.

"Listen, I definitely shouldn't be saying this but ..."

I put my hand up in an unambiguous open palmed gesture. Then I put my finger to my lips to indicate he should stop talking. He followed my sign language.

"Let's take a walk, I hear St James Park is particularly lovely at this time of year."

Chapter 30

At my suggestion, we bought ice lollies at the confectioners immediately opposite the Yard and then headed towards the little cut through from Queen Anne's Gate, across Birdcage Walk and into the park. We started a slow clockwise walk around the lake that would take us past Buckingham Palace. It was a nice afternoon, and the place was busy with hundreds of tourists, most of whom were queuing to take the traditional picture on the small bridge. A few irritating idiots were sunbathing on the grass while playing their music so loudly that there was little peace and absolutely no tranquillity.

On route we had chatted about old times and discussed a dozen old colleagues and what they were up to, now. A couple were or had been in prison, a few had left the Job, but most were still somewhere amongst the myriad of roles provided by the country's largest law enforcement agency. We decided that at Detective Superintendent, Alphabet was the only one of us to have attained any significant rank with, of course, one famous exception. Kitty Young, my old nemesis from both Stoke Newington and Tottenham, was now a Deputy Assistant Commissioner and heralded by all and sundry as the next commissioner. Even without that promotion, she was by far and away the highest ranking black female officer in the U.K.

As we neared the palace, our conversation about the good old days came to a natural close and there were a few moments as we both adjusted our thoughts back to the subject at hand.

"Listen, I'm in a bit of a dilemma. I have a sneaking suspicion there might be more to Marcella Parker's murder than there appears." Alphabet said.

"Your intel?"

"No"

His response surprised me.

"Here's the story. The intel came in yesterday and I genuinely don't know where it came from. I could find out, of course, but I haven't. It came in sanitised so I've no clues as to provenance, but it is graded B2 so its credible, at the very least. Normally, we may not even break that out, I mean, it's pretty unactionable, so what's the point of you having it? But I insisted because there is something I know. But I know this in an unofficial capacity, and it's put me in a really unenviable position. When I explain, you'll understand, I hope.

My wife's ex old bill, she works for Standard Investigations, it's a firm that specialises in countering work-based theft and fraud. Their clients are the big city firms who don't like to wash their dirty laundry in public, if you know what I mean. You know, chief accountant embezzles several million pounds from the big oil company he works for, well they want the irrefutable evidence so they can sack him, and he can't sue for wrongful dismissal. They're not necessarily after a police prosecution. Anyway, of course as it's not the state doing the investigating, they don't have to comply with RIPA or other human rights legislation. Basically, they can do want they want; bug a phone, wire up an office, place them under twenty-four-hour surveillance. No paperwork, no risk assessment, no human rights considerations."

"No bullshit then, I want to resign and work there." I said, only jokingly.

"Anyway, the wife is working for Standard Investigations at Skimmia Investments. It's a long running contract. Quite simply, Skimmia Investments monitor their staff very closely using covert CCTV. Every office, every bathroom has them. Obviously, a few senior members of staff are aware but most of the employees haven't got a clue. Well, this generates hundreds of hours of footage and they sub-contract the review of the footage to Standard Investigations."

"What are they trying to identify?" I asked.

"There's a list of things, but mainly the leaking of information to other investment companies, insider trading, or internal fraud or theft. They had a case last year where one of their employees was front running the company's investments."

I didn't tell Alphabet that I had no idea what 'front running' was.

"Ordinarily, my wife wouldn't have said anything, but when she heard about Marcella's disappearance, she didn't know what to do."

"Go on …" I said.

"About a month ago, she saw footage of Marcella Parker in her husband's office. She was acting very strangely. She was taking photographs; of his desk itself, the carpet; the office walls and the furniture, even the light fittings. The wife didn't know what to make of it." Alphabet said.

"So, Tristram Parker even has his own office under surveillance?" I said.

"Presumably, for exactly something like this." Alphabet replied.

I nodded.

"Did your wife disseminate the information?" I asked.

"Of course, that's her job. She did her weekly report, as she always does, and sent it to her boss. She assumed the boss sent it onto Skimmia Investments. And she really wouldn't have given it another thought, if Mrs Parker hadn't then disappeared and the case been reported in all the papers."

"So, Mrs Parker was routing through her husband's office, but we've no idea why. Your intelligence suggests Skimmia Investments might have been involved in laundering dirty Russian money. My enquiries say Mr Parker was operating a legitimate but wide scale tax avoidance scheme which he probably wanted to keep very secret. And to cap it all, the Portuguese think Mr Parker had his wife murdered by contract killers because he was having an affair and couldn't be bothered to get a divorce. Oh, and I'm still not entirely happy with a hotel waiter and a date that never was."

"Sounds like the proverbial canine feast." Alphabet observed.

"What?" I asked, momentarily lost.

"It's a dog's dinner, old sport." Alphabet concluded.

Chapter 31

I hadn't seen Sergeant Bellamy for ten years, maybe more. He'd been my Street Duties instructor at Stoke Newington and then my Section House Sergeant. Between the two postings, he'd had a massive heart attack, so it was really good to know he was still alive and kicking twenty-five years later. After his coronary event, he'd also lost a huge amount of weight but when I met him that day in the Black Dog at Vauxhall, he'd put it all back on, and then some.

He was sitting in the corner but as I walked in, he jumped to his feet, held out his right hand and made a level V sign with his two forefingers which he then pointed towards my eyes and shook. It was a gesture I'd seen a hundred times and one he always used to greet me.

"Nosrtilsssssssssss" He declared, loud enough for the half the pub to hear.

"Hello, Sarge." I replied, wearing perhaps the first and certainly the widest smile of the day.

I knew he wasn't a sergeant anymore, but PS Bellamy would always be my sergeant. I mean, I used to call him 'Sergeant', even when I was of the same rank. It was out of respect

We shook hands warmly and he called over the landlady to 'get my mate a pint of the dark stuff'.

"Before I forget, there you go."

He handed over a piece of A4.

"I've sent you it electronically, too. Just fill it in, one for each subject, as much information as possible. You can cut and paste the background and justification. I'll do the rest."

"How long will it take to come back?" I asked.

"Depends from country to country; the U.S., two weeks, our European partners can be quicker; some countries, like China, never respond, that's because we don't have a formal agreement with them, so they'll only respond if it's in their interests to do so. African countries are a nightmare, almost impossible, Australia and New Zealand are no problem."

"People staying at a holiday hotel in Madeira, will be mainly European, I'd have thought. The Portuguese ones will have already been done." I replied.

"I bet they'll all be Brits. It was the Porto Mare, wasn't it? I know it well; usually stay down the road at their sister hotel, the Cliff Bay. I've been to Madeira loads of times; the island is heaven on earth." Sergeant Bellamy replied.

The landlady put a pint of Guinness on the table in front of me.

"Cheers, darling." Sergeant Bellamy said.

He raised his glass.

"To Dawn." He proposed.

"To Dawn." I replied.

We clinked glasses.

"Did you hear what happened to that cunt?"

I nodded.

"Two fucking years! For the Preston bombing and yours! Innocent children were killed in the Preston bombing. Cowardly, fucking scum."

"I know." I said, quietly.

"You don't seem bothered, Nostrils."

Just for a second I felt my temper coming, just like in the A.C.'s office a couple of weeks ago, but this was Sergeant Bellamy, I couldn't lose it with him, he'd done way too much for me after the bombing. Instead, I fixed him with a stare, the best 'don't be such a cunt' stare I could muster at four in the afternoon in Vauxhall.

He held a palm up in acknowledgement.

"Sorry, Nostrils. Of course, you're fucked off."

"If I let it, it would destroy me, Sarge. Every day for twenty-five years that event has cast the darkest shadow over my life. If I'd given into it, I'd have died a long time ago. I have to fight it, all the time. It doesn't matter how many years pass. It doesn't get any easier. I try to block it out, to keep myself sane, I have to move on without looking back."

I could feel myself getting emotional. I could hear my voice starting to crack.

"I know, mate. I'm so sorry; don't get upset." Sergeant Bellamy said.

I took a few greedy gulps of Guinness and cleared my throat.

"Don't get mad, eh, get even." I said.

Sergeant Bellamy frowned.

"I've moved in with Dawn's mum." I said, quickly nudging the conversation on.

"Oh, great. I think. You got divorced, didn't you. Someone told me you left your missus for some plonk. That didn't work out then?"

"Nope"

"Idiot! It never does. Cos of course, you were shagging the lovely Sarah, weren't you? That plonk that used to be a model. You thought no one knew but everyone did, well except her husband, the guy that blew his brains out in the downstairs bog."

"Fuck me, Sergeant Bellamy, this is a right old trip down memory lane."

"You were always were a shagger, Nostrils."

"I wasn't, actually." I replied, in all honesty.

"Who's the lucky lady, now?" He asked.

"I had a blind date last week, actually, but it didn't quite work out. Other than that, I haven't been out with a member of the opposite sex in four years."

"Fuck me, I don't know who you are, but can you please fuck off and if you see the real Nostrils, can you tell him I'm waiting for him?"

Chapter 32

It was tricky to trace and interview Miss Sonia Nicholson, the woman with whom Tristram Parker had been on holiday, when his wife disappeared. Her picture had appeared in all the newspapers, so it was hardly surprising she'd decided to go to ground. And where do most people, well, women in particular, go to ground? At their parents, of course.

Sonia was a strikingly attractive black lady, in her early twenties, who worked as a sales rep for a Porsche dealership in Beckton. She lived on her own in a flat in East Ham, but her parents were from Romford, in Essex. I had to go to her place of work and persuade her manager into giving me her next of kin details on the promise that I wouldn't compromise her. It worked.

When she answered the door, Sonia looked rough, like she hadn't slept properly for weeks. I was determined to make the ordeal as easy as possible for her. She invited me in, sent her parents out, and we chatted.

"How long had you been seeing Tristram?" I asked.

"Nearly two years." She replied.

"Tell me how you met?"

"Every year, just about bonus time, there's like a car show in Canary Wharf. We have a stand and several of our like most impressive pieces are displayed to like, get the bankers to spend their bonuses. T bought a 911, fully specced, and I got 1.5% commission, thank you very much. He was chatty, and suave, and like, really nice. I called him a few times over the coming weeks, we always do, you know, like excellent customer service and during one of those calls he asked me out to dinner. I was like flattered. He was very different to anyone else I'd been out with. Where I like used to eat in KFC, he was taking me to classy restaurants. It was like, wow, what is going on? Yes, I knew he was married but I didn't really care. His wife was always away, doing like charity work, and I enjoyed everything about our relationship. I was happy. And then this pile of crap; like, no way has he had his wife murdered, no way."

I said nothing, but Sonia started to cry into a tissue.

"I think you did the right thing to keep your head down."

"Work have been brilliant; they've like given me a month's unpaid leave."

"Oh, that's good." I said.

"Hang on a second, I thought I read in the papers that you worked for him?"

"I read that too, but I don't. I never have. They got that bit wrong."

"What's happening, now, with you and Tristram?" I asked

"T's like finished our relationship. I got a text last week. Said he was sorry, but it was for the best."

I had to admit, I was a little surprised she was bothered but then, the heart wants …

"Had you spoken to him much since you got back from holiday?" I asked.

She shook her head.

"Where did you go again?"

"Estepona, near Gibraltar. We had like a little villa, nothing special. T was always working, anyway. Always on his computer, always on the phone."

"Did you get the impression everything was all right?" I asked.

"He was stressed, but he's always stressed. He gets up at five every day; gym for an hour and then he pretty much works solid until about eight, maybe nine."

I frowned.

"That's not too bad, is it?" I asked.

Sonia looked confused.

"He works like fourteen hours a day!"

I realised she meant eight or nine in the evening.

"What, even on holiday?" I asked.

"Always, like, every day." Sonia replied.

"Well at least he earns the money."

"He certainly did. He once said, he could earn more asleep in one night than the average U.K. wage for the year." She replied.

"Did he buy you nice gifts?" I asked.

"Sometimes, but I wasn't with him just for the money."

I noted the word 'just' – her declaration would have been much more impressive without it, but then, perhaps, not quite as honest.

"Did he talk about his wife?" I asked.

"Occasionally, of course. She was high up in some charity 'Feed the World' or something."

"Did he ever talk about leaving her?"

"For me, you mean?"

"Well, yes."

"No"

"Never?" I asked.

"Never, not once, like." She replied.

"Did you want him to?" I asked.

"Of course, I suppose. But I knew it would never happen. Why does a man, as sophisticated as T, want to be with like Sonia from East Ham?"

I wanted to reply 'love' but said nothing.

It was pretty clear to me that I had learnt one thing from Sonia, there is no way T, as she called him, had had his wife murdered so he could be with her. She was actually really nice and despite the no make-up and the tracks of her tears, really, really pretty. I suspected when she was dressed up, she was' stop you dead in your tracks' gorgeous. But nothing she was saying made any sense of a scenario which put her as the principal motivation for the most serious of offences. It was all rather sad.

"What do you think has happened to Marcella Parker?" I asked.

"She's gone off with her boyfriend."

"Did she have a boyfriend? It's the first I've heard of one." I said.

"T thought so. I think T thought it was someone like that lived in Pimlico. She was often going there to meet someone."

Now, I'd heard 'Pimlico' before!

Chapter 33

I really wanted to have a weekend off. I'd been working quite hard over the past month, and we'd been weekend on the day before I'd got the Portuguese case, so it felt like I'd only had one day off in ages. I wanted to see my girls, well if they weren't too busy; to take Jackie out to dinner, to show I wasn't completely ignoring her in her time of need; move the last of my things out of Starburst and do a deep clean, so I could at least get something back for my money; and, finally, do something really quite illegal just in case I made a certain decision.

The problem was, I still had loads of work to do to sort out the property store so I really should spend at least a few hours there on Saturday morning; besides, if I did four hours work I could re-roster the rest day and get a whole day back, which was an old policeman's trick.

Whether my investigations were complete or not, the final stages of the extradition process were nearing conclusion, at which point the charming Mr Parker would find himself on the big silver bird to Lisbon.

I had no one left to interview, although I was a little disappointed that I'd not had the chance to speak to Cheryl. She was the closest to Marcella, so if anyone of the three women knew what had happened, it was going to be her. With that said, the statement the Portuguese had taken, short though it was, married nicely with what both Lesley and Natasha had said. I'd heard nothing from Brucie for a few days, so I assumed his financial enquiries were proving unproductive. Since Marcella went missing, she hadn't spent any money or made any phone calls – usually, a pretty good indication that she's dead. I got the distinct impression that my small part in this interesting case was beginning to come to an end.

These several thoughts were churning through my mind as I drifted off to sleep that Friday evening. I was vaguely aware that Mrs M had come in, she'd been at the Yard at the Widows and Orphans event and returned much later than I'd anticipated considering they were sitting down to eat at six.

Being woken up unexpectedly at three o'clock by your mobile ringing is never nice. My first thought was that something had happened to one of the girls, but the voice on the phone wasn't Jackie's, said only five words, and then hung up.

"Look out of the window."

I lay in the bed for a few moments working out whether I was still dreaming and then I got up, walked over to the window, and carefully pulled the side of the curtain back. There was a car parked immediately outside and blocking the drive. I couldn't see the colour or make because the yellow streetlight was shining on it, but I did see the headlights flash three or four times before the driver sped off, ridiculously quickly.

I turned the light on and checked my phone, caller ID withheld. No surprise there then.

Brucie had also had a call at three in the morning. It didn't take a genius to work out that whatever we were doing, we'd ruffled some serious feathers.

It was then I remembered the Pimlico connection. Brucie had told me Marcella was regularly meeting someone in Pimlico which he deduced from her spending pattern.

Pimlico was a strange area of London; exclusive yet understated. Squeezed between Victoria, Belgravia, Westminster and Chelsea and on the north bank of the Thames opposite Vauxhall, it was one of London's better kept secrets. It was also, I realised, right in the middle of the headquarters of MI5 and MI6. Was it possible that Marcella was working for them?

Incredible though that thought seemed, it wasn't completely ridiculous. While I was certain she wasn't a fully-fledged, full time operative, there was every possibility that she was what I would call, a covert human intelligence source. Of course, that started to make sense. Marcella worked for a worldwide charity which operated in some of the world's poorest countries. It happens that many of these are Muslim. I knew from a previous enquiry, terrorist funding was often moved around the world through various charity accounts. Of course, the charities weren't complicit, they had no idea what was going on, any more than a bus driver does when he inadvertently carries a passenger who's just murdered someone.

If I was MI5 or MI6, having an intelligence source able to provide account details of a major international charity operating in largely Muslim countries, would be invaluable.

Suddenly, the sound of a car horn beeping loudly immediately outside brought me back to reality. I jumped up and looked out of the window, this time throwing the curtain wide so that whoever was outside was in no doubt that they had my attention, but no sooner had I done so, the car, the same car as before, sped away, again. It might have been a BMW, but I wouldn't swear on oath.

I moved quickly and quietly because I didn't want to wake Mrs M up. I was glad her bedroom was at the back of the house because she probably wouldn't have heard the car horn.

I got dressed, choosing warm clothing as the night looked cold, damp and far from inviting.

I intended to lie low in my car and should the car pitch up again, I'd get out, show out and challenge the driver. Then I'd arrest them for attempting to pervert and call the police. If they drove off, I'd give chase.

But I took half a dozen steps down the stairs and stopped. I couldn't do that. In my car, under the driver's seat, was a Beretta 92, a suppressor and twenty-four live bullets. I didn't want to get into any sort of altercation, when I was carrying a firearm, ammunition, and component parts, all illegal to possess without a certificate under Section 1 of the Firearms Act, 1968. It might be a technicality, but I was also committing a Section 18 offence, possession with intent to commit an indictable offence.

Chapter 34

I was woken later that morning in a much more pleasant way, by the smell of bacon. When I went downstairs, Mrs M had made me a butty and a pint of tea using two teabags, just about my perfect breakfast.

"I heard you get up last night…" Mrs M said, taking me a little by surprise.

"… did you go downstairs?"

"Some idiot was honking their horn; I was going to give them a mouthful, but they drove off." I replied.

"I thought you might be getting up to pay me a visit. You might have been lucky, too, I'd had rather a lot to drink."

"Always helps, if you're going to bed with me." I said.

We laughed but I was just the tiniest bit surprised by the comment; it was a little risqué.

"On a more serious note …" Mrs M said.

"… I've been asked out."

"Wow, I didn't expect you to say that." I replied, perhaps a little insensitively.

My answer clearly deflated my old friend.

"Oh, you're right, it's ridiculous. Ignore me, I'm an old fool. I'll just say no."

I had some reparation to make.

"Don't be ridiculous; I was only joking. You're a really attractive woman. I mean that. Anyone would be lucky to go out with you. You look fifty-five, you're slim, you've even got some of your own teeth and only one wonky eye."

Mrs M laughed.

"Quite a catch, eh?"

"Joking aside, anyone would be lucky to have you."

I couldn't remember exactly, but I thought Mrs M was about twenty years older than me. She had Dawn at sixteen and Dawn was two or three years older than me. I was forty-three, so Mrs M must be about sixty-two? Although, she could easily have been in her fifties.

"It's the first time I've been asked out since that bastard who tried to con me." She said.

"Gosh, that was way back in 85! That's nearly twenty years ago, Mrs M. Time to get your glad rags out of the wardrobe and dusted down. Who's asked you out, anyway?" I asked.

"John." She replied, as if I knew who John was.

"John, who?"

"John King, the policeman from last night."

"The Assistant Commissioner?" I said, in astonishment.

"If that's what he was. A very nice man, quite charming. He bought me home; we were both a little pissed." Mrs M replied.

"He was driving?" I asked.

"No, of course not. He has a driver, doesn't he?"

I know it really wasn't any of my business, but from what I'd heard about the A.C.s previous activities, I wasn't sure I was entirely happy.

"Is he married?"

A hint of doubt flashed across Mrs M's face.

"He didn't say he was." She replied.

"Did you ask him, directly?"

"No"

"Did he give you his mobile number?"

"No, he took mine." She replied.

I shrugged my shoulders, as if to say, 'I'd be careful'.

"Chris, can you find out for me? Please?"

"Why don't you just ask him?" I suggested.

"Please?"

"And if he is married, what will you do?" I said.

"I'll ask your advice. I mean, I don't suppose you've ever been unfaithful, have you?" She replied. Of course she knew full well that I had.

My phone rang, it was Brucie. I politely gestured to Mrs M and went upstairs.

"I was just about to call you." I said.

"What about, matey?"

 told him about what had happened in the early hours of the morning.

"Have you had any more calls or threats?" I asked.

"No, nothing. But Steve Kibble called me. He's been suspended and he's blaming us."

"What happened?"

"He went into work yesterday and his swipe card wouldn't work. Then two guys from HR approached him and led him into an interview room. They read him a prepared letter which informed him he's being suspended because of a data leak."

"What, they know he's spoken to you about the Skimmia Investments' audit?"

"No, don't jump the gun. Apparently, last year he meant to send a very sensitive document to his counterpart in the States. His counterpart's names is Steve Kiba. When he started to type the name in, the email auto-populates, and he presses send. Anyway, two seconds later, his own mobile alerts him to a new email and when he reads it, he realises he's sent the sensitive document to his own private email address by mistake. The auto-populate thing has auto-populated to S Kibble and not S Kiba. Anyway, he immediately deleted the email and then sent an email to his own boss, telling him what he'd done and confirming that he'd deleted the email from his own server. His boss was happy. Steve had to complete a breach form, or something, and he never heard anything more. Anyway, that's what he's been suspended for."

"When did that happen?" I asked.

"Friday, I said"

"No, when did the email thing happen?"

"Six months ago. Steve thinks it's a sham, they're using the email thing as an excuse to suspend him. He wants to meet. You free?"

"I'm at Arbour Square for a few hours this morning. Shall we say the biker's café at High Beech, just off the A11 at the Robin Hood roundabout?"

"That should be discreet enough. I've got more news to impart, and quite frankly, matey, it's all a bit concerning." Brucie said.

Chapter 35

Arbour Square was deserted and this time there were no clandestine smuggling operations taking place. I did another four hours trying to get rid of exhibits that were no longer required. Most I 'destroyed on division' and threw in a large rubbish bin in the yard; of course, only after I'd removed any trace of a connection to the Met Police.

This time I didn't discover any untraceable firearms.

I got a call from Julie who told me Cassandra was devastated when she told her I didn't want a second date, which I thought was a bit of an over-reaction. I mean, we'd had a nice enough evening, but she wasn't the one for me and there just wasn't that spark. I'd been absolutely desperate for sex and yet, when it didn't happen because she was so pissed, I wasn't that bothered, which I think said a lot.

"How's your no sex pact with Luke going?" I asked.

I don't think I'd have normally felt so confident about asking such a personal question, but she had recently asked me about my sex life.

"I'm struggling, babes. Three months isn't natural." She replied.

"How's Luke managing?" I asked.

"He's alright I think, I mean, it was his idea." She replied.

I thought that was strange and if I were Julie, that would set the alarm bells ringing, but I didn't know whether to express my concerns. Three months without any form of sex was unnatural for anyone in the prime of their life. I wondered what it meant. I thought, perhaps, Luke was getting it elsewhere. But then I was transposing my own inadequacies onto another who might not share them?

"You've gone very quiet, Chris. You think I should be worried, don't you?" Julie said.

"Not really; four years without sex tends to screw with your mind." I replied.

"Whatever, babes. Cassandra says you were quite the stud."

There that was again, Cassandra's claim to Julie that we'd had sex. Why would she lie? Perhaps she had sex so often, she couldn't imagine a date without it.

"Any news from the old crowd?" I asked, as if I'd been gone for months, not weeks.

"You don't smoke, do you?" She asked.

"Not anymore, why?"

"Cos Nobby Knocker on team six is selling off some fags really cheaply."

"I wouldn't …"

I was going to say 'touch them with a barge pole' but I learnt a long time ago not to say anything incriminating over the phone, in an office or in your car. Even in your own home, one ought to be very careful.

"… bother." I said, my sentence somewhat petering out rather meaninglessly.

"Do you think Luke's over the side? Have you heard something?" Julie asked, returning to our earlier conversation.

"No and no." I said, firmly.

"Okay, babes, thanks for putting my mind at rest." Julie said.

I wasn't sure I'd done anything of the sort, but it's funny because sometimes people only hear what they want to hear.

"Hang on, I've got another call coming in …" I said.

"Speak laters, babes." Julie called out as I switched.

"Hello"

"Hello"

"Hello"

I knew someone was there. It was just like Brucie had described when he'd told me about his threatening phone call. Then the line went dead.

***

Brucie and Steve Kibble arrived for the meeting in High Beech together. I did recognise Steve, a short, red-headed man in his late fifties with pale, almost albino features. Our paths had obviously crossed at some stage and after a few discussions about where we'd previously worked, realised we'd been at Stoke Newington together back in the eighties, but Steve had been a DS and our paths would have rarely crossed.

It was busy at the café with perhaps a hundred bikers milling about their beloved machines. I'd always found bikers a great bunch of chaps; many, in fact, were ex old bill, often retired traffic cops, but they were still decent people. We stood to one side, nearer the forest itself and while we were clearly not part of this community, it felt a welcoming place to be.

Steve talked us through his suspension, the same tale Brucie had told me earlier. He seemed curiously pragmatic about the whole thing but perhaps he was just the kind of guy who didn't get too melodramatic.

"I know you spoke to Brucie last week about your firm's audit of S.I. but after that conversation, did you speak to anyone else?" I asked.

"I did. I spoke to Becca Benson. She was the chief auditor on the preliminary stage of the contract. I asked her about those wash trades and how we were so certain the activity we had found wasn't money laundering. If I'm being honest, as a retired copper and not a banker or auditor, I'm often a little lost when it gets really technical. I mean, my only qualification is an AML diploma; these guys are all super, super bright. I'm not shitting you, where a work having only a degree is looked down on, you need at least a masters, if not a doctorate to impress."

"How did you get the job?" I asked.

"At the time my brother worked for them, really high up …"

"Thirtieth floor, apparently." Brucie interjected.

"Shut up, you wanker …" Steve replied, jovially.

" … anyway, my brother was Head of their IT department. I'm not saying he got me the job but, well, you know how it works. So, I spoke to Becca, she started talking about wash trades …"

"I know what they are." I replied.

"And push through trades." Steve added.

I looked across at Brucie who shrugged his shoulders indicating that he didn't know what they were.

"Becca talked about something called dividend arbitrage and equities flow."

"For fuck's sake, Steve, what are you talking about?" Brucie said.

"Look, you two. I was as lost as you, but I can't admit that because someone might ask what the fuck is someone with so little financial knowledge doing as a Vice President in the country's biggest auditors? So, I said 'oh I see' a few times and left the matter there."

"And that was it?" I asked, incredulously.

I didn't know Steve, but I did wonder whether there was anything else, unconnected to our enquiries, which was lurking in the background.

I looked at Brucie and just a hint of an expression suggested to me that he was thinking the same. Steve obviously caught the non-verbal exchange because he took a deep, exaggerated breath, and said:

"I know what you're thinking, officially, S.I. is nothing to do with my suspension but I'm telling you it is. The reason I'm fucking suspended is because I asked more questions about their audit. I'm not shagging the

MD's secretary or fiddling my expenses. I haven't pissed anyone off and I got a thirty-grand bonus in March, so they can't think too badly of me. The only fucking reason I can think of, is because I started asking questions about S.I."

"Okay, when they did the audit, did they find anything untoward? Is it possible that S.I. is in fact the next Enron scandal? Have we inadvertently stumbled into a minefield?" I asked.

"Possibly, matey." Brucie replied.

"They do like a preliminary audit. That team discovered loads of money going to and from Luxembourg for no apparent reason. They asked me whether it could be money laundering, and, if I'm being honest, I thought it might. It looked like layering to me." Steve explained.

"I'm murder, not fraud squad." I said.

"Layering is when you pass dirty money through so many different accounts that it becomes increasingly difficult to trace the source of the funds." Brucie replied, helpfully.

"Anyway, I thought 'layering', and articulated my thoughts in a report which I sent to Becca. Becca was quite concerned and raised it as a concern further up the chain. I'd done my bit and didn't think much more about it. Then months later, I had no more than a five-minute conversation with Becca when I read somewhere that the S.I. audit was complete and only a few minor issues identified. I said something like 'what was the Luxembourg connection?' and she said it was connected to equity dividends and something to do with reducing tax burdens by leveraging lawful inconsistencies."

"And you believed her?" Brucie asked, sarcastically.

A slight titter circulated amongst us.

"Of course, I believed her, she might as well have spoken to me in Swahili. I hadn't got a clue what she was talking about. She seemed happy, and she knows her shit, who am I to challenge her? What you've got to appreciate guys is, when you work for a big financial company, it's not about doing the right thing, like it is in the police, it's about protecting the company. That's it. That's what you're paid for. Nothing else."

"That's a sad indictment of the world's biggest financial sector." I observed.

"It's how it is, Chris. It's why many are reticent about hiring ex old bill. They're worried we might still have the Queen's interests at heart."

"Do you think this Becca woman spoke to someone else, after you pulled her?"

"She must have done." Steve replied.

"That would suggest she's also involved in any shenanigans." I said.

"I'd be surprised, but maybe. Fuck! Fuck! Fuck!"

Steve had obviously just realised something.

"What?" Brucie and I asked simultaneously.

"Becca's other half works for S.I."

"What?"

"She's engaged to some Russian guy who's head of their Security & Investigations Team."

"Wasn't that a conflict of interest? Her being involved in the audit?" Brucie asked.

"Yes, it was. That's how I remember it. But she only did the preliminary bit and as her partner wasn't involved in the business side, it was decided she could play a minor role. Fuck, fuck, fuck, fuck. And I'm not meant to know that. It was kept really quiet, and I only got wind of it from a third party. Being honest, I didn't think I gave it a second thought. Fuck, cunting bollocks. She's gone and told her boyfriend that I was asking questions and bang, bye, bye Mr Kibble."

"What's the boyfriend's name?" I asked.

"Not a clue, I just know he's from Moscow because she went on holiday there last year."

"There is something to hide, fucking hell, guys." I said.

"But how does it connect to the missing Mrs P, matey?" Brucie asked.

"Fuck knows." I replied.

"It must, somehow." Brucie observed.

"The only thing Mrs P did was some charity accounts."

"Please tell me she doesn't work for C.W.W.?" Steve asked.

Chapter 36

I felt elated as I drove home because, at last, we were getting somewhere.

A quick internet search identified that two years ago Clean Water for the World had taken nearly three hundred million pounds in donations. I hadn't realised quite how much money a large charity received. It was hardly surprising therefore that C.W.W. should invest some of that money, where better to put it than in your husband's successful hedge fund?

I was also cognisant of the intelligence I'd got that said Marcella Parker was routing around her husband's office taking clandestine photographs. It didn't need a genius to guess that she thought something was wrong. Was her husband really embezzling from her charity? That hardly seemed credible. It's not like he needed the money, but what else could it be? Perhaps S.I.'s financial situation was in fact desperate? Maybe, it was all a giant Ponzi scheme, as one of the hacks outside their home had suggested, all those weeks ago? And no doubt, the report of his wife's behaviour got back to him. I came to the conclusion that Mr Parker was very much back in the frame for her murder.

As I drove home, I got another silent phone call. They were irritating but hardly threatening. It was then I realised I'd forgotten to ask Brucie whether he'd had any more calls.

Was the missing wife anything to do with tax avoidance? That seemed too oblique a connection.

I needed to share this line of enquiry with my Portuguese counterparts but a part of me was weary. I couldn't really drop Alphabet's wife in it, could I? She certainly shouldn't have told Alphabet what she'd seen, and Alphabet shouldn't really have told me. I was also a little conscious that I was perhaps starting to exceed the remit of my liaison role.

I was also waiting on the manifest enquiries to come back. Was there any intelligence to suggest a hired killer had rented the room next to Mrs Parker?

At first this case had seemed quite straight-forward, as the weeks rolled on, it became increasingly like any other unsolved murder enquiry, except I was a team of two, instead of a team of thirty.

After my meeting with Sonia, I'd dismissed the girlfriend motive. Now, I dismissed the tax avoidance connection. I had reluctantly to remove the waiter, as the local police clearly thought that was a moribund line of enquiry. The facts did not support a random and unplanned sex attack, as the body would have been found, by now.

We were left with the charity's money, a corrupted audit and terrorist funding. The link to CT made it likelier that Mrs Parker was in fact working for the Security Services. I needed to bottom that out, but it was a Saturday, everything would have to wait until Monday.

***

I drove into Loughton to pop in on Jackie and the girls. When there was no one in, I called Jackie to learn she was shopping, and we agreed to grab a coffee in the High Street.
It was nearly a month ago that Jackie and George had split up and she looked much better.

"How are the girls? It feels like I haven't seen them for ages." I said.

"Pippa's split up with her boyfriend." Jackie replied.

"Is she ok?"

"She's fine, it was her choice; probably for the best."

"Oh, why? Wasn't she happy?"

Jackie sighed and I guessed something was wrong.

"Was he violent towards her?" I asked.

"Good god, no. There's wasn't a lot about him, to be honest, Chris. It was her first love and I think she did love him for a bit, but she got bored. He never wanted to go out or do anything, he just wanted to sit in his room watching T.V. or playing computer games. He was a nice lad but quite immature."

"For the best then." I said.

"It is, Chris. There's something I need to tell you?'

"She's not a lesbian, too, is she?" I said, half-jokingly.

"No, I don't think so." She replied.

I laughed.

"One's enough in any happy family."

"Listen, please, Chris ..."

I sensed something serious was coming; I'd obviously misjudged the mood.

"What is it?"

"It's really difficult, but ..."

She hesitated.

"Go on, I'm fine, I don't think anything you could say could shock me. Is it Trudy?'

"No, both the girls are fine. Listen, Chris, we're probably moving."

"Oh, okay, I can't afford any more maintenance, Jackie. If that's where this conversation is going. Sometimes, it feels like I work my balls off for really very little."

"It's not a money thing." Jackie said.

"Please don't tell me George owns half the house and you've got to sell? My fucking house."

"No, of course not. It's nothing to do with George. Well, I suppose in a way it is."

"Are you moving down or up?" I asked.

"Away." She replied, and there was a genuine sadness in her voice.

It suddenly dawned on me what she was going to say.

"Where to?"

Jackie looked at me.

"Just say it?"

She started to tear up.

"Look, it's okay. If I can still come and visit. I mean, now you're not with George I can stay over, can't I? It'll be nice, I can have somewhere to go at weekends. I mean, not every weekend, obviously."

I was starting to ramble, and Jackie was now crying, full proper tears were flowing slowly down her face. She didn't make any attempt to wipe them away. I reached in my pocket for some tissues but didn't have any.

"We're going to Perth." She said.

"Jesus Christ, Jackie, fucking Scotland! Why?" I asked.

"No, darling. Perth, as in Western Australia."

I felt a thump in my guts. For a good ten seconds, I couldn't speak.

Jackie was crying again.

"Do the girls want to go?" I asked.

She nodded.

"Really? All their friends are here." I exclaimed.

"Trudy's best mate emigrated there last year. It was her idea. George wasn't interested, what with all her businesses here. But now there's no George, well."

"But there is a Chris." I said, rather pathetically.

Jackie smiled.

"You're married to the Job, Chris. Always will be. Besides, it's the chance of a completely new life for the girls. This country has had it, darling. Sometimes, I feel like a foreigner in my own capital city."

I couldn't be arsed to tell her that if she moved to Australia, she'd always be the foreigner.

"But you haven't even been there." I said.

"I know; but I've done my research. They're trying to encourage trained nurses and there was a recruitment advert in one of the nursing magazines. I think it's a great opportunity."

"But I'll never see my girls." I said.

"You can visit." She said.

"I haven't got that sort of money. I can't just pop back and forth. Please, please, please don't take them away." I pleaded.

Jackie smiled kindly and walked out, without saying a word. I had my answer, I could now add Pippa and Trudy to Matthew and make it all three of my children who never cared whether they saw their father again. I burst into tears but put my elbows on the table and my hand across my forehead to hide my eyes from the other customers and staff. When I looked down my tears were dropping on my Starbuck embossed paper napkin. I think I'd never felt so low.

Chapter 37

In the Starbucks in Loughton, what had started, a while back, as the briefest of passing thoughts, and more recently developed into something of a plan, suddenly crystalised into my destiny. The most dangerous person is one that has nothing to lose and, with my family moving to the other side of the world, that was now me. In that moment of realisation, I decided that my oldest adversary, the one that had tried to destroy me, just to forward their own political agenda, had less than one month to live.

Chapter 38

The Extradition Warrant arrived the following week. A formal request from Portugal's Minister of Interior to Her Majesty's Minister of Justice to arrest and deport Mr Tristram Acton Parker for, on or before 28th April 2007, conspiring to murder his wife, Mrs Marcella Shannon Parker.

Such activity is dealt with by the Extradition Squad who, by coincidence, worked in the office next door to the Special Enquiry Team. They invited me along on the arrest, but I declined and decided to go straight to Belgravia police station, where Mr Parker was going to be detained before being taken to Heathrow and flown to Lisbon.

At the police station I watched him booked in and then took him to the cell. In such cases, and they're rare, there's no interview. Of course, you're not meant to speak to the suspect 'off the record'. All conversations should be in the presence of their solicitor, under caution and be tape recorded, but 'off the record' chats are pretty harmless because whatever the suspect says wouldn't be admissible in evidence anyway.

"So, if you didn't, then who the fuck did kill your wife, Mr Parker?" I asked, politely.

"I don't know." He replied, quietly.

"And why?"

"I haven't got a clue, Detective Inspector Pritchard. I only wish I had because ..."

His voice trailed off and anything else he said was lost amid the jangle of nearby custody keys.

Tristram Parker was about to lose everything, and he knew it. Five weeks after his wife went missing from a hotel room on the tropical island of Madeira, the handsome hedge fund manager was about to be extradited to Lisbon where he would be formally charged before spending anything up to a year in a foreign jail awaiting a trial at which he would, almost certainly, be convicted.

As the trial was to take place abroad, the British press had been unhindered by traditional legislation demanding a degree of impartiality and they had already convicted and sentenced the forty-eight-year-old, former Etonian. They'd uncovered his extra marital affair, ascertained that despite his million-pound income he'd paid less tax than someone on minimum wage, and exposed his large donations to his fellow Old Etonian David Cameron's Conservative party.

On 27th May 2007, one newspaper led with the headline 'But where's your wife, Tristram Parker?' under which they printed a photograph of Tristram and his girlfriend laughing like they didn't have a care in the world. The next four pages told the story and left the reader in absolutely no doubt that the banker had arranged to have his wife murdered. It was only when one read the small print that you realised the picture of Tristram, and his girlfriend, predated the victim's disappearance.

The newspaper portrayed his beautiful wife as the ultimate victim. A charity worker who travelled the world's disaster spots providing help to the most desperate; the picture they painted of Marcella Parker was of a quiet, understated and dignified 'Mother Teresa' type.

As a result, and for a few weeks, Mr Tristram Acton Parker had become the most hated man in the U.K.

When I'd first met him, I can honestly say I detested the man. I thought he was probably the most arrogant, unlikeable individual I'd ever known. As the weeks had passed, I'd gone from thinking he was guilty to innocent and then, with last week's revelations, guilty again.

After making sure the cell door was slammed shut, I turned to walk away.

"Detective?"

Tristram's voice was clear, and I realised I must have left the wicket open, so I turned back with the sole intention of closing it rather than engaging the suspect in further conversation.

"Detective, you have to help me."

I frowned.

"What do you need?" I asked, not unkindly.

"What do I need? You have to prove that I haven't done anything to my wife. I am completely and utterly innocent."

"That's not going to be easy. To the whole of the world, you look as guilty as a puppy sitting next to a pile of fresh dogshit. As I said, a few moments ago, if you didn't kill her, then who did? And why?"

"I don't fucking know!"

His voice was raised in desperation and panic rather than anger.

"Even my lawyer thinks I'm guilty, I know she does. I'm going to be extradited tomorrow, you're going to be my only hope. Please. Look, if you get me out of here, I've got loads of money …"

"Now you're trying to bribe me?"

"No, for fuck's sake, no. I mean, I didn't mean that. Help me, please, just help me. Listen, you know an ex-copper called Ferris, Jill Ferris, don't you?"

Like most police officers, I hated the word 'copper', I didn't mind most colloquialisms, but 'copper', just got my heckles up.

"Jill Ferris? Never heard of her." I replied, impatiently.

'Long, she used to be called Long."

I did know Jill Long, she was my Superintendent at Tottenham but that was ten years ago, she'd be long retired by now.

"How do you know Jill?" I asked.

"She's my aunt, my mother's younger sister."

I nodded.

"I spoke to my mother last night. They let me have a phone call. My mother's distraught and she's been speaking to her sister. Jill told my mother you're a good detective and that if anyone can find out what's happened, it'll be you. I need you on my side, I need you on my side more than I've ever needed anything or anyone in my life."

"I'm not on anyone's side, Tristram."

It was the first time I'd ever used his first name.

"No, I didn't mean that, oh fuck, I'm desperate, please. I keep saying everything wrong."

This was a Tristram Parker I'd never seen before. Where was the overly confident, massively successful, Porsche driving, Canary Wharf top hedge fund manager now?

"I'll do what I can, Tristram, but you've no commented your way through hours of interview and only guilty people do that. Take that from a 'good detective'.

"That's because that's what the solicitor told me to do."

"And that's what they all say." I replied.

"I didn't kill my wife, or arrange to have her murdered, or abducted or anything. I just went on a week's holiday with my girlfriend. Adultery, that's all I'm guilty of. You've got to help me!"

I must admit 'you've got to help me' wasn't the thing most suspects in custody said to the detective dealing with their case.

Chapter 39

When Mr Parker boarded his plane bound for Lisbon, I assumed my role as liaison officer would largely cease and I'd have to go back to the murder squad. It wasn't the end of the world, but I was feeling pretty low, what with Jackie and the girls heading off to a new life in Australia, too.

Jackie was all like 'why don't you see the girls as much as you can, before they go' but I thought that would just make it more difficult when they left.

Life with Mrs M was settling into a nice routine, and it was infinitely better living back on dry land. In all the years I'd known her, I don't think Mrs M and I had ever had a cross word and I wanted it to remain like that. So, when I discovered that the Assistant Commissioner was in fact married, I decided neither to tell Mrs M, because she might already know anyway, or to judge her for what she was doing. She'd only seen him the once, but she was happier than I'd ever known her; she was buying new clothes and getting her hair done and everything else a person falling in love does. I remember when Dawn was seeing a married man, Mrs M was very pragmatic about it and here she was, twenty-five years later, doing the same thing. I hoped it worked out for her, but I wasn't sure if it did, what guise that would take.

I'd heard nothing back from Sergeant Bellamy about the Interpol checks on the hotel guests, but he had said that it might take months.

Time was one thing we did have, because Tristram's trial had been scheduled for the following summer, while he languished in a cell in Prison Monsanto, on the outskirts of the capital. I was really surprised when he didn't get bail, especially as his lawyer offered a twenty-five million Euro security, but the Portuguese judges were having none of it and the hedge fund manager from Theydon Bois found that, probably for the first time, his money couldn't help him.

It was nearly a week after the deportation that I got a message from Brucie calling a meet on. As a result, on that sunny Monday afternoon, I once again met Brucie and Steve up at High Beech, but this was a weekday, so the bikers had disappeared, and the place felt completely different.

"Matey, this is a nightmare." Brucie said.

"What is?" I asked, genuinely thinking I must have missed something.

"Mr Parker has more bank accounts and investments than most third world nations. At the last count, I've now sent Orders to forty-seven financial institutions and identified in the region of fifty million pounds of personal wealth. The thing is, obviously everything leads to and from Skimmia Investments, so I really need to get separate Production Orders on the company. If it was Joe Blogg's painting and decorating business, then no problem; but I suspect we'll run straight into their large, powerful and heavily funded legal department, so, so far, I've held back. Fortunately, Steve's been helping me go through everything. I know technically that's not allowed …"

"… but thanks to you two, I've got cunting all else to do …" Steve interrupted.

" … but he's been a diamond. Especially, his knowledge and experience after five years in auditing. Anyway, matey, a couple of three things stand out."

He paused for effect.

"Go on…"

I said.

"Well, there's an awful lot of money from Eastern Europe, I mean, way too much …"

"… unless he had factories over there, or some other core business …" Steve added.

"Where exactly?"

"Russia. And I'm suspecting they're the kind of Russians that the major banks wouldn't touch with the proverbial."

"So, what are you telling me? He's laundering Russian money?" I asked.

"It's more complicated than that. The money in his personal accounts? Yes, its dirty money, but I suspect they're payments for what his company is doing. That's where the big money is being laundered. His chip of that will be a tiny percentage."

"I understand." I said.

"And it's almost like they're not even trying to hide it. It's almost as if it's too obvious, which sets my alarm system off." Steve added.

"There must be millions, perhaps even billions going through the business accounts." Brucie added.

"What did the audit show, Steve?" I asked.

"I don't know; I was only asked to look at some trades to see if they were money laundering."

"The wash trades?"

Steve nodded.

"But they weren't?" I added.

"No, they were push through trades. I never looked at anything else."

"Okay, where do we go from here?" I asked.

"Well, there's another problem." Brucie said.

"I got a call from my Superintendent the other day. He's come under pressure to get me back to Hornsey."

"Why? Are they short of skippers?" I asked, innocently.

"No, no, not at all. Apparently, D.A.C. Kitty fucking Young is asking why I've not been tenured, as she was promised."

"I heard something about that, apparently, she saw you and me outside the Star, what four weeks ago? She thinks we're conspiring to do her some great injustice. What's your Superintendent said?" I asked.

"Said I wasn't needed, that because I hadn't been in uniform for fifteen years, I was of no use to them and that, as far as she was concerned, I was better employed doing F.I. work."

"He sounds as sound as a pound." I said.

"She, Nostrils, she … is …" Brucie replied.

"But she did also say, she didn't know how long she'd be able to hold that line. So, my time with you might be limited."

I shrugged my shoulders.

"I don't know how long I'll be here, especially as Parker's now been extradited." I said.

"What have you still got to do?" Brucie asked.

"The A.C. wants an interim report, and he wants me to sit in on the trial in case the prosecution requires anything from us, but that's a year away. I'm waiting for some Interpol enquiries to come back on the other hotel guests that were staying there the night she went missing, oh and your enquiries, of course. I'm starting to feel like it's over, but then, if I'm being honest, I'm not certain this case ever got going. Anymore threats?"

Brucie shook his head.

"I get a silent call from a withheld number at least twice a day." I said.

"Really?" Brucie asked.

"I'm starting to think they're nothing to do with this." I replied.

"And Steve's got something to tell us, haven't you Steve?." Brucie said.

206

"My company, bless their little cotton socks, are offering me a settlement of six hundred and fifty thousand pounds if I resign, but only on the condition that I sign a gagging agreement."

'Fucking hell, mate! You must be fucking delighted." I said.

Steve looked solemn and I realised I'd misjudged his mood.

"They must be fucking desperate for me to keep my mouth shut about something." Steve said.

"It fucking stinks, matey." Was Brucie's closing observation.

Chapter 40

Apparently, the contract which the auditors wanted Steve to sign included a clause that said once he'd signed the document, if he disclosed any information about the company to any third person, including law enforcement and the Financial Services Authority, he would forfeit all the money.

Steve said that in thirty years as old bill, he'd never taken so much as a penny; he'd always maintained that he didn't have a price; that no one could buy his integrity. He was going to tell his employers where they could stick their offer. To say I was greatly impressed, is an understatement but there was a part of me, I've got to admit, a big part of me, that thought he must be stupid.

The following day I got summoned to see the Assistant Commissioner. I assumed it was to close the case, or at least to hibernate it until the trial. I was going to ask for another ten days, just to wrap up the loose ends.

I did briefly flirt with the idea of telling him not to upset Mrs M, but Mrs M was a big girl and besides, it really was none of my business.

I'd been allotted fifteen minutes at eleven, but when I got there the A.C. was with the Commissioner so I sat chatting to Erling.

After a few minutes of idle but polite conversation, during which time, Erling kept wiggling his mouse to make sure his computer didn't go into stand-by, there was a distinct ping and Erling's eyes glanced to the bottom right of his screen where, I anticipated, an email had just arrived.

"This might be interesting."

He double clicked his mouse, I assumed to open the email, and then double clicked again, perhaps to open an attachment.

"What's your warrant number?" He asked.

I told him, though I didn't have any idea what the email could contain that would require him to know my warrant number.

"One eight one zero five six?" He confirmed.

"That's me. Is it a one six three?" I joked.

A form one six three was a notification of a complaint or disciplinary action and receiving one, though quite common, was never pleasant.

"No, it's better than that, my friend. You passed the Inspector's exam." Erling said.

"Oh, brilliant. Does it give the actual results?"

"Yeah, it does; the pass mark was eighty percent, right?"

"Yes" I replied.

"You got eighty-point one percent …" Erling declared.

"Eighty-one, Christ, that was a bit close." I said.

"No, not eight-one, eight, dot, one." Erling said, laughing.

"Everyone below you on the list failed. That is what I call a close shave." Erling said.

"I've been in a few of those." I replied.

Erling stood up and put his hand out.

"Chris, well done. Congratulations."

"Still part two to pass." I said.

After passing the written exam, you then had to pass six role-play scenarios, commonly called OSPREY Part Two. In effect, passing the exam just secured you the right to progress to the next stage.

The Assistant Commissioner walked in, and I stood up, in deference.

"Come through, Chris. Erling, put the kettle on and then join us, please." He commanded.

I took a seat on the far side of a large conference table, while the Assistant Commissioner gathered a file from his desk and examined several post-it notes which had been left for him during his absence.

"Dawn's mum is incredibly fond of you." The A.C. said, without looking up from his desk.

"The feeling is mutual." I replied.

I watched him carefully, as he studied each piece of yellow paper. I wasn't convinced he was reading any of them, I think he was waiting for me to say something else, but I didn't.

"I didn't realise you actually lived with her." He said.

"Only moved in last month; she asked me, I saw no reason to say no." I replied.

"She says you lived alone on a boat."

"I did. I have, I had, a barge moored in Docklands. When I got divorced, it's all I could afford. Are you divorced?" I asked.

I had never intended to, but the opportunity was just too good to miss; and the question came out so naturally.

"No" He replied.

I said nothing and he looked up, catching my eye.

"Is that a problem?" He asked.

I couldn't believe it. From the tone and inclination in his voice, the Assistant Commissioner was asking me whether he could go out with Mrs M.

"No" I replied, speaking barely above a whisper.

210

"Thank you." He replied, almost submissively.

Two seconds later, Erling entered carrying three mugs of tea, placed them on the table and the A.C. joined us.

"Extradition went off smoothly, I hear." He said.

"Last week. Yes, no problem. I need a couple more weeks, Sir, to put everything to bed until the trial." I said.

"You'll need more than that, Chris." The A.C. asserted.

I frowned.

"Tristram Parker wants to speak to you."

"Sorry?"

"Tristram Parker has written to the Commissioner from prison. He asks that you visit him in jail in Lisbon. He's asked for you by name."

"Does he say why?" I asked.

"No" The A.C. replied.

"Did the letter come from his solicitor?" I asked.

"No, he has specifically said that he doesn't want a solicitor or anyone from the Portuguese police."

"How long will you need?" The A.C. asked.

I shook my head while I considered.

"I've absolutely no idea, boss. If he wants to confess to the murder, ideally, four, maybe five days. If he wants to whine about how horrible the conditions are, about twenty minutes." I replied.

"Fair point, book a week, book business, you can always change it then, if you need to." He suggested.

"There is one thing." I said.

He nodded.

"If he's going to talk about the murder, I really need to visit the scene, first. You know, to make the interview more effective. I would also like to get a feel for the place."

I thought perhaps the A.C. might think I was taking the piss, but I really wasn't. Any good detective would visit the scene of a murder before interviewing the suspect.

"Forty-eight hours will do?" I said, to emphasise that I wasn't trying to be clever and get a quick week in the sun, courtesy of the job.

"Okay. Obviously, liaise with your Portuguese counterparts and make sure they're happy." He said.

"I'll need someone with me. I can't do the interview on my own." I said.

"Of course. Who do you want to take?"

"Sergeant Bruce Franklin, the F.I. I was telling you about, boss. The only thing is, D.A.C. Young is trying to get him moved off this enquiry and back to Hornsey."

"Oh yes, that's right. She was making a fuss. Erling?"

"Yes, Sir." The staff officer replied.

"Please give the Borough Commander at Hornsey my compliments, she's an old friend. Tell her that Sergeant Franklin is going to be formally seconded to this office for three months. Actually, do the same with Chris's OCU Commander, too. Let's get some top cover over this arrangement and then see what the suspect has got to say for himself."

Chapter 41

I turned the development over in my mind. Tristram Parker must want to tell us about the murder, surely? What else? Perhaps he was going to try to bribe us? Although, as soon as that thought materialised in my mind, I rejected it as after all, he was languishing in a Portuguese jail over which we had absolutely no jurisdiction. Yes, his company appeared to operate some dodgy financial dealings, but didn't they all? Every so often one of the big banks got stuck with a huge fine for allowing some dirty money to pass through their accounts, so that was hardly headline news, was it? Was it the tax thing? Again, I thought that highly unlikely. Tax avoidance wasn't even a crime, so he could get no leverage by revealing any secrets about that. Besides, what did any of these financial matters have to do with the murder of his wife?

As I made my way back from the Yard that day, I tried to play devil's advocate by identifying exactly what case there was against Mr Parker in respect of his wife.

The fact she was still missing kind of worked both ways. First, the prosecution couldn't prove she was dead, and in a British court that might be a significant obstacle, but the fact she hadn't reappeared did also tend to suggest she was dead; as did her failure to use her mobile phone and the absence of spending on her bank accounts. The fact that Tristram personally had an unbreakable alibi, being in Spain at the time she went missing, was also good for him. However, that alibi would highlight the fact he was having an affair, which would no doubt be put be forward as the motive for the crime, so his defence would also play against him. The finding of blood in Mrs Parker's hotel room might also be seen as strong circumstantial evidence that she'd met a violent end. Did they have any additional evidence from the product of the intrusive surveillance which they deployed in his hotel room when he went to the island?

On reflection, my personal opinion was that the case was weak. If I added in what I knew, and the Portuguese authorities didn't - that his wife was caught spying on Mr Parker by his own security team - then things started to look much more sinister. With that said, I still didn't know for certain that he'd been told about that. I know Alphabet's wife put it in a report, but it was only an assumption that report had found its way to the Mr Parker. If you wanted to introduce that into the evidence and propose it

213

as a motive, you'd most certainly have to find the person who told him to give evidence about that conversation.

This train of thought reminded me that, in an ideal world, it would be useful to know whether my suspicions were right and establish whether Marcella Parker was being used by the Security Services to gather intelligence on terrorist financing. I knew however that finding that out would be almost impossible. For very good reasons, MI5 would never confirm or deny that someone was working for them.

Was it just possible that there was something at their home that might assist? I mean, when we'd searched the enormous house, we were looking at evidence regarding the murder, anything linking Mr Parker to Portugal or the island itself, we weren't looking for something connecting Mrs P with handlers and clandestine meetings in Pimlico.

We couldn't get a second warrant just to look for evidence as to whether the victim had been working for the Security Services, could we? No, getting the first one was difficult enough.

Then something somewhere made me think deeper. I was pretty sure, a Section 8 PACE warrant, unlike a Theft Act or Firearms Act ticket, allowed multiple entries. I needed to pull over, but the road was 'no stopping', so I turned left into the car park of the Rising Sun pub between Whipps Cross and the Waterworks Roundabout. It was mid-afternoon and there were no cars about, but I pulled up next to the forest and in what was probably the parking space furthest away from the entrance.

I searched through the paperwork in the boot and dug out the warrant. Bingo, I was right, it could be executed multiple times, as long as the Magistrate hadn't made a specific stipulation. I checked and he hadn't. That was great, and with Mr Parker a thousand miles away in a prison cell, we'd be able to have a really good root around.

I looked around to make sure I was alone.

There was constant traffic noise as well, which would be useful.

Sitting in the driver's seat, I reached between my legs and pulled out what had, for the best part of twenty years, sat unnoticed in a safe in Arbour

Square. I examined the black handgun closely. I felt a little nervous handling it because my knowledge of guns was zero. But I wasn't stupid and showed the item a great deal of respect.

Each side of the handle had a circular etching with fancy lettering and the word Beretta marked centrally at the six o'clock position of the circle. The bottom of the handle had a button which required more than a little pressure to use; so, holding the gun in my right hand, I used my left thumb to push the button. When it was about half an inch in, the middle of the handle dropped down to reveal what I thought was called 'the clip'. Inside the clip were rounds of gold coloured ammunition, which were spring loaded, so I could literally flick them out, one by one. I flicked out ten but there were at least another six, so I stopped and carefully put them back, one at a time. I pushed the clip back home and then further examined the gun. There was a short lever on the left which when pushed up, showed a small green dot, and when down, a red one. Although no expert, I guessed that was the safety, although I had no idea whether red indicated the safety was on or off.

I then reached down again and pulled out a black metal tube. When I was a kid, I'd have called this the silencer, but I'd picked up a few things in the job, and now knew the correct name for this item was suppressor. I screwed it on to the business end of the handgun. It fitted perfectly but looked longer than the barrel itself

I glanced around the car park, no one was around.

I pulled the safety lever down, so it was pointing down and not along the barrel.

I opened the driver's door and slanted the handgun at forty-five degrees to the ground, aiming into the forest and at the base of a tree no more than two yards away. Even if anyone was looking, they'd never see that I was holding anything, my arm and hand were almost adjacent to my right leg.

There was a quiet click, no bang at all, and hardly any recoil.

I looked around again, it was all clear.

I did it a second time, the gun hardly moved. Even someone standing a few yards away would have no idea I'd just shot two rounds.

I put the gun back under my seat, leaving the suppressor on, and walked the few feet to examine the base of the tree. There were two small holes, but the bullets had buried deep and no one would ever recognise the damage for what it was.

I got back in the car and drove off.

I now knew who, how and even, thanks to Mr Parker's timely letter, precisely when.

Chapter 42

I can honestly say, in my twenty-five years in the job, I'd never executed a search warrant twice and I'd have never given it a second thought if Brucie hadn't mentioned he'd seized a front door key 'just in case.' We were on dodgy ground here; I mean the suspect had been charged with conspiracy to murder and was in custody in another country, so what exactly were, we looking for? Truth be told, only the vaguest of a connection with the murder. I wanted to find anything that might suggest Mrs Parker was working for the Security Services as a covert human intelligence source, more commonly known by the acronym CHIS.

Steve wanted to come along, but I said 'no'. I also informed the local police station just in case someone called the police. This was standard operating procedure. We went in the dead of night, too. Due to his legendary penchant for black coffee and roll ups from his café crème tin, we were slightly delayed in leaving to allow Brucie's time for his customary pee and a puff. Fortunately, now Mr Parker was no longer residing there, the press had packed up and gone home.

The house was eerie at three in the morning, very quiet and still.

I was conscious that we'd left ourselves open to all sorts of allegations of theft, especially as there was so much bounty to steal, had we been that way inclined.

We learnt during the first search, Mr and Mrs Parker had separate bedrooms, so we focused our attention on hers. I don't think I'd ever searched so carefully or quietly. There was no concern that we'd be heard, the nearest house was a quarter of a mile away, but it just seemed appropriate and in keeping with our furtive activity.

Although I'd never met her and only seen the occasional photograph in the paper, going through someone's most personal and intimate possessions brings one closer to them. Marcella Parker was one sophisticated lady, and educated, too. She got a 2:1 from Oxford in History, as evidenced by a certificate which, curiously, she hung on the wall in her bathroom ensuite.

On her bedside table I found two books, Agent Zigzag and Operation Mincemeat. I'd never heard of either, but when I read the synopsis on the back, I realised they were both true stories of spies and espionage. I called Brucie over and showed him.

"I'm reading a book on Auschwitz, and I'm neither a Nazi nor Jewish, matey."

While I knew he was right, I still thought it was a strange coincidence. I kept looking. Under the books was a glossy magazine about the latest fashions in office design and furniture, so it appeared Mrs Parker wanted her own workspace to match that of her husband's impressive home study.

Brucie found her 2007 diary but there was barely an entry in it; presumably someone had bought it for her as a present.

In the dressing room was a whole cupboard full of C.W.W. stationery, most quite aged and probably originally ordered just before the world went digital and largely paperless.

The rest of the cupboards in the dressing room, incidentally bigger than most peoples' bedrooms, were overflowing with clothing, coats, and shoes. There were occasional designer labels that I recognised but also a lot from Marks & Spencer, which I found surprising.

It also appeared that C.W.W. wasn't her only charitable venture. I found a drawer full of nametags, badges and identity cards that linked her to half a dozen others. They were a mixture of local, national, and international and for a variety of good causes without any particular theme. Mrs Parker must have been a very busy lady.

We got the shock of our lives about an hour into our adventure when the doorbell rang. It was the local police to inform us that one of us has tripped the silent intruder alarm and to request us, very politely, not to do it again. I assured him we wouldn't but as I'd no idea exactly what we'd done to set it off, my promise was somewhat hollow.

It's funny how things turn; we were just about to leave when I saw a small jacket hanging up on a hook just to one side of the front door. In fact, when the door was open, you couldn't see the coat at all, which might explain how we'd not seen or searched it during our first visit. Without holding out much hope, I reached into the left outside pocket and took out a receipt. Upon closer examination, I noticed the receipt was from a Café 89 in SE1 somewhere. It was for a coffee and sandwich, which was no big deal, but on the back was written a name 'Albert Handler' and a mobile telephone number. I looked for the date, but that part of the receipt had faded and all I could make out was that it was this year.

I handed it to Brucie, whose reply was priceless and right on the money:

"Fucking hell, matey."

***

I knew Café 89 rang a bell, and the following day when I searched it on the internet, I realised it was just up the road from Tintagel House, where I was based when I was at C.I.B. 2. It was also immediately next door to the MI5 building and a short walk across Vauxhall Bridge to Pimlico. Also, curiously, it was on the Albert Embankment.

The significance of the note was the word 'Handler'. In policing, four things have handlers; dogs, people who are in the Witness Protection program, undercover operatives and covert human intelligence sources. I thought the word 'Albert' was also important. When CHIS contact their handlers by phone, they use a codeword, known only to themselves and the handlers, and it has to be something the CHIS can remember and also something they can say in a public place which won't merit any attention. Mrs Parker and her handler had obviously chosen 'Albert' because it was the first thing to come to mind, sitting as they were, in a café on the Albert Embankment.

Coupled with Mrs Parker's reading material, I was now convinced she was a CHIS tasked with finding out how terrorists were exploiting her charity and her husband's hedge fund to finance their illegal activities.

If I was right, her murder may well be linked to these activities, but I knew MI5 would clam up tighter than a duck's arse, if any official approach was made to confirm what I thought. Besides, with her now missing presumed dead, they were even less likely to admit any connection.

To be honest, I was out of my depth. I had the briefest brush with MI5 many years ago when they executed a silent search warrant at the home of Colonel Charles Beaulieu, who had been having an affair with a married royal Princess. They wanted to read his autobiography before it was published. He reported the case to police as a burglary and I traced a vehicle which was involved, ultimately leading to a very awkward meeting at the DVLA in Swansea with two pretty dodgy covert operatives who told me to NFA the job. I did.

This felt completely different.

Should I speak to Alphabet, the Detective Superintendent on the Special Enquiry Team, who'd spent years at Special Branch? Was I under any obligation to inform the Portuguese authorities? And, probably the biggest dilemma of all, in a funny sort of way, what should I tell the Coroner? Albeit, years away, I would undoubtedly have to give evidence at Essex Coroner's Court. As I said previously, I never lied under oath, but I could hardly stand in the witness box and blurt all this out.

I needed sound advice. The obvious, and technically right thing for me to do, would be to raise my concerns with the A.C.? We did seem to get along quite well. I was reticent however because a part of me distrusted senior officers. They put the reputation of the Met before all else, even if that sometimes meant that ethically they did the wrong thing. And another thing, they were all so fucking ambitious that they'd never risk doing something that might negatively impact upon their career. They were all the same. I didn't hate them for it, I kind of understood, but it meant I didn't trust John King to deal with this situation properly. I was worried he would just lift the carpet and look for a large brush.

Chapter 43

Arranging the trip to Madeira and then Lisbon was more difficult than I thought because I couldn't get hold of Vincent anywhere. He'd gone back to Lisbon with Mr Parker, and I kept calling his mobile, but it just went to voicemail. I left several messages for him at the Embassy but heard nothing for days.

When he did eventually get back to me, he seemed delighted that Mr Parker had asked to see me but less enthusiastic about my request to go to Madeira. Instead of saying it was my idea, I took the stance that my boss, Assistant Commissioner King, was insisting and that I'd rather not bother if it was just down to me. He couldn't really say no, but I was convinced he wanted to.

"We just want to visit the scene, Vincent, and generally have a look round the hotel. Just in case Mr Parker starts talking about the murder, we need to be able to judge whether he is telling us the truth."

"How long will you be on the island?" He asked.

"One or two days. Perhaps we could meet up with Adao?" I suggested, to demonstrate that we weren't up to anything untoward or underhand.

He eventually agreed, and the dates were set. We would fly out to Madeira the following Monday, then to Lisbon from Funchal on the Wednesday morning. We would be in Lisbon a week. Our first interview with Mr Parker was scheduled for the Wednesday afternoon. Vincent agreed to make the necessary arrangements with the prison, for which I was very grateful.

When I was off the phone to Vincent, I called Sergeant Bellamy.

"You got the results back on those checks on the hotel guests, yet?" I asked.

"Most of them, not all." He replied.

"Mr Parker wants to see us; flying over next week, thought it might be useful to take what you've got, just in case." I said.

"You've got a trip out of this, Nostrils, you jammy cunt. I did thirty-two years in the job and the only trip I got was to hospital when I had my heart attack."

"Going to Madeira, as well." I said, just to rub salt in his wounds.

"Cunt" He replied, and then hung up on me.

I called him back.

"What is it now, Nostrils? I'm a busy man." He replied, but it was all in jest.

"Have your checks shown up any likely lines of enquiry?" I asked.

"Nothing, Nostrils. Sorry, mate, but you've drawn a blank there."

"No escaped rapists or recently released kidnappers?" I asked.

"Not even a jaywalker, Nostrils." He replied.

I was gutted. I'd thought that was such a good idea.

My next call was to Brucie to update him and finally to Erling so the A.C. was sighted on the very latest developments.

I'd worked from home that day. When I say 'worked' I'd made a few calls and spent the rest of the morning lying on my bed, trying to work out what the fuck had happened to the vanishing hedge fund manager's wife. When I wandered down, Mrs M was still in her dressing gown, which at midday, was unheard of.

We exchanged 'good mornings' before realising it was in fact afternoon.

"Not dressed yet?" I said, asking a question to which the answer was blindingly obvious.

"Late night." She said, pouring out two cups of tea.

"Anyone I know?"

She smiled.

"JK, eh!" I said

She smiled and nodded.

"How's it going?" I asked.

"It's only our second date, Chris, but it's like I'm being swept along on a cloud. I feel dizzy. I feel like I'm sixteen again. He's so attentive, he's funny and interesting and …"

She let the sentence hang.

"That's nice." I replied.

Suddenly, her smile dropped.

"I'm stupid, aren't I? It's just ridiculous."

"No, not at all." I replied.

"I suppose you know he's married?" She said.

I nodded.

"You don't think terrible things about me?"

I shook my head.

"Never, Mrs M." I replied.

"There is something I need to talk to you about though."

Her voice had changed its tone.

"Look, he's not sleeping in your bed, not under my roof, if that's where this conversation is going." I said, jokingly.

But I'd misjudged the moment. Mrs M had her serious face on.

"When I got back last night, there was a car immediately outside. I noticed it because someone was sitting in the driver's seat and for a moment, I thought I was going to be robbed. When I saw it was a woman, I relaxed a bit."

"What time was this?" I asked.

"Just gone two. Anyway, the woman got out and started having a right go at me."

"What about?"

"She was asking who I was? Why I was living with you? And what was going on? Then she asked me whether I knew you were two-timing me?"

"I'm so sorry." I said.

I suspected the silent phones calls I was receiving and the honking car at three in the morning was nothing to do with the Parker case, and I was right.

"What did you do?"

"I was going to say we were just old friends, but I think that would have inflamed her even more. She was really cross, Chris. She even started calling me an old witch."

"So, what did you do?" I asked.

"I said 'I don't know who you are? Or what's wrong but Chris is my son'. I really don't know why I said it, and I know it's not the truth, but the words just came out of my mouth."

"What did she do?" I asked.

"She didn't know what to say. She turned on her heels, got back in the car and drove off, after a very impressive wheelspin. You can still see the tyre marks on the road surface."

"I didn't hear a thing; I must have been out for the count, but I had taken a sleeping tablet." I said.

"Who is she, Chris?" Mrs M asked.

"She's the girl I went out with about a month ago. I told you about her, she lives in Notting Hill, you made the joke about the back of her head." I replied.

"Oh my god! How many times did you go out with her?"

"Only the once, we didn't even have sex." I replied.

"You must have impressed her. She's clearly obsessed."

"I can't think why." I said.

"I can." She said.

It was a nice thing to say, and I smiled.

"Have you heard from her since your one date?"

"No, I asked a mutual friend to tell her I wasn't interested. Julie, my work colleague, she was the one who set up the date. She is a friend of hers."

"She's absolutely crazy."

"I'll need to call Julie. It doesn't make any sense though." I said.

"Why do you say that?" Mrs M asked.

I hesitated because I wasn't sure I wanted to tell her the whole story. Mrs M sensed my unease.

"If you don't want to tell me, that's fine, we're allowed to keep our private lives just that. I mean, forget the fact I tell you everything." She said.

"Okay, okay, no need for that. Listen. Her names Cassandra, Cassandra Marsh. She's a high-class call girl.

"You mean a prostitute? You paid for a night with a prostitute? And your friend arranged this, which makes her a pimp."

"No, it wasn't like that. Julie and Cassandra have known each other from school. Julie set us up on a blind date. There was never any exchange of money, payment, or anything. We went out for a meal; she wasn't used to drinking and got drunk on two cocktails. We went back to her place; she fell asleep, and I went home in the morning. We didn't have sex, or any kind of sex, if you know what I mean. She must be a complete nutter."

"She didn't look like a hooker; she didn't look like anyone who you'd be going out with."

"Why?" I asked.

"She looked too young. What is she, early thirties?"

"She's forty. Well in a few months. I'll phone Julie and put a stop to this. She's done it before. She turned up a few weeks' ago. She was honking her horn and flashing her headlights at three in the morning. I'm surprised the racket didn't wake you up. She keeps ringing me and hanging up. Well, I assume it's her." I explained.

"If she turns up again, don't confront her on your own, come and get me. I'll deal with her. You don't want her making some ludicrous allegation against you, do you?" Mrs M said.

"I'll get you straight away, I promise." I said.

I started to walk off, to go upstairs to my room to make the call, but as I turned, I heard Mrs M say quietly.

"Sad, isn't it?"

"Mad, more like." I replied.

"No, it's sad, Chris. Dreadfully sad. Does she have lots of ordinary dates?"

"No, I don't think she's been out with anyone, like normally, for a few years. I think Julie said five." I replied.

"Don't you see, Chris. Cassandra was hurt by the fact you hadn't wanted sex. After all, with her men it's always a business arrangement. The fact that you hadn't paid and, perhaps in her mind, therefore, didn't want it, probably hurt her. It's almost as if she couldn't give it away." Mrs M explained.

"Of course, with Julie telling her I hadn't had sex for four years, it would be embarrassing for Cassandra to go back to Julie and admit nothing had happened." I said.

"You haven't had sex for four years!" Mrs M said, incredulously.

"Perhaps I've shared too much." I said.

"I had sex …"

Mrs M looked at her watch.

"… twelve hours ago, oh, and eleven hours ago."

I shook my head and laughed.

"I don't need to know! Will you please act more like a mother!"

Chapter 44

The Cassandra stalking threat did create me a potential problem. The last thing I needed was someone seeing me leave the house at three in the morning when I was meant to be leaving at six.

I had always maintained that if anything happened to put my plan in jeopardy, I would cancel it, but now, the evening before, I wasn't prepared to do so.

I had several calls with Julie. I told her what had happened, and she got hold of Cassandra, and called me back. Julie was furious with her friend; Cassandra was embarrassed, and I was relieved that we seemed to have put it to bed. It turned out that when Cassandra's last arrangement crashed and burnt it was her that did the stalking and was subject to the restraining order and not her ex.

I didn't sleep that evening, didn't even try. I had way too much going on in my head.

I got the timing down by doing what most people do who are getting an early flight, working backwards. The flight to Funchal left Gatwick at eight-thirty, so I'd agreed to meet Brucie at the easyJet departure desk at six-thirty. At that time in the morning, the run to Gatwick from Buckhurst Hill would take an hour and a quarter, including parking, so that was five-fifteen. I'd have to give myself two hours for the round trip, although it was only forty minutes each way at that time in the morning, I did have to cycle about ten miles which would add an hour. So, that was three-thirty. Then the deed itself; I could imagine that wouldn't take more than ten minutes, but I'd allow thirty. I therefore worked out I needed to leave my house no later than three.

If Mrs M did hear me, well she knew I was getting up early anyway, but ideally, I wanted her to think I'd left about five, so I slipped a sleeping tablet into the cup of tea which she always drank at bedtime. As she didn't drink much and rarely took so much as a paracetamol, I hoped 7.5mg of zopiclone would knock her out for at least eight hours. I was also pleased she'd had such a late night the evening before, which should make her even more knackered.

I'd packed my bike in the back of my car a few days ago, just so it didn't look ridiculous doing it the night before I went on a business trip abroad.

As I waited on the bed for three to arrive, I was calm. Perhaps calmer than I'd ever been before. I kept waiting for the doubt to start, for the panic attack to kick it, but neither arrived. At five to three I had a careful look out of my bedroom window up and down the street for any sign of mad Cassandra. The coast was clear.

In the dead of the night, I snuck out of the house like a warship slipping her moorings at Scapa Flow and setting sail for battle.

I took my mobile phone, which was wrapped in a freezer bag but still on, in silent mode, and placed it under a rock to one side of Mrs M's drive entrance. If anyone subsequently conducted retrospective cell-site analysis, that evidence would support my alibi.

Once at street level, I checked again. There wasn't a soul about. I started the car and drove off without revving the engine even the slightest.

A curious combination of circumstances had aligned to present me with this opportunity, and I wasn't going to miss it.

I'd dealt with dozens of murders. I didn't count, but maybe fifty. In the few where we didn't have a clue as to who had done it, and these were the minority of cases, we invariably picked up a stroke of luck somewhere along the investigation which pushed us in the right direction. Although I was neither religious nor superstitious, it did sometimes feel like fate had intervened to guide us. I got a similar feeling in respect of today's operation. First, the completely chance occurrence had told me where they lived. Then the shitty task of sorting out the property store had provided me with an untraceable firearm, a suppressor and enough ammunition to take out a small shopping centre.

The final piece of the jigsaw was the trip to Portugal. When someone found the victim's body, the discovery might take place later today, but there was every chance it might be next week. If it was the latter, and if for some reason my name did come in the frame, I could prove that for ninety-nine percent of the time period during which the murder might have taken place, I was over a thousand miles away. It was just perfect.

Chapter 45

When I knocked. I did exactly what I had done a hundred times; rapped loudly and deftly. Over the years, many recipients had said how they knew it was the police at their door just from the style of my knock.

I checked my watch; I was right on schedule.

I knew my victim was in because I'd just been around the back and could hear them snoring.

I knocked again and seconds later heard definite movement from inside. Not two yards from where I was standing, the curtain twitched and then lifted back further.

"Open up, it's Nostrils." I said, not too loudly.

It went quiet inside.

I knocked again, this time a little louder to convey growing impatience.

The letterbox opened and a voice in a hard-Irish accent said:

"Who is it?"

"It's Nostrils from the CJPU. I mean Ruislip Associates." I replied.

I heard several bolts unlock and a key turn.

"Let me see some I.D." The occupant demanded, holding the door ajar on the chain.

I showed him my warrant card, which, of course, was in my real name. Just for a second I panicked inside as I thought he might read the name and realise who I was, but having studied it for a few seconds, he undid the chain and stepped back.

"Where's Donna?" He asked.

"She's on her way, I was told to get here as quickly as I could. I've got some bad news. I need to come in and we need to get going. Donna should be with us in twenty minutes." I said.

"Come in, come in."

He stepped back from the door, and I walked into a small, narrow hall. He shut the door behind me.

"What's happened?" He said.

As he did so, he turned on a switch and the light came on. I don't know who I'd imagined Barry Skinner to be, but this wasn't him. The man before me was in his mid-seventies, no taller than 5'4" and as skinny as a rake. He was wearing only a dark brown dressing gown and a pair of glasses, one lens of which was being held in place by what looked like a medical plaster. And he looked ill, really pallid. It was a small space and I had to let him pass me, as I didn't know where I was going. He walked to the end of the hall and turned left into what was the lounge.

The interior of the place was dreary and tired and stunk of cigarette smoke. He sat down on a settee, and I took a seat in a chair. I put my daybook, the MPS files and the logbook on the floor beside me. He glanced at them, no doubt reassured by their authenticity.

"What's happened?" He asked, again.

"The address has been compromised."

"Fucking hell." He said.

"What's the plan?"

"Just pack a small bag; we can come back for the rest later. The priority is to get you away from this address and to a hotel somewhere."

I noticed his left arm was shaking.

"It's the Parkinson's; it's worse at night. It's because during the night I've got to go the longest time between medication." He replied.

"Donna told me." I lied.

With his shaky hand, he lit a cigarette. It was painful to watch.

"Let me smoke this, then I'll get going; did you say your name was?"

"Nostrils, Barry."

"What? As in ya nose?"

I nodded.

"Fickin' strange name?"

He drew deeply and, as he exhaled, visibly relaxed.

"Barry, can I use the loo, I'm dying for a pee?"

He pointed back to the hallway.

The toilet was directly opposite, and I stepped inside, locked the door and took the handgun from my adapted inside jacket pocket. I checked the safety and confirmed it was off. I waited about a minute, during which I felt every heartbeat. I kept breathing slowly and deeply but I could still feel a rush of nervous anxiety. My hands were beginning to shake as I flushed the toilet. I opened the door and put my right arm down by my side and slightly behind my body just in case Barry came out of the lounge as I was walking towards it. He didn't and when I opened the door, and half stepped into the room, he was lighting a second cigarette. He looked up to his left and briefly caught my eye.

"I've run out of toilet paper, sorry, I was going to get some this morning." He said.

He looked away.

I'd kept my right arm and the handgun hidden behind the door.

"Barry?"

"Yeah?"

He took another drag of his cigarette.

"You know I said this address had been compromised?"

He mistook my meaning and interrupted me.

"I'm coming, just let me finish this."

He nodded towards his cigarette.

"I've got really bad news."

"What?"

"I'm the one who compromised it."

I moved quickly and emerged from the door. I pointed the handgun at his left leg which was only a few feet away from me and fired. A small round hollow hole appeared in precisely the middle of his knee and for the slightest moment it was clearly white inside; and then it turned red and filled with blood.

With both hands, Barry grabbed his lower thigh and started to hyperventilate. He didn't scream, he didn't cry, he just looked shocked.

I aimed again, this time at his right knee but I moved closer because he was starting to really wriggle about in agony which would make the shot more difficult.

Click

I missed and a rip appeared in the settee.

Click click click

The next bullet missed again but then a second and then a third hole appeared on the inside of his right thigh, about an inch apart, and just above his knee.

I stepped back and then sat down in the chair I had only vacated a few minutes earlier.

Barry was squirming and hyperventilating but he still wasn't making any discernible noise.

"Barry, people call me Nostrils, but my actual name is Chris Pritchard. Does that ring any bells?"

I think he was in too much agony to listen.

"Barry?"

"My name doesn't ring a bell. Let me read you a few more."

He was shaking almost uncontrollably and had leaned over on his right side lying on the settee. He was still holding his left leg and his mouth was open but no sound forthcoming. His dressing gown had ridden up and come undone, exposing his penis and testicles.

"Sarah Brighton; she was seven. Justin Holding; he was six; Muhammed Mahmood, he was thirteen. Let us not forget WPC Dawn Matthews, twenty-three, my street duties instructor and my best friend."

"Who are you?"

He spat the words out, each syllable cost him.

"I am one of your many victims. My name is Chris Pritchard. You blew me up and you killed my best friend. I am your Armageddon, your Judge and executioner. I'm here to send you to hell, Barry." I replied.

"What's going on?"

"Barry, let me tell you a story. Many years ago, when I joined the Job, I got some advice. Never, ever, take a step backwards. Go toe to toe with the bastards until one of you goes unconscious. Today, Barry, you're the one going unconscious. Well, when I say unconscious, I mean dead."

He wasn't wriggling as much now. I noticed the multi-coloured settee was becoming increasingly blood stained as his wounds bled heavily.

"This is for Dawn's mum." I said.

I stood up and put the breach of the handgun almost next to his right elbow.

Click

He moved at the last minute and the bullet missed the main joint but caught the tip, blowing it off and splattering a large red blob of blood and splintered bone on the television screen, which was way off to his right. I sat down again.

"I'm sorry, are you in some pain? Dawn was in the most terrible pain when she died too. Perhaps I can get you an Aspirin? Or would you like your mum?" I asked.

"Pit" Barry said.

"Really want to keep you alive, just to watch you suffer." I said, with more hatred than I had ever possessed.

For several minutes I sat and watched him roll around in agony.

"Barry, you look so uncomfortable; can Nostrils get you a pillow?"

I glorified in his slow, tortuous death. He was bleeding profusely, and I almost got a hard on watching him in so much pain. I had untethered a lifetime of anger.

When he stopped moving and was probably dead anyway, I put the handgun to his temple and blew his brains all over the settee and the wall. I dispatched my oldest and most hated adversary with just three words.

"Go fuck yourself!"

Chapter 46

I'm not made of stone.

I had to stop twice cycling back to my car to be sick. Not just a little throaty cough vomit, but the full, stomach emptying works. In fact, I did well to make it. I felt so exhausted, that I seriously regretted parking the car so far from the scene. It took a gargantuan effort to complete the last mile, which was all fucking uphill! I thought Essex was meant to be flat! One emotion I didn't experience was regret.

When I tried to disassemble my bike and take the front wheel off, my hands were too shaky, so I rolled it to a nearby ditch and dumped it there. It was half decent and I suspected the first person to see it in the morning would take it home making it effectively lost forever.

I drove a couple of miles and dumped my postman jacket in a skip, burying it towards the bottom of a pile of household junk.

When I got to the outskirts of Loughton, I pulled to the side of a road and, having wiped it carefully several times to remove any trace of my dabs, threw the handgun, suppressor and ammunition into Baldwins Pond.

I had been careful not to get any of the victim's blood on me but before I'd set off, I'd also taken the precaution of covering the driver's seat and footwell with several black bin liners. My final stop was to throw the bin liners and my disposable gloves into a ditch. I can honestly say, I felt more guilty about littering the highway - I detested people that did that - than I did about killing Barry Skinner.

When I pulled up at home, I recovered my mobile phone and no less than a minute later, was on my way to Gatwick, as if nothing had happened.

It was five past five, my timing was a thing of beauty.

Chapter 47

The drive from Buckhurst Hill to the airport was surreal.

The vision of me putting the handgun to his temple and blowing his brains out, accompanied by me saying, 'go fuck yourself', kept playing repeatedly in my mind, like a short film on repeat. By the time I got on the M23, I thought it might be all I could ever think about again.

I fought to break the cycle and asked myself out loud a series of questions.

'Was I going mad?'

"Did I feel guilty?'

'Did I enjoy committing the most grotesque of murders?'

'Was I some sort of sick sadist?'

'Did I leave any evidence?'

'Will I be arrested?'

"How would I cope with going to prison for the rest of my life?'

No substantial answers came, my mind was mush. I wondered how I'd cope over the following days.

Chapter 48

"You look like shit, matey." Brucie said, as soon as he saw me.

"I love you too, cunt." I replied.

"Why are you wearing a suit? It's six o'clock in the fucking morning." He asked.

"I always travel suit and booted. Traditional attire for a Met detective. Thought an experienced teco like you would know that." I replied.

"Don't be a cunt, Nostrils, this is easyslag. No chance of an upgrade with the giant tangerine in the sky. Did you sleep in that suit?"

I didn't know what to say. I probably did look a mess, after all, I'd already cycled ten miles and committed a horrendous crime wearing this whistle and it was still, technically, first thing in the morning.

As soon as I got to the hotel, the whistle, shoes, even the underwear, were going in the rubbish bin. Any trace of forensic evidence linking me to the murder in Southend, would be just about as far away from the scene as it was possible to get by lunchtime.

I am sometimes a bit of a snob and therefore, I always looked down condescendingly at people who drank alcohol first thing in the morning at airports. And I took that stance even though I was probably, in medical terms, an alcoholic. But not that morning. As soon as I got through security, and while Brucie went off for, what was becoming, his routine puff and a pee, I made my way straight to Wetherspoons.

Three pints of Stella later, I was feeling much better. I felt content that Barry Skinner got exactly what he deserved. He'd lived a life which caused unnecessary death and untold misery to so many families. Not only that, he wasn't even a man of principle because when it all came on top, he was happy to sell his fellow Irish republicans down the river. Why else would he be in Witness Protection? In fact, I felt disappointed that his demise came so quickly but then I couldn't fuck about for too long.

I wondered when his body would be found and what would be made of the murder. Of course, Essex would be investigating the murder, which was good, as they were only a small force and their experience in dealing with such a crime would be limited.

Would anyone link me to the crime? I doubted it. Twenty-four years was a long time for any motive to wait for revenge. Would the Assistant Commissioner put two and two together? Even if he did, I doubted he would risk his career by admitting to a third party that he'd been so indiscreet. The Witness Protection Unit would certainly be embarrassed. In fact, I suspected they'd risk disbandment on the back of this very public failure.

On reflection, I thought I was ninety-eight percent safe. With that said, what if I did get convicted? So what? Mrs M aside, I had no one to miss me. Jackie and my girls were going to the other side of the world. Wendy didn't want to know me. My son, Matthew, was too busy to bother meeting up, and the only woman I'd been out with in four years, turned into a bunny-boiling stalker. On the downside, if I did end up in prison, I'd have very few visitors.

I was forty-four, if I got life, and taking everything into consideration, I'd probably make parole when I was in my late fifties. I'd still have a bit of a life to live. And what's more, if I did get sent down at least I'd know it was for a good cause. Even though I would be ex-old bill, I thought the screws and other cons might respect what I'd done.

My few close friends, well Julie and Mrs M, knew that I'd never really recovered after the bombing. Even all these years later. I mean, the panic attacks had subsided, but they still lurked just under the surface. No one ever knew, but there were times when I was close to losing my mind. There would be a loud noise and I'd be a nervous wreck for days, sometimes weeks. I never shared that with anyone because I had to be a man. More than that, I had to be a police officer. Showing such crippling weakness was simply not an option.

Why had I done it? One word, vengeance. For me? Yes. But more for Dawn and her mum; and for the three young children who had died in the Preston bombing and their families. No doubt too, for other people he'd killed and maimed during his lifetime. It was so wrong that such cowardly scum had been allowed to serve just two years and I'd now righted that wrong.

"Fuck me, matey, you're going for it." Brucie said, as he joined me in Weatherspoon's and saw I already had two empty glasses and had nearly finished my third.

"I was thirsty." I said.

"I can see that; do you want another?" He asked.

"No, I better stop otherwise I'll be bursting for a pee when we're on the plane. What did you buy?"

I nodded towards several small white plastic shopping bags.

"Some designer sunglasses and some swimming shorts."

"Oh fuck, I didn't pack any." I replied.

Brucie put his hand on my shoulder, the gesture was a complete surprise.

"You alright, Nostrils?"

"Fine" I replied.

"Why?"

"Your shaking, matey. Do you have a bit of a drink problem?"

He was right, well almost. I wasn't shaking but shivering. I think I was beginning to go into shock. I had to get a grip of myself fast.

Chapter 49

I was tired, I had missed a whole night's sleep, so as soon as I was onboard, I tried to settle down and get a few hours nap. The problem was the three pints of lager meant I had to keep using the toilet. Eventually, somewhere over Northern Spain I fell asleep. When I woke up, I thought we were going to crash. The whole aeroplane was shaking terribly and when I looked out of my window, we were only a few hundred feet from both the sea and cliffs.

"What the fuck, Brucie?" I asked, unable to hide the panic in my voice.

"Don't worry, the pilot said it would be a lively approach. We're just coming into land. I was chatting to one of the cabin crew earlier, she said Funchal was one of the most difficult places to land in the world; apparently you have to be specially qualified."

The turbulence abated, as the plane levelled out and about a minute later, and much to my relief, we touched down.

We were met in arrivals by Adao, which was a little bit embarrassing because I didn't recognise him. I had only met him the once but still, I'd spent several hours in his company, so it was unforgiveable.

To my surprise, he then put us in a taxi, gave directions to the driver and said he'd collect us from the hotel at three. I just assumed he would take us himself, but I was grateful that I'd have a few hours to clean up, change, and hopefully grab another couple of hours sleep.

The weather was hot but overcast, and a thick layer of cloud hung over the island.

As I didn't get abroad very often this felt like a rare treat. For years I'd had a heroin addiction which I could only satisfy when I wasn't far from home. I tended therefore to avoid foreign holidays. Then, when I came off the gear, I got divorced so I had neither the money nor anyone to go with.

"You been here before, matey?" Brucie asked.

I shook my head.

"I don't travel much. I've only been abroad once before on the job and that was to Thailand." I replied.

"I came here a few years ago on a cruise. Only stayed for a few hours, did the cable car up the mountain and the toboggan ride down. It's a lovely place and I always said I'd come back."

After about thirty minutes, we arrived at a small, unpretentious hotel up a steep hill and when we got out and looked back down on Funchal, the view of the city was quite stunning. It would have looked even better on a bright sunny day. After checking in, we agreed to rendezvous in the reception at ten to three.

I went to my room and removed a black bin liner from my case into which I then put everything I was wearing, including my shoes. I dressed and took a short walk down the street looking for somewhere to dump my clothes. I was spoilt for choice; every bin in the area was out on the pavement; where there was one. I walked a hundred yards until I found a large round metal bin which was set slightly apart. I took a quick look around to make sure no one was watching me, and then popped the bin liner into the bin. As I walked back to the hotel, the garbage truck was coming from the other way towards me. I looked up to the sky in disbelief, it was bin collection day, I couldn't have arranged it better!

But I hadn't accounted for one thing. Unlike mine, Brucie's room was at the front of the hotel, and he was on the small balcony smoking a cigarette. I hadn't noticed him when I'd left but then I hadn't looked back and up, which I would have needed to have done to clock him. If he had been there, he would have seen me walk down the street with a full bin liner and then return, not a minute later without one.

"Alright, matey. I thought you were getting your head down for a bit?" He asked.

I looked up.

"I am, see you later." I said, as I disappeared underneath him and out of his sight.

244

If he had seen me and had any questions, he could ask me later. With any luck, he might just forget. My strategy didn't work. Not a minute went by when there was a knock at my door. I was about to jump in the shower and was only wearing a towel.

"Can I come in, matey?" He asked.

I stepped back.

"Take a seat, do you want a coffee? It's only instant."

"No matey, I just wanted a quick word."

I took the kettle to the bathroom to fill it up, it gave me something to do.

"I'm a bit worried." Brucie said.

"About what?" I asked.

"You, you peckerhead. There's something not right; are you sure you're okay? You don't seem yourself today."

I put the kettle on and opened a sachet of coffee with my teeth.

"No, I'm not, mate. I'm in a right state."

"Do you want to tell me?"

I took a deep breath and nodded.

"I fucking knew something was wrong."

"You are very perceptive. In fact, you are a very perceptive cunt." I said.

He didn't say anything but smiled warmly.

"Okay, I didn't really want to tell anybody but …" I paused, for dramatic effect.

"... I just discovered my ex is emigrating to Australia and taking my two beautiful daughters with her."

"Fucking hell, Nostrils, I'm so sorry. No wonder you're a mess."

'Hook, line and sinker' I thought!

Chapter 50

Adao was nearly an hour late, which was irritating, and he didn't even apologise, which I thought was really rude.

It was a ten-minute drive to the Porto Mare Hotel. From the entrance, off a small side street and next to a small supermarket, this looked an unremarkable place but once inside the hotel was enormous and very impressive. There were three or four bars, even more swimming pools and an atmosphere of sophistication and luxury. It was a shame our miserly Met expense budget didn't allow us to stay here, even for the two nights we were on the island.

Adao and the manager took us to Mrs Parkers' former room which was large and comfortable. It was on the fourth floor and sat in a corner position, overlooking the smaller of the swimming pools and had a balcony about the same size as my bedroom up the hill. I can honestly say that I'd never stayed anywhere as nice.

The room was not in use, the bedding had been stripped and there was a sterile smell and feeling about the place.

Adao pointed to some blood drops on the floor but there were no more than six or seven and, save for one which was about an inch across, the others were tiny. If I was guessing, I'd say Mrs Parker got out of bed and bled a little on the way to the bathroom. Quite frankly, I'd have put that down to a heavy period, not a murder scene. I took a few photographs on my mobile phone but there was really nothing to see.

"Does the waiter still work here?" I asked Adao.

Adao asked the manager, in Portuguese, but the manager had clearly understood English because she started to answer immediately.

"Yes; he works every day except Wednesday.

"Do you want to speak to him?" Adao asked.

I was surprised to be invited to do so.

"Yes, if that is okay with you, Adao." I replied.

He spoke to the manager in Portuguese again and there was lots of nodding and general agreement.

"He is off today, his grandmother's funeral, but he will be here, in the tomorrow. You can see him at five-thirty tomorrow?" Adao said.

I nodded.

"Does he speak English?" I asked.

"Perfectly" The manager replied.

"Do you want to be there?" I asked Adao.

"No, no. But, please, you only speak to him, no testimony."

I nodded.

"I must go now. You make your way back to your hotel? I meet you tomorrow. I meet you at ten. I take you to see the island, it's beautiful. Tonight, go eat in Rua das Portas, you say, the road of the doors. Have the espada, very traditional – beautiful."

We shook hands and he left.

The manager smiled, nicely.

"Excuse me, madam, would you be so kind as to join us for a drink?"

***

Mrs Teresa Neves was a forty something Madeiran, slim, with Mediterranean colouring and short, black hair. Unlike Adao, she spoke excellent English. She'd worked at the hotel for fifteen years, starting as a receptionist and rising to General Manager last year. She admitted to not knowing the four English ladies at all, explaining that they had such a high turnover of guests, she rarely met them individually unless there was a problem, like a complaint about something. She had, she said, made a detailed statement to the local police and provided them with relevant documentation, such as the ladies checking in cards, copies of passports, guest lists and staff shifts. She knew the waiter moderately well; his name was Miguel Ronaldo and she'd never had any problems with him. She described him as good looking and charming, and agreed that he was popular with the guests, especially middle-aged English women. She said it was against company policy to have any personal relationship with a guest and that such an activity would constitute gross misconduct and instant dismissal.

That worried me, but only a bit. Assuming for one second Miguel hadn't murdered Mrs Parker, what if he did meet with her or go back to her room. In such a case, he might have invaluable information for the investigation, but he'd have to keep shtum otherwise he'd lose his job.

Brucie, who seemed to have struck up a bit of a repartee with Mrs Neves, asked whether anything like this had ever happened before; it had not.

"I cannot remember the last time we had so much as a theft." She asserted.

"Is there any crime on this island?" Brucie asked.

Mrs Neves shook her head.

"We have the arson, sometimes, the stupid boys set light to the forests." She replied.

"No murders or assaults?"

She shook her head.

"The husband hits the wife, maybe. Sometimes the wife hits the husband." She replied.

We laughed.

"No robbery, burglary?"

"Burglary?"

"Break in house, steal, theft, in building?" Brucie clarified.

"No, never, never." She replied.

"What do you think happened to Mrs Parker?" I asked.

She shook her head, blankly, and then shrugged her shoulders.

She recommended a couple of restaurants for dinner but unlike Adao, she suggested we go to the Rua da Carreira.

"Rua das Portas is for tourists." She said.

Brucie made a note of the recommendation and we made our way back up to our hotel.

"You were very quiet …" Brucie commented, in between deep breaths, as the climb got steeper and steeper.

"… still thinking about the wife and kids?"

"Yes, mate." I replied.

Of course, the truth was, I just couldn't get three words out of my head.

Go fuck yourself

Chapter 51

"My father was in the Job." Brucie said.

We were just about to try the espada with banana in a small but charming restaurant in Rua da Carreira.

"Is he still with us?" I asked.

"Oh yes, he lives in Wokingham, now. It's just south of Reading."

"Where did he work?"

"South West London, Wandsworth, Battersea, C.11, the Flying Squad."

"Career detective?"

"Through and through. Terence Franklin; he's eighty-seven and the finest man who ever worked for the Metropolitan Police."

"That's a lovely thing to say; you're obviously close." I said.

"Very. I told him about this case; he's been following it closely in the news." Brucie said.

"Does he have any theories?" I asked.

"He does. He worked on the Muriel McKay case back in sixty-nine and reckons this job is strikingly similar."

"I don't think I've ever heard of it." I replied.

"Her husband was the CEO or something of News Limited, which was owned by Rupert Murdoch, the Australian media fella. She was kidnapped by two West Indian brothers, the Husseins, or something. They thought she was Murdoch's wife and broke into her home in Wimbledon. She was never seen again, and the court case became famous because it was the first time someone was convicted of murder where the body was never recovered. They reckon the brothers, who owned a farm in Hertfordshire, cut her up and fed her to the pigs."

"Was your old man on that case?" I asked.

"He was the deputy S.I.O." Brucie replied.

"When did he retire?"

"1981, three years after I joined."

"Is he fit and well?" I asked.

"He's survived two heart attacks, two strokes, prostate cancer and, worst of all, my mum dying in 2004 but he was diagnosed with Parkinson's last year." Brucie replied.

It's the Parkinson's; it's worse at night. It's because I've got to go a long time between medication

I'd heard of Parkinson's disease, of course I had, but I'd never known anyone who'd got it. In the last sixteen hours, I'd learnt of two! It's strange how sometimes that happens. You know, like when you've never heard a particular word before, and then, fuck me, you hear it three times in one week!

"Are you alright? You've gone all distant again." Brucie asked.

"Sorry mate, I'm tired. Hardly slept at all for about a week. What were you saying?"

"I was asking what you think of the kidnap theory?" Brucie said, clearly repeating himself.

"I'll tell you what's been bothering me. The victim's room was up four floors and miles from the lift. How on earth did anyone get her out of the hotel unnoticed? And reception is manned twenty-four hours a day. She can't have been carried out screaming, kicking and shouting, that's for sure."

"I agree." Brucie replied.

"And, what the fuck was that blood thing? That wasn't a murder scene."

"More like the wrong time of the month." Brucie said.

"I completely agree. I thought the same, myself." I replied.

"She could have been drugged and then kidnapped. I mean, she's the perfect victim, her husband's fucking loaded. There's more than one way out of that hotel, you don't have to go through reception. They'd have needed someone on the inside. You know, someone from the hotel to tell them where her room was, perhaps to facilitate the kidnap itself. Who was on duty that night? We should find that out."

"That would mean the charming Mr Parker is completely innocent." I countered.

"So what?" Brucie responded.

"What the fuck does he want to see us for then?" I asked.

"To complain about the food."

"And what about the fact he discovered his wife was spying on him? No, he's fucking involved. I'd put my mortgage on it." I said, with more confidence than faith.

I think I just wanted to see how it sounded to be so assertive.

"Do you have one?" Brucie asked.

"Actually, no." I replied.

"I have two, do you want one?" He asked.

"No, you're good." I replied.

***

I was pissed when I got in. Not slaughtered but I'd drunk way too much. I downed two pints of water, to keep the ever-present threat from gout at bay and put two Aspirin next to the bed.

Perhaps I can get you an Aspirin

I took a large sleeping pill.

I'd slipped a 7.5mg Zopiclone into her night-time cup of tea

I took out my mobile and logged into the internet which was more difficult than it should have been. I couldn't find my glasses to read the password on my room key pouch.

I opened the BBC News App and looked, without any success, for any stories of Barry Skinner's demise. That was good, the longer before they found him, the better for my alibi. There was however an article about Mr Tristram Parker and Skimmia Investments. I had been in bed but sat up and turned the light on. I still needed to find my glasses so I could read more than just the headline.

Chapter 52

The BBC would never have written such a prejudicial story had Mr Parker been standing trial in the U.K., but he wasn't, so they did. They destroyed him. They'd interviewed Sonia and secured several quotes, which, having met her, I'm sure were taken completely out of context. They insinuated that Skimmia Investments was a corrupt company with highly suspicious connections to corrupt Eastern European crooks. They identified key members of the S.I. senior management team, who were from Russia, or had connections to that country. The general inference was that the city was corrupt and S.I. was simply the tip of the iceberg. It was so carefully and cleverly written that while the piece said nothing, it suggested everything.

I read it through twice, turned my light off and fell asleep.

***

I suppose I shouldn't have slept so well, but I did.

No nightmares; no night sweats; no panic attacks; no guilt, absolutely no fucking guilt.

I woke refreshed, ready to start the rest of my life over.

I met Brucie for breakfast at eight, but the place was only just opening which was a pain in the arse and meant we had to rush if we were going to meet Adao on time. Then, again, Adao was an hour late turning up, which was absolutely infuriating. Madeirans were a very tardy people.

We spent the day being driven around Madeira. We went up several mountains, saw the northern coast, stood on a glass platform high above a cliff, visited Winston Churchill's favourite fishing village and went up, what must be, the longest cable car ride in the world. Madeira was truly stunning. Adao was a great host, giving a running commentary on everything we saw and did. For the first time in my life, I realised that I might want to retire somewhere abroad. Friends and colleagues would often talk about that, but the idea had never crossed my mind until now.

At five thirty we were waiting at the Porto Mare reception but at six there was no sign of either Miguel or Mrs Neves, who was going to help translate, so, while Brucie went for a puff and a pee, I went to speak to the lady on reception and ask where they were.

"But it is only five o'clock." She replied.

I showed her my watch.

"It is six o'clock." I replied.

"No, no ..."

She held her own watch up in a gesture that mimicked my own.

"... it is five. When you arrive from the U.K. you needed to put your watch back one hour."

That explained why everyone on the island was always an hour late!

When we eventually got to speak to Miguel, I understood why everyone thought he was nothing to do with Mrs Parker's disappearance. He was a polite, quietly spoken young man, in his early twenties who possessed just the right balance of confidence and concern. It was hard not to take to him, and I felt sorry that, for a few days at least, people thought he might have been involved in something quite horrendous.

Over the years, I occasionally thought someone might be guilty of a crime, only later to discover they were innocent, but I don't think it had ever happened the other way round – that is to say, I thought they hadn't done it, but it turned out they had.

Miguel was innocent and I was quickly coming around to the position set out by the Portuguese police at the outset. The origin of this incident was nothing to do with the peaceful, almost crime free, island of Madeira. I was now convinced that Mrs P must be dead. If she wasn't, there was no way she could disappear so effectively unless she'd slipped into a Witness Protection programme. Hang on! Was Witness Protection a possibility? But as quickly as the thought emerged, I dismissed it. No one would let an innocent person stand trial for murder if they knew the victim was safe and well, that would just be perverse. Besides, you're meant to go into a Witness Protection programme before you're murdered, not afterwards. I concluded Mrs Parker was dead and that Mr Parker must be involved. The key that ultimately convinced me was that he knew his wife had been snooping around his office. If she was taking photographs, an obvious reason sprung to mind, whoever she was working for wanted to deploy a probe in the office and needed to know the lay-out of the place and what sort of furniture there was, so they could decide where to deploy the device.

We were flying from Funchal to Lisbon first thing tomorrow; we had a meeting with Mr Parker at four and I suspected by five we would have the solution to the riddle.

Chapter 53

Prison Monsanto was not only Portugal's highest security jail, it was also the country's most notorious penal establishment. Even I'd heard of the place, and I'd never previously been to the country. When our taxi pulled up at the gate, the grey concrete building before us was impressive, in an austere, foreboding way. It was everything a prison should be, uninviting, cold, and gritty. The mere sight of it should have been enough to put anyone off a life of crime.

On the way in, we were strip searched. Brucie looked more worried than I had ever seen when the guard deprived him of his café crème tin.

We waited for an hour in a small interview room while the guards collected Mr Parker. When he walked in, he was barely recognisable from the man I'd only seen a few weeks ago at Belgravia police station.

"Hello, Tristram. This is Detective Sergeant Franklin. How are you doing?" I said, with just a hint of sympathy.

He shook his head.

"This is hell." He replied.

"Are you in solitary?" I asked.

He shook his head, again.

"No; I'm in a cell with an Englishman. A guy called Steve."

"What's he here for?" I asked.

"He's awaiting trial for assaulting a policeman. He's a Chelsea supporter and was arrested in January after a fight before a European football game. He works for a German bank in Canary Wharf, so at least we can have a half decent conversation."

Brucie kicked me gently under the table. I knew why. He was thinking, 'that's a bit of a coincidence'. So was I.

"You look tired." I said.

"What do you expect; it's impossible to get any sleep. This place is always noisy and, if that wasn't bad enough, my cell backs on to a kennels where the dogs bark all night."

Brucie and I exchanged a glance; I nodded. Brucie said:

"Before we go on, Tristram, you can assume there is a recording device in this room."

"Can we move rooms? I'd rather speak in private."

"No. Everything you say is admissible in evidence and Brucie and I won't be saying anything we wouldn't want our Portuguese colleagues to hear. Just to make sure you know, if at any time you want legal advice, just tell us and we'll arrange it. Are you sure you still want to talk to us? You can say no, and we'll get on the next plane to old blighty." I replied.

He put his head in his hands and didn't move for well over a minute. Brucie and I said nothing, in fact, I don't think we even moved.

"I'm completely buggered; completely buggered. Rock and a hard place. I've nowhere to turn. How did this happen so quickly?" He asked.

We said nothing. This was the ideal interview scenario, a suspect desperate and beginning to ramble.

"In April, my company reported record profits. We got an all clear from the auditors, I had a wife and a stunning girlfriend and so much money I didn't know what to spend it on. Not six months later, my wife is dead, my business in the control of others and I'm looking at twenty-five years in a Portuguese hell hole for something I haven't done."

I was just a smidgen disappointed because that sentence didn't seem to suggest he was going to admit having his wife murdered.

"So, you're still saying that you had nothing to do with killing your wife?" Brucie asked.

"Of course not!"

He spat those words out with a sudden flash of real temper and he banged his right fist down hard on the table.

The guard opened the door and frowned.

"It's ok, its ok." I said to him.

Mr Parker grimaced and held his right hand in his left.

"Fuck" He said.

"Fuck, fuck, fuck, fuck, fuck, fuck!"

I wasn't entirely sure whether he was exasperated at his current predicament or had broken his hand.

"I'm not doing twenty-five years for something I didn't do."

"But you said your wife was dead; how can you be so certain, if you're not involved? I asked.

"Because I'm not stupid. If she's not dead, then, where is she?"

"Is it possible she's done a moonlight?" Brucie asked.

"Why?" Mr Parker replied.

"You were having an affair." I replied.

"Really? Run away? Leave everything for nothing? Why the devil wouldn't she just divorce me?"

"Look, whatever my wife thought of me, and yes, our marriage was far, far from being perfect, but then whose is? Whatever she thought of me, she wouldn't let me go to prison for life for murder. She's not that evil, who would be? If she has, as you said, done a moonlight flit, by now she would have surfaced again, wouldn't she?"

I had to agree.

"Look guys …"

Mr Parkers tone had changed, softened.

"… is it possible she's been kidnapped?"

"No ransom demand." I said.

"I get that but what if it all went wrong, you know, they used too much chloroform and killed her by accident; then panicked and got rid of …"

Mr Parker couldn't bring himself to say the last word.

"It is possible." I replied.

"We've actually discussed it." Brucie added.

Mr Parker frowned.

"You don't think I did this either, do you?"

"That's not what we said. We don't know. You having her murdered is the most likely scenario but we've considered everything." I replied.

"I'll tell you why I don't think she was kidnapped …" Brucie said.

"… while she is a very likely kidnapping victim, if that was going to take place, it would have happened back home, where she spent forty-eight weeks a year, not a thousand miles away in a place she'd only just got to. No, I don't buy the kidnapping. It's like the idiots that think Princess Diana was murdered by the authorities. Even if that could happen, and take it from me it couldn't, it would have been a mock suicide in Kensington Palace, not an orchestrated car accident in Paris, where no one knew she was going to be, until, like, the day before. Same applies here. Your wife would have been kidnapped from your home in Theydon Bois, not the Hotel Porto Mare." Brucie concluded.

"That makes sense, when you put it like that." Mr Parker replied.

"Listen, Tristram. I'm going to be absolutely straight with you…" I said.

"Okay" He replied, a little nervously.

"… we know that you know your wife was spying on you."

"What the devil are you talking about?" He asked, with astonishment.

I was impressed by his acting.

"You employ Standard Investigations to undertake security assurance at S.I. …"

He nodded.

"… we know that they captured evidence of your wife secretly photographing your office."

"I know they saw her taking pictures, yes." He replied.

"So, she was spying on you." I said.

"Or …" He replied.

"… she was going to redecorate my office, as I'd asked her, and was taking photographs to help her do the designs and pick some new furniture."

In that one sentence my own very personal prosecution case against Mr Tristram Parker collapsed.

Chapter 54

We were staying in a small but nice hotel in Lisbon just outside the city centre. Vincent met us for dinner in the dining room and explained that he had just heard from the Prison Governor that Mr Parker was at hospital having his broken hand plastered.

"Were you listening to the interview?" I asked, candidly.

Vincent nodded.

"He's still denying the murder." I replied.

"You must get him to admit it. It will be easier for him, ten years; maybe eight." Vincent replied.

I hadn't anticipated Vincent would take that approach. Perhaps that was why they allowed us to come and see him? So, we could convince him to cop a plea."

"I am pleased with you, Christopher." Vincent said, as he started to eat his fillet steak.

I frowned by way of a reply.

"And a little disappointed." He added.

I didn't say anything, I knew I didn't have to. Vincent was clearly going to explain, or so I thought, but I was wrong.

"You are clever, Christopher. A very clever Scotland Yard detective. Are all Scotland Yard detectives as clever as you?"

I put my knife and fork down, quite deliberately. Out of the corner of my eye, I noticed that Brucie had also stopped eating. I felt like I was about to be ambushed but tried to appear as relaxed as I could. All those years ago, when I first walked the beat at Stoke Newington, my street duties instructor had told me, 'when walking down the street, the more nervous you feel, the slower you walk.' I applied that advice often. I applied it in that restaurant. I smiled coolly and came to a metaphorical stop.

"Most are much cleverer than me. Brucie for example, I think he's even got a master's degree."

"From the University of Life and out of the School of Fucking Hard Knocks, matey." Brucie replied, with a chuckle.

"What's on your mind, my friend?' I asked, but there was a hint of steel in my voice. I was determined not to feel intimidated.

"Today, I listen to your conversation with the suspect. So did my capitao, my boss. But you are smart, why were we pleased?"

"Because we declined Mr Parker's request to move interview rooms." I replied.

"Si, obrigado."

Thanks to *Portuguese for Dummies,* I knew that meant 'yes, thank you'.

"And why were you disappointed? Is that your second question?" I asked.

Vincent turned to Brucie and tapped the side of his own forehead.

"Si, smart. Yes, Christopher, why was I annoyed?"

"Because you didn't know about the victim taking photographs in the suspect's office." I replied.

Vincent tapped his head again and said to Brucie:

"Si, very smart."

"Would you like me to explain?"

He nodded.

'It's simple, I discovered that information from a personal friend. His wife works for Standard Investigations and had the job of looking at the footage. It was not from the investigation. I couldn't formally tell you because my friend's wife would have got the sack." I explained.

"The Sack?"

"Made to resign." I replied.

"Ah, you mean, dismissed." Vincent said.

"Yes."

"I think, perhaps, you could have told me, we are best friends, are we not?"

I wanted to point out that I didn't even know Vincent's real name and that they had yet to tell me about the covert surveillance in Mr Parker's hotel room, but I didn't. I had also noticed, since we'd been in Portugal, Vincent's attitude to me had changed. He was in charge here, and he showed it.

"Anyway ..." I said

" ... Mr Parker has explained that."

"And you believe him?" Vincent asked.

"I do." Brucie replied.

"So do I." I added, quickly.

Of course, Brucie and I both knew that there was evidence at the Parker's house which supported Tristram's account, namely the office furniture magazine on his wife's bedside table.

My mobile phone rang, and I took a quick glance at the screen, 'unknown caller' flashed up.

I excused myself and stepped outside.

"Chris Pritchard." I said.

"Chris, it's John King."

I felt a sudden rush of blood to my head, my knees went to jelly, and I started to get tunnel vision. I felt myself fainting but managed to stumble to a sitting position on the pavement, propped up by the hotel wall. This was it – the call where he tells me about Barry Skinner and tells me to return immediately.

"Chris, are you there? Hello, hello."

"Sorry, boss, bad line, I've stepped outside now. Is everything all right?" I asked, recovering my composure.

"Just seeing how you're getting on?" He asked.

That didn't make sense; an Assistant Commissioner simply does not ring up a Detective Inspector to see how he's getting on. I knew that was bollocks.

"Fine, boss. We saw the suspect today. He's still denying the murder." I replied.

"That's what I wanted to talk to you about ..." He said.

"... I've got a message from the Minister of Justice; he's been speaking to his counterpart in Lisbon. The Minister instructed me to get you to agree a deal. Tell Mr Parker they'll offer ten years for a guilty plea to second degree murder."

"I'm out for dinner with the Portuguese officer, he's just said the same thing. What's going on?" I asked.

"Between you and me, and I mean that Chris, don't even tell the DS you're with ..."

He waited for me to acknowledge the instruction.

"Okay"

" ... between you and me, I think they've fucked up the investigation so badly, they don't want this going to trial. But that's not the official line, it's just my best guess. And of course, Mr Parker will be able to afford the best counsel money can buy. I suspect that might concern them. I think they're worried about their international reputation." He said.

I was still coming down from my panic attack about Barry Skinner and although I was listening, I wasn't taking it all in as quickly as I should.

I said "Yes" but then had second thoughts.

"Hang on, boss. What if he hasn't done the murder?" I said.

"They're convinced." The Assistant Commissioner replied.

"I'm not, boss." I said.

"Just do as you're told, Chris, put the offer to him."

"Yes, Sir." I replied.

I wanted to tell him to stick their offer up his arse.

Chapter 55

I had to force myself not to keep checking the BBC News App on my phone; I was at risk of doing it so often that it might look bad if I ever got to trial.

Three days after my trip to Southend, I thought I was dealing with it quite well. I could only assume his body hadn't been found. Every day that went by improved my chances of getting away with it. I kept running through events, not just on the day, but in the weeks leading up to it, and I couldn't identify making any mistakes. Even when I looked up the name of the children who died in the Preston bombing, I did so on a Wandsworth library internet terminal. My own internet search history was clear, my phone record would support my alibi, there was no forensic evidence at the scene. If I'd taken any away with me on my clothing, that was now a long way from the scene. I hadn't spoken to a soul or confided in anyone. To find any trace of my car, they'd have to look a long way from the scene and while that was possible, it was highly unlikely. I'd have to come into the frame first before they would follow that line of enquiry.

Brucie might recall that I was acting a bit strangely, but I had explained that credibly.

No, I assessed my chances of being caught at less than one percent.

***

The following day, we were back in the jail.

Mr Parker had his right hand in the most enormous plaster cast.

"Does it hurt?" I asked.

"Like mad, it's throbbing but they won't let me have any painkillers." He replied.

He looked truly awful; absolutely and utterly defeated. And he stank, too, like he desperately needed a shower.

"How's your Chelsea cell mate?" Brucie asked.

"They moved him yesterday. I'm on my own. They also think I'm a suicide risk, so they've got someone checking on me every fifteen minutes, all day and through the night. And because I was at the hospital, I've missed dinner and breakfast." He said.

"Why breakfast?" I asked.

"Because breakfast comes with last night's dinner. It's only bread, butter, and jam but the bread is baked in the prison and is lovely. I'm fucking starving."

"Shall we see if we can get you something?" Brucie asked.

"Please"

Brucie went and spoke to the guards, returning a few minutes later with two Mars bars and a bottle of water.

"Listen carefully, Mr Parker. We've been authorised to offer you a deal."

"Go on." He said, looking just slightly hopeful.

"You plead guilty to second degree murder, and you'll be sentenced to ten years. The bloke we spoke to last night said, if you do all the educational courses which they offer to convicted prisoners, and behave yourself, you could be out after seven. If you plead not guilty, they'll go for first degree murder and a mandatory twenty-five years."

He leaned back in his chair, tipped his head up and stared at the ceiling. He took a deep breath in and then a long exhale.

"Not a bad offer." Brucie said.

"Unless you truly didn't murder your wife." I said.

"Get me painkillers and I promise you I'll tell you …"

He paused, apparently searching for the right word.

"… oh just get me fucking painkillers, please."

Brucie stood up and went back to the guard.

Mr Parker tucked into both bars of chocolate with the enthusiasm a starving dog would show if thrown a meaty bone.

Not two minutes later, Brucie returned with two white tablets.

Perhaps I can get you an Aspirin

Mr Parker threw them down the back of his throat and gulped down the last two inches of water.

We sat there, awaiting his next move.

"Are you in any way connected to your wife's disappearance or murder?"

"I don't think so."

I thought that was a strange reply.

"I didn't ask anyone to abduct or take her or anything." He said, adding more clarity.

"Okay"

"Let me say one thing at this point, Tristram. If you want our help, you must tell us the truth from now on and all the way through. If we catch you lying, if we even think you're lying, we'll get up and walk out of here, and you won't see us again, ever."

He nodded.

"My company does a lot of business with Eastern Europeans, Russians mainly, but also some Poles, Albanians, Romanians, Slovakians. I also do a lot of business with some very senior …"

He let the sentence hang. I think he was unsure what noun to use.

"At first the Eastern European investment portfolio was only a side line, but we were very good at what we did, and we made our clients a great deal of money. To cap it all, we discovered a way that meant they could avoid paying tax. That bit's lawful by the way."

"If that bit was legal, the other bit, the first bit wasn't. Is that correct?" I asked.

He nodded.

"They were putting so much business our way, they wanted to have some of their own people in. They said it was to demonstrate our commitment and that their people would just be there to keep an eye on their money. But it didn't play out like that."

"What was illegal about it?" I asked.

"Perhaps we didn't conduct sufficient due diligence in respect of the source of the money."

"Money laundering." Brucie said, shaking his head.

"How long has it been going on?" I asked.

"Eight years, but at first it was very minor. Only on a serious scale in the last three years."

"Give me some numbers?" Brucie said.

"It's tricky to be exact." He replied.

"Humour me, give me a ballpark, the total amount of dirty money going through Skimmia Investments over the last five years." Brucie asked.

"Ten maybe fifteen, not more than that." He replied.

"Fifteen million?" I asked, incredulously.

He shook his head.

271

"Fifteen billion." He whispered.

Chapter 56

Such ridiculous amounts of money meant nothing to me. Over dinner that evening, Brucie explained.

"The Annual Met budget is about three and half billion. So, what Skimmia Investments have laundered is enough money to pay every police officer, every civvy, rent and rates on every building, every police car in every station, all the fuel. And Skimmia Investments have been cleaning that amount through their books every year for the last five years. It's the net asset value of a big high street bank. Fuck me, over five years it's the GDP of a small African nation. It's a phenomenal amount, matey. Apart from the Columbian drug cartels of Pablo Escobar, it's the biggest money laundering scandal I've ever heard of. Fuck me, the biggest U.K. bank got done last year by the Feds in the States, it was a huge fine, like a billion pounds and all they'd laundered was a mere two hundred million!"

"What do we know about who he's doing this for?" I asked.

"Not a great deal, matey. Faceless Russian oligarchs with false passports, operating with the assistance of the Russian Secret Service, all working under the protection of diplomatic immunity." He replied.

"Sounds like a job for the Fraud Squad." I replied, mimicking the 'this is a job for Superman' catchphrase which I'd used so often as a kid.

"This job is way too big for the Met Fraud Squad, or the City of London one, for that matter. This is a Serious Fraud Squad, Financial Services Authority, multi-agency, international piece of work. No doubt Uncle Sam would want to play, too. Hell, it might even involve our own Security Services."

"Explain to me why so many Russians have got so much money, and why does everyone say it's all bent money? We wouldn't say that if some rich Texan oil magnate came to London to invest a few million, would we?"

"Back in eighty-nine, when the Soviet Union collapsed, the main reason for that collapse was bankruptcy. The fiscal system they operated was completely corrupt, with corrupt officials nicking a slice of the money at every opportunity. The whole system was so inefficient that every enterprise lost money. This meant there was no reinvestment and therefore no research and development. Communism, and the five-year plan, was a disaster and lasted only until all the money, stolen from Eastern Europe after the war, ran out. The collapse of the Berlin Wall wasn't a political event, it was a financial one.

Anyway, after the Soviet Union fell there was an enormous power vacuum in the country. For a few years, the country became like the wild west where the person with the biggest balls, the largest gang, and the most powerful gun, dominated. Roving gangs took over oil wells, coal mines, shipyards, food distribution networks, the bigger shops, garages, transport companies. Where the state had failed, organised criminal gangs ruled. But the good thing was, these gangs got the country working again. People were fed, able to heat their homes and food was put on the table. It was humanity at its best, but also, it's worst. Move the clock forward from eighty-nine seventeen years, and the criminals who took over the essential services are now the Russian government."

"Sounds like the U.S. after prohibition. Isn't it right that the Kennedy dynasty made its vast wealth from the illegal trade of alcohol?" I asked.

"It's precisely the same. You could even draw similarities between the British Empire, the slave trade and some of this country's wealthiest families." Brucie replied.

We'd also brought away from the interview a list of twelve Russians who were officially working for Skimmia Investments. All of these held key positions and had important connections. Three for example, apparently did nothing but look after personal investments of the President himself. Others had very specific but key roles, with several working in legal.

The other Eastern European investors had to do business through the Russians and Tristram admitted he'd largely lost control of his company. Only recently, one of the most intimidating individuals had suggested to him that he might like to spend more time at home.

"What makes this even more of a problem is the tax avoidance." Brucie pointed out.

"He hasn't explained that yet, so how do you know that?" I asked.

"Because most clever money laundering schemes pass the ill-gotten gain of crime through a legitimate business, and that business pays tax. That looks good, obviously, for all concerned and helps to avoid detection. And hell, at least some of the bad money is being recovered by the Treasury and put to good use."

"Like paying our wages." I suggested.

"Exactly, matey. But, if our little plaster armed friend has not only discovered how to launder billions but also how to avoid paying any tax, then fuck me, this will be the biggest financial scandal since Enron."

"But what about the murder? I'm a murder squad detective, not a Fraud Squad pen pusher." I said.

"Remember the Fraud Squad motto mate, The Pen is Mightier than the Sword." Brucie replied.

And then it hit me. I knew why Mrs Parker had been murdered. I also knew Mr Parker was innocent. I wouldn't say anything to Brucie yet. I needed a little bit more clarity to turn a few more permutations over in my mind and I'd had too much to drink, but by the love of god, I thought I'd worked it out.

Chapter 57

It had been a fascinating day, but not the day either Brucie or I had expected when we first got on that plane to Funchal.

The food in the hotel was lovely and just opposite was a large café that served custard cakes in their thousands, other desserts, and alcohol too. It was like a kind of late evening heaven. We sat up drinking in the café discussing the case until gone one. When I went to bed I was nicely pissed.

I was just nodding off when I received a text message from Mrs M, it read 'Is everything alright, darling?'

When I turned the words of the text message over in my head, I thought it didn't sound disastrous. Perhaps they just found his body. Well, they were going to anyway at some point. I resisted the temptation to text her back until the following morning, by which time I thought, the story would be in the news anyway.

As soon as I woke up, and despite a very decent sized headache, I checked the news – nothing.

I texted Mrs M saying hi and I hoped she was well. I didn't respond directly to her question, I thought it would look better if I responded as if I'd hardly noticed. Two paracetamols ...

Perhaps I can get you an Aspirin

... a breakfast, three cups of black coffee and thirty minutes in a cab, and we were back in Prison Monsanto sitting opposite the suspect.

"Did you manage to do any checks? With the names I gave you?" Mr Parker asked, eagerly.

I got the impression he thought this was the key to his release. He couldn't have been further from the truth but there was no point in disillusioning him, not when he was telling us everything.

"No, not yet. When we left you yesterday, you agreed to tell us about the tax evasion scheme you were operating." I said.

"How good is your understanding of the financial world?" He asked.

"Brucie's good and I'm learning fast. I mean, I now know the difference between a wash trade and a push through trade and how that can be used to hide money laundering. And remember, we police officers are stupid." I replied, having a dig at his previous comments.

"Do either of you own shares?" Mr Parker asked.

We both shook our heads.

"Shares are also called equities; it might help to know that."

"Shares are equities, got it." I replied.

"If you own shares in a company, you literally own a part of that company, albeit a very small part. If your company makes a profit, because you own a part of that company, usually twice a year, sometimes four with bigger companies, you are owed some money, a proportion of the profit. This is called a dividend.

"Got it." I said.

"Now, to qualify for the dividend, you must be the lawful owner of that share, on a particular day. As that day approaches, the share price will usually rise and when it passes, the share price falls because it goes, what is called, ex-dividend."

"So, I could own a share for six months but if I sell it the day before the dividend day, I don't get any money, right?" I asked.

"That's it, exactly. You wouldn't get a penny, even if you'd had it all that time. The new share owner would profit."

"Even if the new share owner sold it two days later?" I asked.

"Yes. Now dividends are taxable. If you get a £1 dividend, you pay standard rate tax on it, assuming of course, you already earned your tax-free allowance, which, now, is about nine thousand pounds a year."

So far, I was following quite easily but I suspected things were going to get much more complicated.

"Now let me tell you about tax laws. Each country in the E.U. has slightly different tax laws. We all know that and most of us exploit them whenever we go on holiday and bring back cheap alcohol and fags. That's not illegal because, if you've followed the tax laws of the country where the goods or service was purchased, you don't have to pay any more tax."

"And you've found a way to exploit a difference?" Brucie asked.

"I did, and it concerned tax on company dividends. Some of the smaller E.U. countries want to attract businesses by offering lower corporation tax rates. That's why lots of big multi-nationals are based in Ireland, their corporation tax undercuts everyone; well, apart from Gibraltar. And then there's Luxembourg. They decided to abolish tax on share dividends. If you live in Luxembourg, when you get your £1 dividend, you don't have to pay any tax.

I was rather surprised to discover I was still following him.

"We set up a specialist company in Luxembourg, we called it Flow Equity. The day before your company dividend is due, you and Flow Equity sign a contract transferring ownership of your share to Flow Equity for just forty-eight hours. The contract includes a condition that the share, and any money made from it while in their possession, is returned to you after forty-eight hours. The contract obligates Flow Equity to comply with all local tax laws in respect of any profit made.

If you do this, Flow Equity claim the dividend, which is tax free. The following day, they return ownership of your share and the tax free £1 dividend."

"How do Flow Equity make any money? Or don't they?" I asked.

"For their services, they charge 1.5% of the dividend."

"Fuck me!" Brucie said.

"Is it lawful?" He asked.

"One hundred percent." Mr Parker replied.

"Fuck me. How much money did Flow Equities make last year?"

Mr Parker scratched his ear.

"Just shy of one." He replied.

"Billion?" Brucie asked.

Mr Parker nodded.

"The U.K. government is out at least twenty billion pounds?" Brucie said.

"At least."

"Is this a bigger scandal than the Russian money?" I asked Brucie.

"I think so." Brucie replied.

"Did you do this with all the Russian money?"

"Yes. But we also did this for, well, the rich and famous."

"Who, exactly?" I asked, incredulously.

"If you're going to want another list, might be easier to name those who we aren't doing it for." Mr Parker replied.

***

One thing was surprising, we hadn't heard from Vincent for a couple of days. We did, however, have a conference call with the Assistant Commissioner that evening. I could have been a little nervous but when

Erling said the A.C. was happy for Brucie to join us, I knew it was nothing to do with the other matter.

I'd heard no more from Mrs M which was another plus. Whatever she was concerned about had clearly past and obviously hadn't been that important.

"Upshot is, you've uncovered a massive money laundering operation run by Skimmia investments?" The A.C. clarified, after I'd given him a short briefing.

"And the murder?" He asked.

"I think I speak for both of us. We're not convinced Mr Parker is guilty, but we do think the two are linked." I said.

"Agreed' Brucie added.

"Tell me how?" The A.C. asked.

"We think the Russians discovered Mrs Parker had been sniffing around. They may have thought she was spying on them because she was filmed taking photographs by a covert camera in Mr Parker's office. Now we know that was for a legitimate reason, she was going to decorate the place, but if the Russians thought, like we did, that she was doing that for more clandestine reasons, they may have thought she was an informant." I replied.

"You're saying it's more likely the Russians killed Mrs Parker than her husband?" The A.C. asked.

"Yes" Brucie interjected.

"They had a great deal to lose, and you know they've got previous for assassinating people overseas whom they perceive as threats. And the money laundering goes right to the top of the Kremlin." I added.

"What? That tall spire?" Brucie interjected.

I laughed, but quickly covered it up with a fake cough.

"Good work, chaps." The Assistant Commissioner said.

I took that as the cue that he wanted to end the call.

"One more thing, Sir." Brucie said.

"Yes, go on."

"There's a big tax avoidance scam going on. Mr Parker was telling us …"

"Avoidance or evasion?" The A.C. interrupted.

"Avoidance, legal apparently." Brucie replied.

"Is it connected to the Russian money?" He asked.

"Yes, but it's much wider than that." I replied.

"Forget it, focus on the Russian money laundering, that's what you're there for. I'll see you when you get back."

The line went dead.

Brucie and I looked at one another.

"That was a bad call." Brucie said.

"Wasn't too bad, was it?" I replied.

"Not the phone call, you peckerhead. Not wanting to know about the tax avoidance - the A.C. made a bad call there."

"Perhaps, but we're not from the Inland Revenue, are we?" I replied.

"Still a bad call. That's got huge ramifications and is what these Bramshill guys are taught to recognise."

"What's that?" I asked.

"A critical incident, a fucking critical incident, matey."

"You don't think he's part of it, do you?" I asked.

"What? The tax evasion thing? Wouldn't have thought so. I just think he's made a bad call. But we've told him, so we're in the clear." Brucie said.

"That's not what's worrying me." I replied.

"What is then? The link to the murder? I know we've chatted it through but when you gave that explanation about the Russians finding out about her taking pictures in his office, it didn't sound too convincing. Were you thinking the same?"

"Yes, I was, but that's not what's worrying me, either." I replied.

"Then I've no idea, matey." Brucie said.

"Right at the end of the call, did you hear what Kingy said?"

"He said 'I'll see you when you get back'." Brucie replied.

"No, before that, you cunt. He said something like 'focus on the Russian money, it's why you're there'. I thought we were here to investigate a fucking murder. Has the A.C. forgotten about poor Mrs Parker?"

Chapter 58

We got pissed again that evening; not dreadfully but enough. I was certainly drinking more to block out certain recent memories. That was one reason, but the other was that we just got on well. I liked Brucie. He was smart, smarter than me, and very grounded, too. He was amusing and great company and quite frankly, if I'd only been gay, we could have made a lovely couple.

I phoned Mrs M just to make sure everything was all right. She didn't mention the text, which was just fine, so neither did I. She told me she was going out with John again. This was, she said excitedly, their third date. He was taking her to the oldest restaurant in London, somewhere called Rules, which was in Convent Garden. I'd never heard of it. I can honestly say, I'd never known her so happy. I hoped the Assistant Commissioner didn't let her down; if he did, exalted rank or not, I was quite capable of punching his lights out.

We spent the next two days interviewing Mr Parker. That sounds a long time, but we were only allowed in the prison for three hours every day, so in reality, it was only one day's work. We took a forty-page statement detailing the money laundering practices and those involved, although without access to the company records, he did, on occasions, forget the finer details, like the spelling of some of the foreign names.

In line with the A.C.'s directions, we didn't include anything in the statement about the tax avoidance, but Brucie took extensive notes. He said he'd draft a detailed report when he got back. I have to say, I was more than a little worried about the political fall-out from the tax scheme. The list of clients using S.I.'s services read like an extract from the latest Who's Who. There were members of the royal family; celebrities, including two previous James Bonds; politicians; even cabinet members; Lords and Knights of the realm; a tranche of sports stars, footballers and F1 drivers; rock stars, both old and contemporary; and a whole list of people whose names I recognised but whose precise role in society escaped me.

Mr Parker convinced us beyond doubt on two points. One, he didn't have anything to do with his wife's disappearance and, two, there wasn't any connection between the money he invested for his wife's charity, C.W.W.

and terrorist financing. Although he did admit that several years ago, and after his wife had been interviewed by the Charity Commission about that very thing, he'd asked Standard Investigations to conduct a comprehensive review.

The A.C. had wanted fortnightly briefings from me. When he commissioned these, he said 'no longer than a page and a half'. I wrote my next briefing to him in less than two hundred words.

On 8th June 2007 Mr Tristram Parker, a U.K. national was extradited from this country to Portugal. He has been charged with conspiracy to murder his wife, Mrs Marcella Parker, and is in custody awaiting trial.

On 10th June 2007 and without solicitation, he wrote to the Commissioner requesting to speak to police.

From 21st to 25th June 2007, at Prison Monsanto in Lisbon, accompanied by DS Bruce Franklin, I interviewed Mr Parker.

It is relevant to this briefing that Mr Parker is the majority shareholder of Skimmia Investments Ltd, a hedge fund based in Canary Wharf, London. This is regarded as a highly successful investment company whose clients include members of several royal families and senior international politicians.

Mr Parker denied any knowledge of, or connection with, the unexplained disappearance of his wife, Mrs Marcella Parker, who was last seen in Funchal, Portugal on 28th April 2007.

In connection with his business dealings, Mr Parker admitted numerous offences, including money laundering, false accounting, forgery, and conspiracy to defraud. These offences occurred over an eight-year period on an almost unprecedented scale. He is willing to cooperate unconditionally with any investigation.

Mrs Parker was the accountant for a registered charity called Clean Water for the World. This charity has invested money in Skimmia Investments. Mr Parker claimed his company's dealings with these investments were entirely lawful.

It was, if I say so myself, a masterpiece in precision.

***

When I arrived back at Gatwick, I had a lovely surprise. Pippa, my eldest daughter, was waiting for me as I came through arrivals. I'd never been one of those travellers who'd been met at an airport. Mind you, I didn't really go anywhere, so that might have been why.

Pippa was eighteen and had just finished her A levels. She was bright but a bit lazy and had largely abandoned her studies when she fell in love with her first boyfriend, a young lad called Danny. She'd recently dumped him. Now she had a part-time waitressing job in Buckhurst Hill, while she was awaiting her exam results. Whereas her sister, Trudy, was painfully shy, Pippa was personable, and people took to her immediately. It was a great trait to have, and my eldest daughter had it in spades. I know I am biased, but she was attractive. Sometimes I got frustrated because she didn't require half the make-up she wore.

Our relationship had been brilliant when she was younger but since the divorce we'd grown apart.

"Hello, darling. What a lovely surprise." I said.

She gave me a huge cuddle.

"Hello, daddy. I've passed my driving test. I've driven all the way here to pick you up."

I introduced Brucie and threw him my car keys, told him where my car was parked and offered to call him tomorrow. He was grateful, having had to get the train to the airport as his old Audi was in for a service.

I thought having someone else driving my car for a few days might help confuse any subsequent forensic examination and cloud any DNA or fingerprint evidence. Hell, if the case didn't come to court for years, I might even be able to suggest Brucie had the car at the time of the murder.

On the way to Pippa's car, we chatted about her test and the journey down in great detail. She'd been having lessons, but it was all a big secret about the test because she didn't want to have to tell people if she failed. It probably sounds awful, but when I saw her, my first thought was, 'oh my god she's come to tell me she's pregnant'. It was a blessed relief when she told me about the driving test.

The journey home was nothing short of terrifying and it was the closest to death I'd been in many years. Like most police officers who had been taught to drive to the highest of standards, I hated being driven by civilians, let alone an eighteen-year-old who passed her driving test less than twenty-four hours ago. But I was brilliant, I only screamed like a little girl twice.

We hadn't even got on the M23 when the real reason for her picking me up became clear. Pippa was upset.

"Dad …" She said, like only a daughter can say to her father.

I knew instantly something serious was coming.

"Mum told you about Perth, right?"

"She did." I replied.

"She told you, like, three weeks ago, right?"

"Yes" I replied.

"Then why haven't you come to see me about it, Dad? Why haven't you asked me anything? Mum said you'd want to see us a lot before we went, but apart from the odd text, you've not spoken to me, visited, taken me out to tea, not anything. It's like you don't care."

She was right, of course. I'd been so busy with this case I'd not really had any time, but more than that, it would just hurt way too much. I love my daughters as much as any father does, but why get even closer to them now? That would just be even more painful.

"Because it's too agonising, Pippa." I replied.

"But you could have come and seen us, it's like you're already cutting us out of your life."

I turned to face her.

"Pippa, you're going to the other side of the world. I'm a poor police officer, I can't even afford a week in Spain once a year. How do you think I really feel about you going? I'm devastated, blown away, unable to sleep, distraught with grief. Only two days ago, Brucie, the guy at the airport, asked me why I was so quiet and was I upset about anything. I told him you and your sister were going to Australia. He asked me how I would ever cope with that, and I told him I would never get over it."

I was stretching the truth a little, but the sentiment was right.

"When your Mum told me you were going, I burst into tears. In Starbucks in Loughton, of all places!"

"What ... "

I hesitated because I didn't, as a rule, swear in front of my girls.

"... the fuck, do you think, I think? I'll have no one, no family, nothing. And knowing that, you think I can just pop round and see you, like it's not happening?"

Pippa started to tear up. I didn't want to hurt her, I really didn't. It was however important for her to know the truth.

"I can't stop you going. I wouldn't stop you going if that's what you want to do."

Tears were running down her cheeks and she wiped them with her sleeve. The car swerved ever so slightly every time she did.

"Do you want to go?" I asked.

"No, but I don't want to upset Mum. Since George left her, it's all she's talked about."

"What about your sister?"

"Trudy wants to go because her best mate is there; that's the only reason."

"I suspect your Mum is still missing George and this is a kind of escape." I said.

"I agree, thank you. That's what I think, too."

"Dad, can I stay here? I mean, I can live with you, right?"

Chapter 59

I was delighted my daughter didn't want to go to Australia but very conscious of the fact that her decision might have a devastating impact upon Jackie's plans. I also thought that, as I'd just got settled at Mrs M's, it would be a little disappointing to move out again. What's more, I hadn't lived with Pippa for four years, so I hoped we'd get along now she'd made the transition from child to woman. Finally, if I had to rent a two-bedroom flat somewhere, I'd go back to having no money again. With all that said, there was absolutely no doubt in my mind that I would do everything, and spend anything, to make my Pippa happy.

I had planned to call on a meeting with Jackie to discuss the latest development with Pippa but, first thing the following day, I was summoned to see the Assistant Commissioner. I had no idea whether he was going to arrest me for murder, ask my permission to marry Mrs M or thank me for my work in Portugal and send me back to the Murder Squad. I wasn't especially keen on any of the possibilities.

When Erling showed me into the A.C.'s office, I was surprised to be introduced to a white male about my age who was also attending the meeting.

"D.I. Pritchard, this is D.C.I. Simon Bowyer, he's from the Witness Protection Unit ..."

My heart started to race; this was it. They were going to tell me about Barry Skinner. I had to put on the best acting performance ever. I sat down and braced myself.

"You'll be working together closely over the coming months." The A.C. said.

I nodded and Simon got out a slim orange docket which he opened. It contained my last briefing note. I had no idea what was going on.

"The Portuguese authorities have dropped the charges against Tristram Parker." The A.C. declared.

"Why? They were absolutely convinced of his guilt." I said.

"You need to return to Lisbon and bring him back to the U.K. He'll be released first thing Thursday. Meet him at the prison and get him on the first plane" The A.C. ordered.

"But we don't want you flying to Gatwick, we need you to fly via Belfast and then to Birmingham. You can collect the tickets from Travel Bureau, they'll be ready this afternoon. We'll meet you at Birmingham International and get you booked into a hotel, whilst we make the necessary arrangements." Simon interjected.

"The necessary arrangements for what?" I asked.

"Mr Parker will be entering the Witness Protection programme. He needs to be debriefed. I've got representatives from half a dozen agencies queuing up to speak to him. Five and six, the F.S.A., Customs & Revenue, Immigration, and the Serious Fraud Office, to name just a few." Simon replied.

"Congratulations, Chris, you did an excellent job turning him. Get him home, get him safe and then hand him over to Simon. Your job is almost over, very well done."

The door opened and Erling stuck his head around the corner.

"Boss, the Commissioner's on the phone, I'll put him through."

"Wait outside." The A.C. said.

I was a little stunned and more than a little confused, but I did as I was told.

Erling put the kettle on, and Simon sat down at the desk opposite. I looked out of the window, trying to make sense of it all.

Before the kettle was boiling, Erling answered a call on his desk phone.

"Simon, go back in."

I went to follow him, but Erling stopped me.

"Just Simon, Chris. Not you." He said.

I sat down in the chair Simon had just vacated.

"Do you know what's happened?" I asked.

"No, the boss just told me to send Simon back in. He'll call you when he wants you."

"No, I meant about Tristram Parker and the fact the Portuguese have dropped the charges?"

He shrugged his shoulders, but I didn't believe him.

We sat in an awkward silence for a few moments and then the door to the A.C.'s office opened with urgency and without saying a word, Simon marched out and off down the corridor.

The A.C. emerged momentarily and with a deft movement of four fingers, waved me in.

I sat down in the same seat.

"I've just had the Chief Constable of Essex on the phone. I've got some news for you."

I gulped.

"The terrorist that planted the bomb that killed Dawn and injured you ..."

"Barry Skinner." I interjected.

"He's just been found dead."

"Good" I responded.

"He's been murdered. Looks like a classic assassination, typical I.R.A. style. You know kneecapped first and then shot through the head. He had turned Queens and was in Simon's programme."

"Good. Best news I've had all day." I replied, coldly.

"Embarrassing for the organisation, though. We were protecting Skinner for PSNI. He was giving evidence against several of his old colleagues. We'll probably lose those cases now, so not ideal. But I understand your feelings, Chris."

"Does Mrs M know?" I asked.

"No, the news has only just come in." The A.C. replied.

"We need to tell her before she hears it on the T.V." I said.

"I'll tell her." He replied.

"No, it shouldn't be you or me."

He stood up, walked over to his desk, and picked up his phone.

"I need to see the Deputy Commissioner." He said.

Chapter 60

I was in the lift on the way down when my mobile rang, which is a bastard because the signals terrible. I couldn't hear who it was, so I told them to ring me back in one minute.

As soon as I got out of the foyer, my phone rang again.

"I was in the lift at the Yard." I said.

"D.I. Pritchard?"

"Yes" I replied.

"It's the Deputy Commissioner's staff officer here. The Deputy Commissioner would like to see you in his office, as soon as possible."

"Eighth floor, right? Five minutes." I replied.

Getting ordered to report to the Deputy Commissioner is a once in a career call. In fact, it's probably rarer than that. I felt nervous but also a little excited. It was obviously about Mrs M.

The Deputy Commissioner's office was in the corner of the Broadway building and impressive. It led immediately into a large conference room, where they probably held all the important meetings, like Management Board. I'd never met the Deputy Commissioner before. He wasn't as popular amongst the rank and file as the Commissioner, as he had a reputation as a bit of an academic. I knew someone that was in his class at training school. He reckoned the Deputy Commissioner was one of the nicest gentlemen ever to wear the blue. Even back then, my mate said everyone knew he was destined to be head of the Met one day.

As I entered his office, the Deputy Commissioner got up immediately and came around the desk to shake my hand. I thought that was nice.

"Sit down, sit down, Christopher." He said.

"Thank you, boss." I said.

Perhaps I should have used the pronoun, 'Sir', but I was long in service teco and saying 'boss' came very naturally to me.

"John has told you about the murder of Barry Skinner?"

I nodded.

"How are you feeling?"

I was genuinely surprised because I wasn't expecting such a personal question.

"Honestly, boss?"

"Of course." The Deputy Commissioner replied.

"Absolutely fucking delighted." I replied.

Perhaps I shouldn't have used 'fucking' but I was …

"It seems like only yesterday, the Stoke Newington bombing. I was a D.I. at West End Central. We were all shaken to the core. I can't imagine what it was like for you."

"It took me a while to get over it." I said.

"I can't even begin to imagine. Weren't you going out with the poor WPC who was killed?"

"No, boss, we were living together but only as mates. She wouldn't have gone out with me. I was just a kid, she was a beautiful, sophisticated woman."

I knew that wasn't technically accurate, whilst Dawn was attractive no one would describe her as beautiful, but it didn't matter because to me she was so beautiful.

"You got the QPM for Gallantry, didn't you?"

"No, boss, everyone thinks that, but I got that for rescuing an old gentleman from a burning building."

"What about the bombing? Didn't you get recognised for your part in that?"

"No, but I didn't do anything, boss, I just took a very ordinary call to what we all thought was a bomb hoax and got blown up. Any one of my colleagues would have done the same."

He nodded in agreement.

"I'm going to see WPC Matthew's mother. John tells me you know her. Any tips, you know, so I don't say the wrong thing?"

"Are you going now?" I asked.

He nodded.

"Just so you know the full picture, I live with Mrs Matthews. We've been friends since before the bombing. She's lovely. She's spent twenty-five years waiting for justice. I think she'll be happy when you tell her. But tell her everything, even the fact he was in Witness Protection. Don't let her find out anything from the media that you could have told her."

"I'm waiting for a briefing from the Essex SIO who's on the scene." He replied.

"Do we know anything about what's happened?" I asked.

"Skinner had turned super grass and his killing has all the trademarks of an assassination so it's not hard to work out that he probably told someone he thought he could trust where he was, and the rest, as they say, is history. It's a shame because, apparently, he was giving us some fantastic intel on the Real I.R.A. and was due to give evidence in half a dozen historic murders cases. They'll all have to be dropped now."

His phone rang and he returned to his desk to answer it. I stood up and gestured as if to say, I'll go. He pointed back to the seat. I sat down again. He said, 'yes', several times, and then hung up.

"Sky News are breaking the story. I need to get to Mrs Matthews."

He picked his uniform jacket off the back of his desk chair. As he walked towards the door, I said.

"Do you know where you're going?"

"My driver does. I'll tell him its blues and twos all the way."

I didn't move because I'd misunderstood what was going on. I thought the Deputy Commissioner was going on his own. Two seconds later, however, he reappeared

"Well, are you coming, Pritchard?"

***

The blues and twos run in the Deputy Commissioner's Range Rover with two traffic police motorcycle outriders, was surreal.

It was two o'clock and the fourteen-mile journey from the Yard to Buckhurst Hill would normally take an hour. That afternoon it took us thirty-five minutes. As we neared the house, I politely suggested we lose the outriders and kill the siren. I was worried poor Mrs M would have a heart attack.

"When we arrive, please go in first and ask Mrs Matthews whether she would be kind enough to see me."

"Of course, boss. But you could just go and knock at the door, she won't bite." I replied.

"If you think that's best."

"I do. I'll wait in the car. If she gets upset, come, and get me." I replied.

The plan was a sound one, except Mrs M wasn't in. The Deputy Commissioner returned to the car and got it.

"Well, that was a waste of time, but at least I tried." He said.

"It wasn't a waste of time, boss. I know exactly where Mrs M will be."

***

It was sort of fitting that the Deputy Commissioner met Mrs Matthews at Dawn's grave. I remained in the car. If I'd tried to be any part of that conversation, I would have gone to pieces. I don't even think Mrs M knew I was there, which was just fine.

They were together for about an hour, sitting on the bench chatting. At one point they hugged. I might have been mistaken but I'm sure I saw, on more than one occasion, the Deputy Commissioner wiping away a tear.

Eventually they parted, and I watched Mrs M walk away along her well-trodden path.

The Deputy Commissioner then saluted the grave, it was a lovely touch. It's a shame those officers that spent so much of their time slagging him off hadn't seen that moment.

When he got back to the car, the Deputy Commissioner seemed really subdued. He asked me whether I needed a lift home, but I politely declined. I had to have a chat with my old friend.

> WPC Dawn Jayne Matthews
> Born 24th February 1957
> Killed in the line of duty
> 28th July 1983
>
> No parents were ever prouder
> Or a daughter more missed.

The grave was immaculate and there were two large fresh bunches of flowers. I knew every week Mrs Matthews brought a bucket, sponge, and washing-up liquid to clean the stone.

I sat on the bench adjacent to the grave and broke one of my own cardinal rules by telling my old partner and best friend exactly what I'd done to her murderer.

Chapter 61

I'd just left the cemetery when my phone rang. It was Brucie and there was excitement in his voice.

"Have you heard the news, matey?"

"Yes, mate. The Deputy Commissioner has just told Dawn's mum." I replied.

"What? Why would he do that?" He asked.

"He wanted to do it before the news broke." I replied.

"Why? And why is she interested?" He asked.

I was confused.

"Okay. I'm detecting a crossed wire. Let's start again. Have I heard what news?" I asked.

"Mrs Parker's alive."

"What?" I asked.

"Marcella, Mrs Parker, Tristram's wife, she has been found alive."

"Fucking hell. I had a meeting with the A.C. a couple of hours ago. He told me the Portuguese authorities were dropping the charges and that I had to go and get Mr Parker tomorrow. Fuck, I've left the tickets at the Yard. Fuck!"

I realised that by turning down the Deputy Commissioner's offer of a lift, which I should have taken, I'd now have to make my own way to the Yard which, without a car, would take hours.

"So, you knew? You could have told me, matey."

He sounded really pissed off.

"No! I didn't know she was alive! It's not like that, at all. Listen Brucie. I got an urgent call to go to the Yard and see the A.C. At the meeting, which was only two hours ago, there was a D.C.I. from Witness Protection. I was told the Portuguese were dropping the murder charge and releasing Mr Parker, but not why. The A.C. told me to go to Lisbon tomorrow and fly back with Mr Parker. When I land, I'm handing him over to the Witness Protection Unit so he can be debriefed about all the money laundering stuff. I was going to tell you, but something came up. In fact, I completely forgot that my plane tickets are at the Travel Bureau. I've got to go fucking back to the Yard and get them."

"Don't worry about that. I'll pick 'em up. I'm in the Feathers where they've got the BBC News channel up. I just saw the tickertape headline at the bottom of the screen, I don't know anything else."

"What did it say? Exactly?" I asked.

"Something like, 'Hedge Fund Manager's Missing Wife Found Alive and Well'. I've stepped outside to call you. It was only on a few seconds ago."

"Can you get my plane tickets, please? But stay vicinity only. Don't have any more to drink. I'm coming up to the Yard. We need to see the A.C."

"If he'll see us. We can't just go barging in." Brucie replied.

"I'll call Erling on route. He'd better fucking see us." I said.

"You alright matey? You sound really pissed off."

"I'm starting to realise that we've been really fucked about here."

"What do you mean?" Brucie asked.

"We've been played like a couple of complete cunts. What's more, we've swallowed it hook, line and fucking sinker."

***

It took me nearly two hours to get back to the Yard, a twenty-five-minute walk to the station and then the slowest underground train in the world with two changes. On the way, I spoke to Erling, but he said the A.C. was busy for the rest of the day. I asked him what time his last meeting finished, and he replied 7.30.

"Put my meeting in his diary at 7.30 then." I demanded.

"He'll spot it, chastise me and then delete it, anyway." Erling replied.

"Tell him, if he ever wants to see Jenny again, he'd better not move or delete that appointment."

"I don't think threatening is appropriate, Chris. You sound angry. I do appreciate it's been a difficult day and that you've had some news that must have brought back a lot of bad memories but please, don't threaten an Assistant Commissioner. Who's Jenny?"

I sort of knew Erling was right, and I didn't want to put him in an insidious position.

"Just put the meeting in his diary, please Erling. Tell him it's urgent."

"Okay" Was Erling's one-word answer, and then he hung up.

***

Four of us sat in his office; Brucie and I, on one side of his small circular coffee table, and the A.C. and Erling on the other.

"They said you were sharp." The A.C. said.

"Not sharp enough." I replied.

"How annoyed are you?" He asked.

"Upset more than annoyed, boss. You could have told us. I feel like we've been treated like a right pair of wankers."

"Have you worked it out, too?"

The A.C. addressed the question to Brucie.

"I think so, but only because Nostrils reacted like he did when he heard Mrs Parker was alive. I didn't realise at first but then I didn't know the charges had been dropped because somebody …"

He looked at me.

"… forgot to tell me. I just thought, they'd dropped the murder charge because they'd discovered Mrs Parker was alive." Brucie replied.

"No, they dropped the murder charge because there was no murder. The whole plot was all a complicated deception to get Mr Parker to spill the beans on the Russians, wasn't it?" I said.

The A.C. nodded.

"Quite clever actually, peckerhead." Brucie said to me.

"Mrs Parker was working for MI5 then?" I asked.

"And 6. They approached her saying her charity was being exploited to fund terrorism and they needed her to report anything suspicious."

"But it wasn't, was it?" I said.

"No. The finances of Clean Water for the World is, well, as clean as the water it provides to disaster areas." The A.C. replied.

"They just wanted someone close to Skimmia Investments, didn't they?"

The A.C. nodded.

"Having gained her trust, they turned her by showing compromising photographs of her husband's infidelity. She wanted out of the marriage, anyway. What's more, she is, apparently, a very decent person, and when they explained that putting an end to her husband's company's dirty tricks would save dozens, if not hundreds of lives a year, she agreed." He explained.

"Operation Mincemeat." I said.

302

The A.C. frowned.

"Operation Salcombe, I think." The A.C. responded.

"No, boss, Mrs Parker was reading Operation Mincemeat. We found the book by her bed when we spun her drum. It's a true World War Two story about a brilliant military deception. It involves a dead body of a British army Major on which they planted false invasion plans. As a result, Germany moved their defences from Sicily to Greece. Come to think of it, the similarities are startling. How did they persuade the Portuguese to get involved?"

"I suspect Portugal is facing similar threats to national security from dirty Russian money." The A.C. replied.

"It was the perfect way to bring pressure on Mr Parker. I mean, he thought he was facing life in prison for a murder he knew nothing about." Brucie said.

"The press did their part too; with some well-placed leaks I suspect." Brucie said.

"Yes, Fleet Street had him tried, convicted, and sentenced. Of course, that was one of the advantages of using a foreign prosecution, they weren't bound by the usual U.K. reporting restrictions."

"Very clever. Pritchard's upset, I'm quite impressed, but then he is rather an emotional creature." Brucie said, with a smile.

"We knew she hadn't been murdered. Didn't we, Brucie? And we fucking knew he wasn't anything to do with her disappearance." I said.

"I know you did. That bit was starting to worry everyone."

"Not as much as the tax avoidance scam though." Brucie said, with a wry smile.

"You're not wrong." The A.C. replied.

"Where was she?" Brucie asked.

"At first light, and before anyone knew she was gone, Mrs Parker was taken off the island by a Portuguese naval vessel. They took her to the mainland and straight into hiding."

"What are we going to do about the tax avoidance scam? The wonderfully named 'Dividend Arbitrage'?" Brucie asked.

"My instructions are to put that to one side."

"That's bollocks." I said.

"Too many powerful people are caught up in that." The A.C. replied.

"That's shocking, boss. That's not right. Besides it's all going to come out in the wash, surely?" I said.

"My experience is the press have got a way of finding these things out. I'm not suggesting anything, but ..." The A.C. said.

We all knew what we were being told to do. I made a mental note to call Laura Shewan from a TK in the, not too distant, future.

"What about Vincent? Did he know?" I asked.

"He's Portuguese secret service." The A.C. replied.

"For fucks sake, I knew he was. I found his real identity card. Fucking hell, boss."

"I know you're annoyed, Chris. But you two did your part brilliantly. We couldn't let you in on the secret, otherwise it would never have worked. Skimmia Investments were operating in such a way that some of the largest organised criminal networks in the world had access to almost limitless laundering facilities. It made them untouchable. That money was funding terrorism, drug dealing, the supply of illegal firearms, human slavery and trafficking, and prostitution. The crime this money was enabling was causing misery on an unimaginable scale. And you two did your part in bringing it down. You have saved far more lives today than you can ever imagine. Don't be annoyed because I had to lie to you. It was a necessary fiction. You have my apologies but not my regret. Whatever else you two have done before, or will do in the future, believe me, in investigative terms, your key part in bringing down Skimmia Investments is your crowning glory."

Chapter 62

One week later.

When I told Mrs M about Pippa, she immediately suggested that she come and live with us, but I wanted to make sure she'd thought that through. We chatted at length, and it became clear she was absolutely determined that was what she wanted. I thought perhaps she'd like having another lady in the house.

During our conversation, the six o'clock news had been on the T.V. and we hadn't paid any attention until an article came on about the Barry Skinner murder. Mrs M reached for the remote and turned the volume up.

The black BBC presenter in a pleasant but discernible Welsh accent read his auto script, as a series of pictures came up on the screen; first, an old photograph of the victim shaking hands with a senior Labour politician. Skinner's face was highlighted.

The Real I.R.A. have claimed responsibility for last week's murder of former I.R.A. bomber, Barry Skinner. Skinner was shot dead at his house in Southend-on-Sea, Essex.

Then, in quick succession, the BBC showed different photographs from the scenes of several bombings.

Last year Skinner, who was sixty-eight and suffering from Parkinson's disease, was convicted of the 1983 Stoke Newington shopping centre and the 1988 Preston Remembrance Day bombings in which four members of the public were killed. The BBC Crime Correspondent understands he had agreed to provide evidence in respect of other historic bombings, both in Northern Ireland and the mainland U.K.

A spokesperson for the Real I.R.A. described Skinner's murder as a lawful execution.

Next the BBC broadcast several grainy photographs, taken from a CCTV camera, of an indeterminable male on a bike, cycling along a road.

Police are appealing for witnesses and are particularly keen to speak to a white male seen riding a black bicycle on the A127 in the early hours of Monday 3rd September.

The newsreader paused and a telephone number came up under the words Incident Room.

Anyone with information, please call the number on the screen now.

I stood up and asked Mrs M if she wanted a tea.

She smiled.

"Thank you." She said.

I turned around to walk to the kitchen.

"Chris …"

Her voice was slightly louder.

"I don't want tea. I said thank you."

I put on my best 'I'm confused' expression.

"I've no idea what you're talking about." I replied.

"I think you do."

She looked at me and, in that moment, I knew she was talking about Barry Skinner.

I put my finger to my lips to indicate she shouldn't say anything and then I pointed to the back door. I had probed up too many houses to make that rudimentary mistake. A minute later, we were standing in the garage, a room I'd only visited twice in the two months I'd been at Mrs M's.

"Is there washing in the machine?" I asked.

She shook her head.

"Can you put it on fast spin, anyway?" I asked.

She turned a dial and pressed a button. The drum immediately started turning and emitted a whirring sound.

"What are you talking about, Mrs M?" I asked, keeping my voice low just in case a probe in the house could still pick up any trace of our conversation.

"Thank you for killing that bastard."

"What on earth makes you say that. You heard the news; the Real I.R.A. have admitted it."

"Of course, they have. It's in their interests to do so. You know, to send a message out to others, this is what will happen if you betray us, and we can find you wherever you are."

"It was, perhaps for them, a necessary fiction." I said, aping the words of the A.C. when he justified why he'd lied to Brucie and me.

"I agree; but the Real I.R.A. didn't kill Barry Skinner, you did." Mrs M said.

There was clearly absolutely no doubt in her mind, but I wasn't ready to admit anything, not until I knew why she was so certain.

"Why do you think that?"

"Because on 7th September you left this house at one o'clock. I thought, that's early for the airport, I mean, your flight wasn't until eight-thirty. I thought that crazy woman might have come back, what's her name?"

"Cassandra"

"I thought Cassandra might be giving you grief and, if she was, I was going to come and help you. Besides, where mad women are concerned, it's useful to have a witness, so she couldn't allege anything untoward. I looked out of the spare bedroom window but there was no sign of her. I saw you hide something under a stone by the gate and drive off. And do you know what? I could just make out you were wearing gloves, the blue plastic ones that the doctors wear on Casualty. Curiosity got the better of me. I got some clothes on and went outside to see what you'd been doing. When I saw your phone, wrapped in one of my freezer bags, I knew you were up to something clandestine. I stayed up for hours. I saw you come back at about five. You retrieved your phone, but you didn't come in which I thought was doubly weird. Then when the A.C. told me about the murder, I remembered that night and thought, I wonder. All day they've been talking about the man on the bike. Where's your bike, Chris? It's usually here."

She pointed to the space in the garage.

I didn't know what to say.

"And another thing, a few days before all that happened, I noticed you'd used some of that black masking tape to hide the manufacturer's name. I was going to ask you why, but it clean slipped my mind. Then a few days later, you put your bike in the car. You had to take the front wheel off to get it to fit. I watched you do it. I assumed you must be going somewhere and didn't give it another thought. But now, everything fits together perfectly."

"You should be a detective." I said, quietly.

"You killed that bastard and I'm glad you did. I hope you made him suffer. I hope he begged for his life. I hope he pleaded for forgiveness. I hope you gave him nothing but hate and vengeance. I hope he died slowly, and painfully and in fear. He stole my daughter's life, he deserved to die."

"He killed three children as well, in the Preston bombing."

She nodded.

"How did you know where he was living?" Mrs M asked.

"About a month ago, and by chance, I found some paperwork in the Assistant Commissioner's office. Skinner was in the Witness Protection programme and the Assistant Commissioner had to sign off an invoice for a washing machine or something, which the Met had purchased for him.

They'd given him a new identity, but I knew that when they did that, they always keep the same first name. Apparently, it's just too difficult to get used to a new one. I also know, they give you a very common surname to make it more difficult to find you. When I saw the name on the invoice, Barry Kelly, I guessed that was Skinner. I'd seen his photograph a few times over the years, so I knew it was him as soon as I had eyes on. Of course, if I'd been wrong and the door wasn't opened by a seventy-year-old Irishman, I could have made my excuses and left."

I explained.

"Fate was leading you to him."

"I have to agree." I replied.

"You did tell him why he was going to die, didn't you? You didn't just shoot him? He did know it was coming?"

"I did. In fact, I read the names of each of his victims to him before the final bullet."

"After twenty-four years of the most unbearable pain, you have made me happier than I can say. I love you, Christopher Pritchard. You brave, brave man. That bastard messed with the wrong police officer when he blew you up."

"There was nothing brave about shooting a sick old man, Mrs M. Nothing at all." I replied.

It was the first time I'd considered my actions objectively and it dawned on me that there was a heavy element of cowardness about what I'd done. In fact, I decided, it was very much a case of one coward dispatching another. The sordid business was neither glorious nor admirable. It was, however, necessary. It bought my world back into balance. Sometimes, only the immoral can defeat the wicked. I felt some shame but no remorse.

"You are my hero, Christopher Pritchard. You braved the aftermath of the bomb, and your own terrible injuries, to be with my daughter when she most needed someone. Now, you have avenged her murder and at great personal risk. If they catch you, there is no Good Friday Agreement to keep your sentence to just two years."

"Only the risk was brave, not the act itself, Mrs M. There was nothing courageous about that." I replied, my voice barely audible.

"The devil took my only child, Christopher, but god sent me his avenging angel in the guise of you."

"I don't know about that." I replied, with genuinely humility.

We hugged for minutes, and Mrs M sobbed her heart out. For once, not a tear touched my cheek. When we eventually let go of each other, I said.

"It worries me sick that you know, Mrs M. That makes me, us, really vulnerable. I wish you'd never worked it out. We must never talk of this, ever." I said, almost pleading.

"Don't look so worried, Chris. Your secret is safe. I will never mention it again for as long as I live. The night of the murder, you never left this house. That is the story I shall tell until I join my daughter in heaven. What expression did you use, just now? A necessary fiction? That is exactly what this will be."

I smiled but my smile quickly dissipated when Mrs M said:

"Only three people will ever know what happened."

"Three!" I said, panic rising.

Fucking hell, had she told her boyfriend, the Assistant Commissioner?

"Yes three, and that's the way it will always be …" Mrs M replied.

"… you, me, and my beautiful Dawn."

Printed in Great Britain
by Amazon